'You can't stay in here,' she said.

'You would not turn me out, would you?'

'But it is unseemly.'

'You should have thought of that before you stowed away.'

'Yes, but I did not think…'

'That is your trouble, Miss Giradet, you do not think. I recall you promised to be good if I brought you.'

'Good, yes. Wanton, no.'

'Touché!' He laughed.

'You could have told him I was not your wife.'

'I could, but then he would have drawn his own conclusions, to your detriment. Besides, I could see the advantages…'

'I'll wager you could.'

'Do not be so waspish. Let me finish. If we pretend to be man and wife you will, as a British citizen by way of marriage, be safe from arrest even if it is discovered who you really are—or were before you married me. You will be able to go out and about openly. Otherwise you will have to stay in hiding. You may not care for your reputation, but I certainly care for mine.'

'So what happens tonight?' she asked.

AUTHOR NOTE

If you have been following the fortunes of *The Piccadilly Gentlemen's Club* series you will recognise the name Drymore. Captain James Drymore, later Lord Drymore, was the instigator of the club in THE CAPTAIN'S MYSTERIOUS LADY, the first book of the series (short-listed for the Romantic Novelists' Association Love Story of the Year award). The Commodore in this story is his son, carrying on the tradition of the Gentlemen and rescuing damsels in distress—this time the daughter of a French count in Revolutionary France, where the Gentlemen are a thorn in the side of Robespierre. Naturally, she doesn't make it easy for him. Sir John Challon, Lady Drymore's father, appeared in the first book as a follower of the Young Pretender, who was forced into exile in France, but here he plays a part in the rescue and is reunited with his daughter.

I hope you enjoy reading it.

IN THE COMMODORE'S HANDS

Mary Nichols

Published in Great Britain 2013
by Mills & Boon, an imprint of Harlequin (UK) Limited.
Large Print edition 2014
Harlequin (UK) Limited, Eton House,
18-24 Paradise Road, Richmond, Surrey, TW9 1SR

© 2013 Mary Nichols

ISBN: 978 0 263 23946 1

Born in Singapore, **Mary Nichols** came to England when she was three, and has spent most of her life in different parts of East Anglia. She has been a radiographer, school secretary, information officer and industrial editor, as well as a writer. She has three grown-up children, and four grandchildren.

Previous novels by the same author:

RAGS-TO-RICHES BRIDE
THE EARL AND THE HOYDEN
CLAIMING THE ASHBROOKE HEIR
  (part of *The Secret Baby Bargain*)
HONOURABLE DOCTOR, IMPROPER
  ARRANGEMENT
THE CAPTAIN'S MYSTERIOUS LADY*
THE VISCOUNT'S UNCONVENTIONAL
  BRIDE*
LORD PORTMAN'S TROUBLESOME WIFE*
SIR ASHLEY'S METTLESOME MATCH*
WINNING THE WAR HERO'S HEART
THE CAPTAIN'S KIDNAPPED BEAUTY*

*The Piccadilly Gentlemen's Club mini-series

**And available through Mills & Boon®
Historical eBooks:**

WITH VICTORIA'S BLESSING
  (part of *Royal Weddings Through the Ages*)

**Did you know that some of these novels
are also available as eBooks?
Visit www.millsandboon.co.uk**

Chapter One

Early summer, 1792

Lisette could see the crowd from her bedroom window, marching towards the château, pulling a tumbril containing a tree decorated with flowers and ribbons in red, white and blue, and although they were singing and laughing and banging drums, she did not think they were coming in a spirit of friendship. Since the King had been forced by the National Assembly to accept the new constitution, the peasantry seemed to think they were no longer required to pay taxes and they were insisting that the seigneurs, among them her own father the Comte, should remit those already paid, not only for this year, nor even for the period since the beginning of the Revolution, but for many years previously. Naturally her father had refused. He had his own taxes to pay and many of the privileges he had enjoyed before the Revolution had been abolished. Times were hard for everyone.

She left the window and hurried downstairs to alert her father, who was working on papers in his library, though he could not have failed to hear the noise. 'Go out of the back way and fetch help from the *maréchaussée*,' she urged him. 'I'll try to delay them.'

'I will not be driven from my home by a mob,' he said and set his jaw in a rigid line of obstinacy. 'And I will not give in to demands.'

Comte Gervais Giradet was a third-generation aristocrat. His grandfather had become very rich through colonial trade and bought his title and lands in the village of Villarive close by Honfleur in Normandy for 60,000 *livres,* an enormous sum, enough to keep two hundred working families alive for a whole year. The village was part of the Giradet estate. It had a village green with a fountain from which the women drew their water, one church, two inns, a leather worker who made the harnesses for the horses and the shoes for the villagers, a blacksmith and a vendor of comestibles and candles, although most of the shopping was done in Honfleur. The village showed no sign of prosperity—except, perhaps, the surrounding apple orchards which provided most of the inhabitants with their living and the Comte with his wealth, though that was declining.

Until the Revolution Gervais had lived quietly in his château, an autocratic but benign seigneur, minding his own business farming and growing apples to be made into cider and Calvados, and not interfering in anyone else's. Now everything was in turmoil. The aristocrats were the people's enemy. Hundreds of them had already fled the country, mainly to go to England.

'But you cannot stand up to a mob like that, Papa,' Lisette protested. 'They will lynch you.'

'Do not be so foolish, Lisette; they will not harm me. I shall speak to them. After all, we are all equal now—or so they say.'

The crowd had reached the courtyard and had set up the tree in the middle of it. There was a traditional belief that if a May Tree was put up in the lord's courtyard and hung with small sacks of grain and chicken feathers, the peasants were telling their seigneur they thought his dues excessive and if it was kept standing for a year and a day, they would be free of their dues to him. Lately the May Tree had become the Liberty Tree and now it symbolised the freedom given to the people by the new Constitution and their contempt of the lords of the manor.

They were calling on the Comte to show himself and Lisette repeated her plea that he should leave. 'You can come back when they have gone away again.'

He smiled, adjusted the lace frills of his shirt sleeves and straightened his shoulders to go and meet them. On the way out he passed a gilded mirror and stopped to straighten his wig and give a tweak to his neckcloth, settling the diamond pin more securely in its folds. Then he nodded to a footman who opened the door for him.

His appearance at the top of the steps seemed to inflame the mob. They all began shouting at once. 'Give us back what is due to us,' one man yelled. 'You have been bleeding us dry for years, you and the rest of your aristocratic friends. You are rich and we are poor and that situation has been denounced by the new government. Even

King Louis thinks it is wrong. The rich can afford to pay, we can't…'

'I have to pay taxes too.' The Comte attempted to make himself heard, but they were in no mood to listen.

'You have no right to our taxes.' The speaker was a big man, dressed in a faded black suit and wearing the red cap of the Revolutionaries. Lisette knew him as Henri Canard, a lawyer and ardent Revolutionary who led the local peasants, rousing them from their apathy to take part in demonstrations against the nobility. 'You have no title to the land you hold.'

'I certainly have. My grandfather bought it…'

'Obtained by trickery,' Canard said, taking a step or two towards the Comte, his dark eyes gleaming, a threat in every gesture. 'We demand restitution.'

'I cannot pay what I do not have.'

'Then we'll take what we want in kind,' someone yelled. 'I'll have that diamond pin in your cravat.'

'And I'll have the silk cravat,' cried another.

'I think we should lock him in prison until he

pays,' added a third. 'See how he likes prison fare. No more fat pigeons until he pays what he owes.'

'*À bas les aristos!* Down with all aristocrats!' This became a growing chorus and they milled round Gervais and began pulling at his fine clothes. Lisette ran to intervene, but was pushed roughly aside. Having divested him of everything except his breeches and shirt, they put him in the tumbril while others entered the house and began gathering items they thought they could use or sell and piling them into the cart alongside the Comte. Some went into the cellars and emerged carrying bottles of Calvados, still more invaded the pigeon loft and wrung the necks of several birds before the remainder flew off to safety. Lisette watched in horror as they set off again, taking her father with them. One of the crowd was even wearing his wig and laughing at his own cleverness.

She ran after them, pulling on Henri Canard's arm. 'Let him go,' she cried. 'He is an old man and has done you no harm. You can keep the other things, just let him go.'

'He needs to be taught that the old order is gone,' the man retorted, shaking off her hand. 'We are all equal now. If prison is good enough for those of us who cannot pay our taxes, it is good enough for him who will not.'

She continued to run alongside him. 'What are you charging him with?'

The big man laughed. 'Withholding what belongs to the people, plotting against the State, hiding a refactory priest. I am sure we can find something.' The National Assembly had confiscated all Church property and stripped the clergy of their rights, requiring them to sign an oath of loyalty to the new regime. Those who did so were allowed to remain at their posts and paid a stipend by the state, making them virtually civil servants. Those who refused were not allowed to practise; they could not say mass or officiate at funerals, baptisms or weddings. They either fled the country or went into hiding and practised secretly. The Comte was known to have sheltered one of these until recently when the poor man had died—of a broken heart, so her father maintained.

'And you would do that to an innocent old man?'

'Innocent, bah! Now out of the way, before we put you in the cart along with him.'

She fell back and the crowd passed her and bore her father away. She needed help and the only person she could think of was her twin brother, Michel. He was an equerry at the court of King Louis. If Louis ordered the mob to release her father, they would surely obey.

She returned to the château and set the servants clearing up the mess, then made preparations to leave for Paris. Hortense, her faithful duenna, packed a small portmanteau and Georges, their coachman, prepared the travelling carriage and harnessed the horses. She would travel faster without a large entourage, but Georges insisted two of the grooms should ride alongside, armed with pistols. It was not going to be an easy journey and would take at least three days.

Lisette had always been close to her brother. There had been no families of equal status close by as they grew up, no children with whom they could associate, so they had spent all their time in each other's company, especially when their mother died. Their father had been too immersed in his grief to pay attention to them and it was Michel, miserable himself, who had tried to comfort her.

Physically they were very alike, though she was an inch or two shorter than her brother, and good living at court had made him heavier. They both had fair hair and grey-blue eyes. She was unusually strong, probably due to the rough games she played with Michel when they were children, and because she had taken over her mother's role in the household she was used to giving orders and having them obeyed. Michel laughingly called her bossy and perhaps she was. She had tried, in her rather confused way, to take the place of her mother and her brother in her father's life and feared she had failed on both counts.

She was convinced that was the reason for her single state at the age of twenty-five. Five years before Papa had taken her to Paris and introduced her to any number of eligible young men, but nothing had come of it. Perhaps she was too particular, perhaps reluctant to give up the independence she was used to, or perhaps, as she later suspected, they were put off by her unfashionably lean figure and self-sufficiency. They had come home again with Papa grumbling he had wasted his money and she might as well have married Maurice Chasseur in the first place.

Maurice Chasseur lived in Honfleur and his parents had earlier talked to her papa about a possible match, but when the young man was approached after they returned from Paris, he flatly refused to co-operate, saying she was too hoydenish, more boy than girl, and he was not at all surprised none of the Parisian eligibles had wanted to take her on, not even for a fortune. The remark had come to her through a servant in his father's household who had relayed it to Hortense.

'He is simply annoyed because your papa hoped to do better for you and, when nothing came of it, went back to him and he didn't like the idea of being second-best,' her maid had told her by way of comfort. But it had hurt far more than she cared to admit and left her firmly convinced she was unmarriageable. It had become even more imperative to maintain her life at the Château Giradet and hang on to whatever privileges that still remained.

She was not an ardent royalist; she deplored the extravagance of the King and his court, the secret whisperings of scandal, the way favours could be bought and sold and the courtiers indifference to the suffering of the poor, made worse by the Revolution that should have eased it. Neither did she like the way the country was being run, the summary justice and injustice, the constant edicts that confused rather than enlightened. Surely, she thought, there must be a middle way, something like the English system where King George ruled in a democracy, though it was said he was mad.

The countryside they passed through was showing signs of poverty and neglect. The fields were not tended as well as they once had been, the livestock grazing on the meadows was thin. Everywhere had an overgrown, neglected air and the people who watched the carriage pass were poorly clad. Some looked on with the dull eyes of dejection, others were angry and spat at the coach as it passed. Lisette was thankful for their escort, especially when they stopped each night at posting inns.

Paris, when they reached it three days later, was seething with discontent. Everywhere—in the crowded narrow alleys, in the wider main streets, in the squares and public buildings—noisy crowds gathered, sporting red caps or wearing a red, white and blue cockade in their hats. The carriage made slow progress, being frequently stopped and searched on its way to the Tuileries

Palace, where the King held court. He had been forced to leave his preferred home at Versailles by a mob of women who thought he should be with his people in the capital where they could keep an eye on him. Lisette was thankful when the carriage drew up in the main courtyard of the palace and she was able to go in search of her brother, followed by the rather nervous Hortense.

There was an air of agitation mixed with despondency in the demeanour of those she encountered as she hurried through the maze of corridors to reach Michel's apartment. People were either hurrying from one place to another or huddled in groups, whispering. They stopped their chatter as she approached and watched her pass without speaking. No one challenged her.

She was admitted to the apartment by Michel's valet, Auguste, who invited her to be seated and went off to tell his master she was there. The room, not one being in the front of the building where the public were admitted, was shabby. Whether that was a sign of the times she could not tell.

'Lisette, what are you doing here?' Michel demanded, emerging from his bedchamber in nothing but breeches and a silk shirt, followed by Auguste with a fancifully embroidered waistcoat into the sleeves of which he was endeavouring to put his master's arms. 'I am about to attend the King. And where is Papa?'

'Papa has been seized by a mob and taken to the prison at Honfleur.'

'*Mon Dieu!* Whatever for?'

'For refusing to remit the taxes he has collected over the years. They seemed to think they had the King's blessing to demand them back. They stole pictures and plates and bottles of Calvados and wrung the necks of some pigeons as well.'

'That's ridiculous, the King would never sanction that. He is not in a position to sanction anything. Since his failed attempt to flee the country, he is no more a free subject than our father.'

Lisette's heart sank. 'I was hoping for his intervention.'

'Not possible, I'm afraid.' Auguste had succeeded in putting on the waistcoat and tying his master's cravat and was now in the bedroom fetching his wig and coat.

'What are we going to do, then? I can't leave Papa to rot in gaol, can I?'

'You could ask the Citizen Deputy for Honfleur to intervene. Let him earn his keep.'

'I did that on my way here. He refused on the grounds that justice must run its course. Is there no one in this benighted country that can do anything but rant and rave?'

Michel was thoughtful for a moment. 'You could try Sir John Challon.'

'Sir John! What can he do?'

'He's English, he might know someone in authority in England who could be persuaded to help, especially since our dear mama was English.'

Sir John Challon was a neighbour and lifelong friend of her father's. He had been a firm supporter of the exiled King James of England and came to France shortly after the abortive uprising of the Jacobites.

'But he's an old man, older even than Papa.'

'What is that to the point if he can summon others to our aid?'

'Then I must return home.'

'Yes, you must, Paris is not safe for you. The outcry against the aristocracy is becoming more vociferous. It does not look good for any of us.'

'But what about you?'

'I stay by my sovereign's side. It is my privilege and my duty.' He was fully dressed now in a blue-satin coat with a cutaway skirt, wide revers and silver buttons. His formal white wig was firmly on his head and his high-heeled shoes put extra inches on his height. He bent to kiss her cheek. 'Go now, sister dear, and God go with you. Let me know how you fare with the Englishman.'

Lisette returned to Villarive more dejected than ever. Her beloved papa was in prison and there didn't seem to be anything she could do about it. She felt somehow that she had failed him, that she ought to have been able to do more. The château when she reached it already had a neglected, unlived-in air. That once-great house was no longer a home and it took all her self-control not to burst into tears.

'We will go and see Sir John tomorrow,' she told Hortense as they unpacked. 'He is our last hope.'

John James Drymore, known to friends and family as Jay, rode into the stable yard at Falsham Hall at the side of his ten-year-old son, Edward.

Behind them rode Anne, who at eight, promised to become the image of her dead mother. He
liked to take them with him when he rode round
the estate; it was good for Edward to learn that
with wealth and property came responsibility and
Anne must learn the gracious demeanour which
was the mark of a true lady.

Jay adored his children, nothing was too good
for them, and he loved his home, but just lately
he had begun to feel unsettled. It might have been
the threat of war with Russia which had made the
government increase the size of the navy and, as
a naval man, he felt he ought to be involved instead of resting on his laurels in the quiet Norfolk
countryside. Or it might have been the calamitous
events in France, which had everyone worried
whether such a thing could happen in England.

He handed his white stallion to the care of a
groom and left the children looking after their
own ponies and went indoors. The house was not
large, but solidly built, with spacious lofty rooms
downstairs and deep windows which let in the
sun. The furniture was, like the house, solid and
useful. The wide stairs were made of oak and led
to half-a-dozen bedrooms on the first floor and

servants' quarters above them. The household was perfectly managed by his housekeeper, Mrs Armistead, and a small army of servants; he was not necessary for its smooth running.

The children were another matter. Since their mother's death three years before, he had made a point of spending as much time as he could with them. It was a time he valued, but was it enough to keep his mind and body occupied?

He had hardly divested himself of his riding clothes and dressed in a plain suit of fawn silk when he heard the sound of carriage wheels on the drive below his window. He looked out to see his father's travelling carriage pulling to a stop outside the front door. He slipped his feet into buckled shoes and ran lightly down the stairs, just as a footman admitted his parents.

'Mama, Papa, I did not expect you. Is something wrong at Highbeck?'

'No, all is well there,' Lord Drymore said. 'We have come on another matter.'

'Then come and sit down and I will have refreshments brought in.' He turned to give the order to the waiting footman before leading the way into the withdrawing room. His parents settled on a sofa and he seated himself opposite them. 'Now, what's afoot that brings you over here without warning? Not that I am not pleased to see you, you know you are welcome at any time.'

'As you are at Blackfen Manor,' his father added.

'We have had a letter from my father,' his mother put in. 'He hasn't written to me since poor Mama passed away and then it was only a letter of condolence, but now it seems he is wishing to leave France.'

'I can hardly blame him for that,' Jay said. 'Is he asking if he might be pardoned?'

Amy laughed. 'I rather think he is taking that for granted. What he is asking is a little more complicated. He has a friend, the Comte Giradet, who has been thrown into prison by the mob for not giving in to their demands and his daughter is distraught that he might lose his life. He requests help from us in securing his friend's release and getting all three out of France.'

'He has apparently heard that others have been helped in that way by some Englishmen,' James added with a laugh. 'It seems the Piccadilly Gentlemen's fame has spread to the Continent.'

'I thought you were going to wind up the Society,' Jay said. 'After all, you are none of you as young as you were when you started it. How long ago was that?'

'It was just after you were born in '54. And you are right, it has had its day, but recently Harry Portman and some of the younger ones have kept its spirit of adventure alive. They have been over to Paris to help those being persecuted by the new regime to escape, but Harry's wife has finally persuaded him to retire after the narrow squeak they had when they were there the last time.'

'Lord Portman knew Grandmother Challon well, did he not?'

'Yes, they trod the boards together.'

'Did he ever meet my grandfather?'

'Once, I believe. I recall he had little sympathy for him.'

'He is my father, after all,' his mother put in. 'And I think he should be helped to come home. I am sure no one thinks he is a threat to the monarchy now.'

'Then your visit is to ask me to go to France.'

'Would you?' Amy's voice was a plea which was hard to resist. 'The children can come and stay with us while you are gone.'

'You can take the *Lady Amy*,' James added. 'It will save having to take the Dover packet and you can sail directly to Honfleur.'

Lord Drymore had never quite abandoned his love of the sea and had bought the yacht to sail up and down the coast and make an occasional trip to France before the troubles began. Jay and his siblings had also used her to take their children on pleasure trips, so the vessel was always kept seaworthy and the crew on call. She was moored at King's Lynn, only a day's ride away.

While servants came in with the refreshments and his mother took over the serving of them, Jay considered the proposal. It might very well furnish the antidote to his *ennui* and he had a curiosity to meet the grandfather after whom he was named and who had been exiled in disgrace the year he had been born. 'What do you know of this Comte Giradet?'

'Nothing but what Sir John tells us in his letter,' his father answered. 'He is a third-generation seigneur who has always treated his people well. His estate is at Villarive, not far from Honfleur. He is a widower whose home is managed by his unmarried daughter. There is a son, too, who is in the service of King Louis.'

'Can he not help?'

'Apparently not. The King himself is virtually under house arrest.'

'The people of France are becoming more lawless every day,' Amy said. 'We cannot leave Papa to their mercies.' She was naturally thinking more of her father than the unfortunate Comte and his daughter. 'He is an old man and should be enjoying his declining years in the bosom of his family. I am sure that old misdemeanour is long forgotten.'

'Of course I will go.' He did not need to think twice about it. His parents had always stood by him, even when he had gone against their advice and made himself the subject of gossip; he would do anything for them. 'Shall you take the children back with you now?'

'Yes, if it is convenient. Where are they?'

'I left them grooming their ponies.' He rang a bell on a table at his side and a footman appeared almost at once. 'Fetch the children here, if you please,' he said. 'Then tell Cook there will be two extra for luncheon and after that, send Thomas to me.'

'Will you take Thomas with you?' his mother asked.

Jay laughed. 'I think not. He will be forever worrying me about the cut of my coat and tweaking my neckcloth. I can valet myself. I would rather take Sam Roker if you can spare him.'

'Of course, if he agrees,' James said. 'He will be an ideal choice.'

Having made his decision, the preparations went ahead at lightning speed. Jay, when in the navy, had always been used to packing up at a moment's notice, and it was as if he were back in the service as he issued his orders and explained to the children that he was going away, but they were to stay at Blackfen Manor in his absence. They took this news without a qualm. To them, being spoilt by Lord and Lady Drymore and playing with the cousins who also frequently visited the Manor was a great treat, and they happily set off with Miss Corton, their governess, in their grandparents' coach in the early afternoon.

* * *

Jay had finished his preparations and was instructing Mrs Armistead and his steward about carrying on in his absence, an instruction they did not need, having done it countless times before, when Sam Roker arrived, sent by James.

'Did my father explain why I need you?' Jay asked after they had greeted each other.

'Yes, sir. We're to fetch Sir John Challon and his friends out of the hands of those froggies. Not that I—' He stopped suddenly.

Jay smiled, realising the old retainer was about to commit an indiscretion and say what he really thought of Sir John. 'Will you come?'

'Try keeping me away.' Sam had been in the navy with Lord Drymore when he was a sea captain and had served him ever since, both in an unspecified domestic capacity and as an associate member of the Society for the Discovery and Apprehending of Criminals, popularly known as the Piccadilly Gentlemen's Club. He had known Jay all his life and was allowed a familiarity others would not have dared.

'And Susan doesn't mind?'

'Susan does as she's told,' Sam said firmly.

''Sides, she'd do anything to please her ladyship, as you well know, so we go with her blessing.'

'Good,' Jay said. 'We sail on the *Lady Amy* on tomorrow's tide. Can you be ready?

'I am ready now, Commodore.'

'You can forget the formality of address, Sam. I do not think an English naval officer will be welcome in France at this time. I shall go as a private citizen on a visit to my grandfather and you will simply be my servant, Sam Dogsbody.'

'Yes, sir.' He laughed suddenly. 'It is an age since I went on an adventure for the Gentlemen and longer still since I set foot in France.'

'This isn't being done at the behest of the Gentlemen,' Jay said. 'It is a personal errand.'

'I know, sir, I know. Let us hope we are in time.'

'Amen to that,' Jay said fervently.

Sir John lived in a small villa on the outskirts of Honfleur, a picturesque port on the south bank of the Seine estuary. It had once been a transit point for trade from Rouen to England, but the blockade imposed by Britain had put a stop to that. Perhaps that was why Sir John had chosen to live there; in the early days of his exile it had offered a tenuous link with home. He was an old man and English to boot, but because the locals were unsure what the attitude of the new government was with regard to aliens, he had so far been left unmolested.

Lisette had known him all her life and now felt as if he were her only friend and ally, and though he had not promised he could help free her father, he had written to his daughter and son-in-law on her behalf. 'I think it is about time I went home myself,' he had told her. 'France is a cauldron about to boil over.'

She had called on him almost every day to ask if he had had a reply and each time she had received the same answer. 'Not yet. It takes time, my dear. The wind and tide might not be favourable for the mail packet and my son-in-law might be from home. You must be patient.'

'How can I be patient with Papa locked up? They would not let me see him when I took fresh clothes for him. They inspected them minutely in case I had hidden something in them.'

'And had you?'

'Only a note to say I was trying my best to have him released. It caused some hilarity when the guards found it. If only I could rely on the servants, we might storm the prison and set him free, but they have been drifting away one by one. Of the men, only two of the seven indoor servants are still with me and only the housekeeper and Hortense of the sixteen women. Georges, our coachman, is still with me and still loyal, but as for the rest...' She shrugged. 'They are afraid...' Her voice faded.

'And what would you do if you could set your father free?' he asked her now. 'You could not take him home, they would come for him again and you too.'

'I don't know.'

'There you are, then, we must await help.'

'How do you know there will be help?' She was beginning to give up hope and his complacent attitude was making her tetchy.

Before he could respond, a servant knocked and entered. 'There is a man at the door who says he is from England,' he said. 'Shall I admit him?'

'Anyone from England is welcome,' Sir John told him. 'Did he give you his name?'

'He said it was John Drymore, Sir John.'

Sir John suddenly became animated. 'Then

don't stand there, man, go and show him in at once.'

The man who entered the withdrawing room was exceedingly tall and well built, dressed in a cut-back dark-blue coat, white breeches and stockings and a lighter blue waistcoat. His sun-bleached hair was tied back with a ribbon and he carried a *chapeau-bras* beneath his arm.

'John!' Sir John rose to greet him, a huge smile of pleasure on his face. 'We meet at last.'

The newcomer was about to sweep him a bow, but found himself being embraced instead. He disentangled himself with a smile. 'It is good to meet you, too, Grandfather, but I am known in the family as Jay.'

'I never thought your father would send you to our aid.' Sir John paused in his exuberance. 'You *have* come to our aid?'

'I am at your service, sir.'

Sir John suddenly remembered Lisette, who had been silently watching them, studying the man who had entered. He certainly had an imposing figure and was handsome in a rugged kind of way. He reminded her of Sir John before his hair had turned snow-white. 'Lisette, my dear, this is my grandson, Commodore John Drymore. John, this is Mademoiselle Lisette Giradet.'

Jay gave Lisette a sweeping bow. *'A votre service, mademoiselle.'*

She noticed he had deep blue eyes which raked her from head to foot, as if sizing up the trouble she might cause him. That intense, cool gaze unnerved her a little and she would have been her haughtiest self in any other circumstances, but as she did not intend to be any trouble if he were prepared to help her father, she afforded him a deep curtsy. 'Commodore.'

'Let us not be formal,' Jay said, offering his hand to help her to rise. 'I left the navy three years ago and British naval officers are not exactly welcome in France at the moment. Plain *monsieur* will do.'

Sir John ordered a meal to be prepared and invited Lisette to join them. 'For we have much to discuss,' he said.

Lisette could still feel the pressure of a warm, dry hand on hers, though it had lasted no more than a second or two, but pulled herself together to accept.

* * *

'We will be informal,' Sir John said as they ate. 'You two must deal well together if we are to achieve our aim.' He looked from one to the other, smiling. 'Lisette has been like a grandchild to me, Jay, and has, in part, made up for the fact that I could not be with my own grandchildren.'

'God willing you will soon make their acquaintance,' Jay said.

'Remind me, Jay, how many are there?'

'Four,' Jay said. 'But I am sure Mama has written to tell you of them. I have two sisters, Amelia and Charlotte, both married, and a younger brother, Harry, who is a first lieutenant in the navy. And you have six great-grandchildren, but we must not bore Mademoiselle Giradet with family matters and I need to hear from her the details of her father's arrest and imprisonment.'

Lisette had been taught English by her mother. It was one of the reasons she and Sir John dealt so well together; she afforded him some light conversation in his own language and made him feel a little less homesick. The account she gave of the circumstances in which her father had been hauled off in the tumbril to the gaol in Honfleur was spoken in faultless English. 'I have been frequently to the prison to take delicacies and clothing for my father,' she said. 'They would not let me see him and I am not at all sure the things were given to him. I have tried reasoning with the Public Prosecutor and appealed to our local deputy on the National Assembly, but they will do nothing. Michel, my brother, who is in the service of King Louis, says he cannot help either. Since His Majesty's abortive attempt to flee the country last year, he is a virtual prisoner himself and being watched all the time. Michel is determined to remain at his side.'

Jay had heard of the King's attempt to leave the country, but it was not his main concern at the moment. 'What is the charge against the Comte?'

'So far there has been no formal charge, but nowadays they don't seem to need one. It only takes someone to denounce him as an enemy of the Revolution and he is condemned.'

'Has someone denounced him?'

'I believe Henri Canard has done so. He is a lawyer and the leader of the local peasantry.'

'What has he against your father?'

'Apart from the fact that Papa is an *aristo,* you

mean? Nothing that I know of, but he is an ambitious man and all too ready to use the grievances of the poor for his own ends.'

'It sounds as if you do not think your father will be released as a result of a lawful trial.'

'We are sure of it,' Sir John broke in.

'Then what you are asking is that we break him out of prison and spirit him away.'

'Do you think you can?' Lisette asked. It was a great deal to ask and she was not sure she should ask it, but there was no one else to help them.

'I cannot tell until I have investigated further. If it can be done, I will endeavour to do it, but we will need a careful plan.'

'You are welcome to stay here, that goes without saying,' Sir John said. 'How have you arrived?'

'I used my father's yacht, the *Lady Amy*. It is moored just off the coast. When the Comte is free we can all go aboard and sail for England.'

'You make it sound easy,' Lisette said.

'That part of it is. It is the getting of him out of gaol which might try our ingenuity.'

Lisette, who was well aware of that, gave a deep sigh and pushed her plate away from her, half the food untouched, though Sir John's cook was a good one. 'What do you propose to do?'

'Knowing the layout of the prison would be a good start,' Jay said. 'And the number and routine of the guards. I think tomorrow I will pay it a visit.'

'Under what pretext?' his grandfather asked.

Jay was thoughtful for a moment. 'I am a wine merchant and have bought cider and Calvados to take to England and have some to spare, that is if you can provide me with a few bottles, *mademoiselle*,' he added.

'Of course,' she said. 'A few bottles of Calvados is a small price to pay for my father's liberty, but I have to tell you I have tried that already. The guards take what I bring, but do nothing for Papa. I think I am become a great jest to them.'

'Then they have a strange sense of humour,' he said gallantly, raising his glass to her.

He had all the hallmarks of a chivalrous gentleman, his manners were irreproachable, he smiled a great deal, but it was a smile that did not reach his eyes. Underneath his cheerful demeanour, she sensed a wariness, a kind of distrust she had done nothing to bring about that she knew of. Had he been coerced into what to him was an unwanted errand because his grandfather wished to leave France and his mother was anxious to have him back in the bosom of his family? Was the fact that her dear father was part of the deal abhorrent to him? Or had he simply taken an aversion to her? Well, she did not care! So long as he helped them, she would be polite but distant.

'I will have a case of Calvados ready tomorrow morning,' she said. 'And a carriage to convey us to the prison in Honfleur.'

'You wish to accompany me?' Jay asked in surprise.

'Naturally I do. If you think of a way of freeing my father, I want to be the first to hear of it and do my part to bring it about.'

'You would be wiser to stay at home and wait.'

'I am quite hopeless when it comes to waiting,' she said, laughing. 'Sir John will tell you that. Patience was left out when the angels decided on my virtues.'

'Which I do not doubt are many,' Jay said with that same gallantry he had displayed before. She wondered how he could say all the right things, yet his cold eyes told another story. 'If you insist on coming, then so be it, I only ask that you stay in the carriage some distance away while I reconnoitre. It is not a good idea for the prison authorities to know we are acquainted with one another.'

She did not think they were acquainted at all; it would take more than a conversation over supper to get to know him, to tear down the barrier of ice he seemed to have built around himself. She surprised herself by wondering what he would be like if he were to let a little warmth into his soul. 'I will do as you suggest,' she said meekly.

There was a pause in the conversation while the cloth was removed and several dishes of fruit and sweet tartlets brought in to conclude the meal. When it was resumed, Jay seemed to set aside the business of freeing the Comte and enquired about the latest news from Paris.

'It was in turmoil when I was there,' Lisette said. 'And so dirty and dismal. Everyone is worried what the King's supporters will do next and since the death of Mirabeau, the most moderate of the Revolutionaries and the most popular, there is no telling what the mob might do.'

'I met Mirabeau when he came to England,' Jay

said. 'He seemed anxious to learn about our British democracy.'

'Yes, that is what he advocated for France, but I do not know how much support he had. He maintained that for a government to succeed it must be strong, but to be strong it must have the support of the people, that was why he was so well liked, in spite of his dubious past. Now...' She shrugged. 'Who knows? The political clubs like the Jacobins, the Girondins and the Cordeliers are becoming more influential and extreme. The people are being encouraged to turn their hatred on to the nobility, whether they deserve it or no.'

'Then the sooner we have you and your father out of France, the better,' Jay said.

The evening broke up after that and Jay offered to escort Lisette home, which was only a few minutes' walk away.

Chapter Two

The night was balmy with a slight breeze that did no more than ruffle Lisette's shawl and it was so still they could hear the distant sound of the sea breaking on the pebbles of the river estuary less than a couple of kilometres away. Above them a new moon hung on its back and the stars made a pincushion of the dark sky.

This peaceful country lane gave no hint of what was going on in Paris, the main seat of all the troubles, where the parks had been given over to making arms and uniforms for the army in the war against Austria, where Revolutionaries in red caps manned the barricades at every entrance to the city and stopped people going in and out to search them for contraband or for *aristos* taking money and valuables out of the country, which was strictly prohibited. They could expect no mercy.

She was thankful that Monsieur Drymore had had the foresight to bring his yacht to Normandy and they would not have to brave the mob to leave the country by the usual route from Paris to Calais. Even so, they still had to overcome the guards at the prison and spirit her father safely to the vessel. For that she needed the enigmatic man at her side.

At last he was constrained by politeness to break the silence. 'You speak excellent English, *mademoiselle*.'

'My mother was English. My father met her on a visit to London in '64 and they fell in love on sight. Her parents disapproved. You see, she came from an old aristocratic family and, in their eyes, he was only the grandson of a merchant who thought he could buy his way into the nobility and French nobility at that, which hardly counted.'

'But they married anyway.'

'Yes. She came to live with Papa in France and never went home again. She rarely spoke of her family. She told us Papa and Michel and I were all she wanted and needed, but sometimes I wonder if she was simply accepting what could not be helped and would have liked to be reunited with her parents. It was not to be. She died of a fever she caught when travelling with Papa in India.'

'I am sorry to hear that. Please accept my condolences.'

'Thank you. But I should warn you, it has left my father bitter against the English and he will feel mortified to have been rescued by one of them.'

'But he is my grandfather's friend, is he not?'

'Oh, yes, but Sir John has lived in France so long, he is almost French.'

'I do not think he regards himself in that way. He is anxious to return to his homeland.'

'Yes, I know,' she said with a sigh. 'It is Papa who will be exiled, if we go to England. Their roles will be reversed.'

'The Comte will not refuse to go, will he? I will not force him if he does not wish it.'

'Let us see what he says when we have set him free, but I do not think he will argue. For all his defiance, he is a frightened man. And so is your grandfather, or I miss my guess.'

'What about you?' he asked softly. 'Are you afraid?'

'I would be a liar if I said I was not, but for Papa's sake, I will try to be strong.'

'Methinks you have already shown that you are,' he said. 'But there is a difference between being strong and being foolhardy. I beg you to remember that.' He spoke so earnestly she turned to look at him in surprise, but he was looking straight ahead and she could read nothing from his profile.

'Indeed I will. But tell me about yourself. I know only what little Sir John has told me. Are you married?'

'I was once. My wife died.'

'I am sorry, not for a moment would I add to your grief.'

'It was over three years ago. An accident while I was away at sea.'

'And have you not thought to marry again?'

He looked sharply at her, then turned away again. 'No. Once is enough. I would not put myself or my children through that again.'

'You have children?'

'Yes, Edward is ten and Anne is eight. They are staying with my parents while I am away and making mischief with their cousins, I do not doubt.' His voice softened when speaking of his children, which made her realise this seemingly cold man must have a heart.

'Your parents being the daughter and son-in-law of Sir John?'

'Yes.'

'It must be lovely to have so large a family,' she said, a little wistfully. 'I only have Papa and Michel.'

'Perhaps we could find your English relations for you.'

'I doubt they would accept me. They never once wrote to Mama.'

'But it was all so long ago. My mother is longing to be reunited with Sir John, so why not you and your grandparents?'

'Let us wait and see, shall we?' she said.

They had entered the gates of the château. In the light of a torch set in front of the door they could see the Liberty Tree casting a long shadow across the gravel of the drive. Its leaves had fallen and were scattered on the ground, but the decorations still hung there. 'What is that?' he asked.

She explained it to him. 'I dare not have it taken

down,' she added. 'It will only inflame the mob further and I do not want to make it more difficult for my father.'

'Or be arrested yourself,' he added.

'No.'

They reached the door, which was flung open by Hortense. 'Lissie, I have been so worried about you. You have been so long gone. I should not have let you go alone. Anything could have happened to you.' She glared at Jay as if her anxiety were all his fault.

'I have been perfectly safe with Sir John and Monsieur Drymore,' Lisette said. 'We have been talking of ways and means to free my father.' She turned to Jay. 'Hortense is my maid and she worries about me. I thank you for your escort, *monsieur*. I bid you *bonsoir* until tomorrow.'

She held out her hand to him; he took it and bowed over it. 'Your servant, *mademoiselle*. I will be here at ten o'clock.'

He turned and left them. He did not look back, but heard the door shut behind him. The flame in the torch flickered and died, leaving the drive and the ghostly tree in darkness.

Striding along the country road back towards

Honfleur, he mused about the task he had been set and the woman who asked it of him. She was not what he would call womanly; she was too tall and thin for a start, her features a little too sharp, but her blue-grey eyes revealed intelligence and a stubbornness which might cause problems. He smiled to himself, anticipating squalls. So be it, he was used to squalls and having his commands obeyed.

But could you issue commands to a woman? He knew from sad experience how difficult that could be. Marianne had objected to simple requests, to pleas to think of her children, to consider the consequences of her wilfulness, by simply laughing and going her own way, with tragic results. When she died, it was left to him to tell Edward and Anne, who had loved their mother and knew nothing of the secret and not-so-secret life she led. Naturally he could not say anything of that and they had been broken-hearted at her loss.

Comforting the children and pretending all had been well between him and their mother had been difficult and accomplished only with an effort of will that left him dour and uncompromising—he would not put them or himself through such an experience again. Lisette Giradet had brought the memories back with her questioning and he had found himself resenting it. He shook his ill humour from him; better to concentrate on the task in hand.

Instead of going back to his grandfather's villa, he went to one of the town's hostelries where he had arranged to meet Sam. It was a squalid place, low-ceilinged and dingy, but it had the advantage of being very close to the prison. Sam, who had spent the day exploring, was already there, sitting in a corner with two men in the blue uniform of the National Guard, who were apparently enjoying his hospitality. They had several empty bottles in front of them and were drinking cider from tumblers.

'Ah, here is my friend, James Smith,' Sam said in excruciating French, using the alias they had decided upon. 'Jimmy, this is Monsieur Bullard and Monsieur Cartel.'

Jay shook their hands and sat down, pulling a tumbler towards him and pouring himself some cider. He took a mouthful, made a face of distaste and spat it out on the floor. 'No better than vinegar,' he said. 'Sam, my friend, couldn't you find anything better than this to give our friends?'

''Tis all this Godforsaken place had,' Sam said in English, then added under his breath, 'They are prison guards.'

'What did you say?' Bullard demanded. He was the bigger of the two men and he had a very red face and broken teeth. 'Speak French, why don't you.'

'I am afraid my friend's language skills are not up to it,' Jay explained. 'But I will translate. He is sorry that the Black Horse does not have anything better to offer you.'

'It is good enough. Who are you to find fault with our cider? And how did two Englishmen come to be here?'

Jay laughed. 'Trade, my friends, trade. I buy good Calvados to take home.'

'Smugglers,' Cartel said, laughing. 'Even in these times it still goes on.'

'Yes, more so in these times, when legitimate trade is difficult,' Jay agreed. 'How else are we to drink the good French brandy we are accustomed to? But I will not be taking any of this rotgut back home. I can get much better at the Château Gi-radet.'

'Château Giradet! Why there?'

'I am told it makes the best Calvados in the area and Comte Giradet will sell it to me cheap.'

'What do you know of Comte Giradet?'

'Nothing. He was from home when I called there. I spoke to his daughter, who told me he was locked up.'

'Locked up!' Both Frenchmen laughed uproariously. 'Yes, he's locked up and like to hang when Henri Canard has done with him.'

'Not before I have had time to deal with him, I hope,' Jay said. 'His daughter is disinclined to sell to me without the Comte's consent. She did let me have a couple of cases, but what good is that to my thirsty friends in England?'

'When he is convicted his goods and chattels will be forfeit,' Bullard said.

'Then I must act before that. Tell me, who is in charge at the gaol?'

'We are,' Bullard said.

'Then I have struck lucky.' He looked round and called out to the landlord to bring Calvados to replace the cider. 'You will let me see him, will you not?'

'Hold hard, there,' Cartel said. 'What's in it for us?'

'Money, good sound *louis d'or,* not that new paper money.'

They gasped at this. The gold coins had been withdrawn in favour of the paper *assignat,* and they could not legitimately spend them, although there were always people who would take them. Cartel looked at Bullard and back at Jay. 'It might be done.'

'When are you on duty again?'

'Tomorrow, all day,' Bullard said.

'Then I will come in the morning.' He left his drink untouched and stood up. 'Are you coming, Sam?'

'No, I think I'll enjoy the company a little longer,' Sam said, winking at him.

Jay left him, glad to be out in the fresh air again and, making sure he was not followed, returned to his grandfather's villa.

He found Sir John in his parlour waiting for him. 'How did it go?' he asked.

'How did what go?' Jay was still thinking of the gaolers.

'Your conversation with Lisette. Was anything decided?'

'No. Until I have been to the gaol and seen what we are up against, I can formulate no plan. I have, however, made the acquaintance of two of the gaolers. They think I am a smuggler.' He laughed suddenly. 'But then, I suppose I am, although it is not brandy I'll be smuggling, but people. If the Comte agrees to come, that is. According to Mademoiselle Giradet, he is no lover of the English.'

'You cannot set him free simply to go home or even to go anywhere else in France. He will be picked up again in no time.'

'I know. I am relying on *mademoiselle* to persuade him that he will be welcome in England. There are already hundreds of French *émigrés* making new lives for themselves there, they will not be alone.'

'Lisette is a lovely girl, not the most handsome, it is true, but she is a good daughter and she and the Comte have been good friends to me, exiled as I am.'

'How did that happen?' Jay asked. 'My parents never speak of it.'

'No, they would not.' Sir John laughed. 'I am the black sheep of the family. I dared to side with the Pretender and voluntarily left the country shortly after the '45 rebellion, but when the Young Pretender went to England to try to drum up support I went with him. It was a foolhardy thing to do and the only reason I escaped was because your father and Sam Roker helped me, and that on condition I never showed my face in England again.'

'Sam Roker? You know Sam?'

'Yes. He is the one who saw me safely on board ship.' He chuckled. 'Mind you, he had to knock James out to do it.'

'Why?'

'James was in King George's navy and helping a fugitive would have gone ill for him had it become known. He was only prepared to do it for the great love he had for Amy, but Roker stopped him.'

'Yes, he is a good man, a trusted retainer. I have brought him with me.'

'I fancy he has no great affection for me.'

'Perhaps not, but he will do anything for my parents.'

'Your parents, they are happy together, are they?'

'Very. Mama is one in a million and my father adores her.'

'It has not been an easy exile,' Sir John went on. 'I settled here in Honfleur because so many English merchants used to use the port and I could learn a little of what was happening at home. Now, with the blockade, that doesn't happen and I grow more homesick.'

Jay detected a wistful note in the older man's voice and realised how hard life must have been in France when everyone he loved was in England. No wonder he had been glad of Lisette's friendship. 'Mademoiselle Giradet told me her mother was English.'

'Yes. She was a Wentworth, daughter of Earl Wentworth.' He looked up as a startled gasp escaped from Jay's lips. 'You know the family?'

'I know of them.' Jay pulled himself together. 'Go on.'

'The Earl was furious when she told him she wanted to marry Gervais and live in France. They cut her off without a penny, hoping it would make her change her mind, but Louise was made of sterner stuff.' He chuckled. 'In any case, money was not a problem because Gervais was as rich as Croesus. What he found so hard to bear, and he told me this many, many times, was that she was cut off from a family she had loved, particularly her mother, and though she never complained he knew she felt it deeply. We had that in common.'

'And what about her daughter? Does she feel it too?' The revelation that the woman he had come to rescue was related to the Wentworths had shocked him to the core. He felt again the fury that had engulfed him on coming home from a long voyage to find his wife absent and children alone with their governess. Miss Corton had said her mistress had been gone some days, but she did not know where she was.

'The children have been told she is taking a little holiday with friends,' she had said. It had been left to his mother to tell him the truth.

'I believe she has gone to live with Gerald Wentworth at his home in Hertfordshire,' she had said. 'They seem not to mind the scandal.'

How Wentworth had seduced his wife he did

not know, but the man could not be allowed to go unchallenged. His mother had advised against it, telling him to let sleeping dogs lie, but he had been so furious, he would not listen. The duel had been fought in the grounds of Wentworth Castle, the choice of his opponent and a poor one for him because his adversary's friends and family were there. Nevertheless he was the better swordsman and no one interfered until he was standing over the disarmed Wentworth, sword raised to deliver the fatal blow. He found he could not do it and had walked away in disgust, with the man's threats ringing in his ears.

The gossip had raged for months; a man did not fight a duel and then refuse to deliver the *coup de grâce* when it was within his power. Many laughed at him, others said he was in hiding, fearing Wentworth's revenge for the humiliation, for it was humiliating to lose and be spared simply because one's opponent did not have the stomach to finish it.

None of that was Mademoiselle Giradet's fault, he scolded himself, and ought to have no bearing on the task he had been set. Once he had accomplished it, they need never meet again.

'Lisette?' his grandfather said, in answer to his question. 'A little, perhaps. I can only guess. Like her mother, she does not complain.'

'What about her brother? What can you tell me of him?'

'He is Lisette's twin and has been in the service of King Louis ever since he finished his education, first as a page and then a gentleman of the bedchamber. I believe it took money and influence on Gervais's part to obtain the post for him. After all, they are not the old nobility. It was an unselfish act on the Comte's part; he was devoted to his son and hated parting from him, but he wanted him to make his way at court and encouraged him to go. Michel is loyal to the King and, according to Lisette, would not dream of deserting him. She worries about him, but is convinced the King will be able to protect him.'

'Do you believe that?'

Sir John shrugged. 'Who knows? The King embraced the new constitution and that pleased the people, but then he chose to try to flee, no doubt to drum up foreign support, and that sent his popularity plummeting. He might just as well be in prison himself. I suppose while the legislature

is divided on what to do about him, he is safe
enough and that goes for Michel too.'

'So *mademoiselle* is content to leave him behind?'

'I think it will be hard for her, she and her
brother were close as children, but her first concern at the moment is to free her father.'

'Then we must do what we can to bring that
about.'

'What would you like me to do?'

'Nothing at the moment, except to put your affairs in order and gather together whatever you
want to take to England, but bear in mind we
cannot accommodate large or heavy items; everything will have to be carried aboard the *Lady
Amy* and we must not attract undue attention. I
shall tell Mademoiselle Giradet the same thing.'

'You mean I am to be welcomed back?'

'That is Mama's wish.'

'And it is mine. I will do anything to be reunited
with my daughter. You may count on me.'

Lisette was ready for Jay the next morning, with
the horses already harnessed to the carriage. She
suspected she had been allowed to keep the equi-

page simply because no one had thought to take it from her. And the peasantry would not know what to do with it if they had it. Riding about in a carriage would be far too ostentatious and would bring down opprobrium on their heads. It was fashionable to be poor and dirty even if you were not. In deference to this and so she did not stand out in the crowd, she had donned the plainest gown she could find, a deep-blue cambric over which she had tied a scarf in the bright red of the Revolution. Unwilling to don the Phrygian cap with its Revolutionary cockade, she chose to go bare-headed, tying her thick blonde locks back with a red ribbon.

She met Jay in the vestibule when Hortense admitted him to the house. All the servants except Hortense and Georges had abandoned her. She dipped her knee in answer to his sweeping bow. 'Good morning, *monsieur*. I am ready. And there is a case of our best Calvados in the boot. I hope that will be sufficient.'

'It will do for the moment.' He handed her into the carriage and climbed in beside her. 'We may need more later.'

They settled in their seats for the short ride to

Honfleur. 'I have met two of the gaolers already,' he told her. 'They think I am a smuggler and buying brandy from the Comte to take out of the country. For a bribe, they will let me speak to him.'

'The bribe being brandy?'

'And money.'

'How much money?'

He shrugged. 'I have yet to discover their price.'

'And then they will free Papa?'

'Nothing was said of that. I am simply being allowed to speak to him.'

'Oh.' There was dejection in her voice. Why she had expected more of him, she did not know. To pay large sums simply to speak to him and leave him where he was did not sound like a good deal to her. 'What happens after you have spoken to him?'

'I have not yet decided. It all depends on what I discover.'

'What do you want me to do?'

'Nothing for the moment. I do not want those gaolers to think we are in league with one another, it will make them suspicious. I suggest you do a little shopping after I have left you and then go home and wait to hear from me.'

'Wait! Is that all? I am in such a ferment, waiting will be purgatory. Surely I can be of use?'

'Later, perhaps. You will need money in England, so when you go home, collect up your most valuable items, gold and silver, all your jewellery, nothing too big, and pack it ready. And make sure the horses are fresh. We may need to move swiftly when we do.'

'I will do that. We will not leave Hortense behind, will we?' she asked anxiously.

'Not if you do not overload the coach and she can be ready at a moment's notice.'

'We will both be ready.'

They had arrived at the end of the street where the prison stood and he called to Georges to stop the coach. 'I will leave you here,' he told Lisette. 'Go and do your shopping, buy food as if you were going to be at home for the immediate future.' He took the case of brandy from the boot and the carriage pulled away again, leaving a thoughtful Lisette to continue into the centre of the town.

Jay carried the brandy into the prison and deposited it on the desk in front of Bullard who was busy writing in a ledger. He looked up at

the sound of the bottles clinking. 'Ah, the Englishman.'

'I said I would come. We made a bargain.'

'Let us see the colour of your money first.'

Jay produced six *louis d'or* from his pocket
and put them on the table where they gleamed
golden in a shaft of sunlight coming through a
dusty window. Before leaving London, he had
obtained them from his bank, which had been
taking them from *émigrés* in exchange for sover-
eigns. He guessed the banker was only too pleased
to reverse the process. To these men, they repre-
sented undreamed-of wealth.

Bullard picked one up and bit into it, then he
called Cartel and the other man on duty. 'Seems
he's as good as his word,' he told them, indicating Jay. 'Do we let him have a few words with
the prisoner?'

'Can't see it will do any harm,' Cartel said, gaz-
ing hungrily at the money. 'Philippe can take him
through.'

'I'll have my share afore I do,' the third man insisted, picking up two of the coins and stowing
them in his waistcoat pocket. Then he beckoned
Jay to follow him.

The prison was not large and contained only half-a-dozen cells. No doubt before the Revolution there was comparatively little crime in the town, but now it was full of political prisoners crammed together in squalor. Jay, who considered himself used to poor living conditions from his time in the navy, found himself wrinkling his nose at the smell.

The guard stopped outside one cell and shouted, '*Citoyen* Giradet, you are wanted.'

Nothing happened immediately and then there was a movement among the inmates who parted to allow a frail old man to make his way slowly to the bars. Jay was shocked by his appearance. He was filthy and in rags, his white hair a tangled mass. He had obviously not shaved since his arrest and his beard was lank. It was clear to Jay that he would be too frail to run, or even walk, and that getting him out and away was going to be more difficult than he had imagined.

'Who are you?' the old man croaked.

'My name is James Smith. I am from England.'

'Never heard of you. What do you want?'

'I want to buy Calvados, but your daughter will not sell it to me without your consent.'

The old man's tired eyes lit up. 'You have spoken to my daughter?'

'Yes.'

'Is she well? They have not harmed her?'

'She is unharmed and looking after everything until you can be reunited. But what about the brandy?'

'*Merde,* is that all you can think of, you English, money and your stiff-necked pride?'

'You know nothing of my pride,' Jay snapped. 'But I do have money to exchange for Calvados.'

'*Louis d'or* at that,' the gaoler said with a grin, which told Jay quite plainly that any money handed to the old man would be taken from him.

'My daughter can do as she pleases and she knows it, so why come here to bother me?' Gervais paused, peering up at Jay. 'Unless you have a message from her.'

'Only that she is doing her best.'

'That's enough,' the gaoler put in. 'You have the permission you wanted, the interview is at an end.' He put his filthy hand on Jay's sleeve.

Jay shrugged him off. 'You do not need to manhandle me, man. I am leaving.' He turned back to the Comte. 'I will tell your daughter she may deal with me with your blessing, shall I?'

If the Comte understood what he was trying to say, he gave no indication of it. 'You leave my daughter alone, do you hear me? I won't have her going off with any damned Englishman.'

Jay laughed softly and followed the gaoler back to the office where the other two were already making inroads into the brandy. 'Is that one of the richest men in Honfleur?' he asked, jerking his head back towards the cells. 'He is a sorry specimen if he is.'

'He will be even sorrier before long,' Bullard said. 'His crimes are so great Henri Canard is having him indicted in Paris. We shan't have the pleasure of seeing him hang. He will lose his head to that new contraption they call a guillotine. I haven't seen it at work, but they do say the head lives on minutes after it has been severed from the body.'

'When will he go?' Jay asked, trying not to show his disgust at the casual way the man had spoken. 'I hope it will not be before I have made my deal with the Comte's daughter and taken delivery of the merchandise.'

'We have to wait for the summons from Paris.

Henri Canard has gone himself to get the necessary papers for his transportation.'

'Then I will do my deal as soon as may be and hasten my own departure.' He produced three more gold coins and put them on the table. 'For your co-operation,' he said and left them.

He strode back to his grandfather's villa in a pensive mood. The Comte was barely more than skin and bone and much older than he had imagined. He had assumed that he had fathered Lisette in his twenties and, as she was surely no more than twenty-five or six, then her father would be in his fifties. But he was seventy if he was a day, about the same age as his grandfather. Sir John was hale and hearty, but the Comte looked as though a blow from a feather would knock him over. Had he been like that before he was thrown into prison or had prison itself aged him? How on earth was he to get two old men and a young lady out of France and on a boat to England without one or the other of them collapsing on him?

He found both Sam and Lisette with his grandfather. 'I thought I told you to go home and wait,' he said.

'I did not choose to. I knew you would come back here and I wanted to hear what went on.'

Jay threw himself into a chair. 'Nothing went on. I paid the dues and had a few words with the Comte.'

'What did he say?' she asked eagerly. 'Did you tell him we were going to try to get him out?'

'No, of course I did not. We had an audience.'

'Then it was a waste of time.'

'Not at all. I established that he is going to be sent to Paris for trial. Henri Canard is too impatient to wait for the summons and has gone to fetch it himself.'

'Oh, no! We are lost. We will never get him out of a Paris prison.'

Jay heard the distress in her voice and found himself wanting to reach out to comfort her. The feeling was so alien to him, he was taken aback. He could not allow her to penetrate his reserve—sympathetic to her plight he might be, but that was all it was. Nothing would be achieved by becoming soft. He pulled himself together. 'Pray, do not distress yourself, *mademoiselle*. If I have my way, he will never reach Paris. He will not leave Normandy, except on the *Lady Amy.*'

'You have a plan to break him out before they come for him?' Sam queried, his eyes lighting up.

'I do not think breaking him out is a good idea,' he said thoughtfully. 'There are other ways, but I need more information. I need to know how the Comte is likely to be transported and when.' He turned to Sam. 'Do you think you can continue your comradeship with those gaolers?'

Sam laughed. 'It is a good thing that my understanding of French is a deal better than my speaking of it, then. And I can hold my drink better than most.'

Jay turned to Lisette. 'Now, *mademoiselle,* I will escort you home. You have still to make yourself ready as I suggested and keeping your horses out late is not going to help if we have the call tomorrow morning.'

'I do not need your escort,' she said haughtily, standing up and shaking out her skirt.

'I beg to differ. I will see you safely home and I will repeat my instructions to your maid, then I may be sure they will be obeyed.'

Lisette did not answer, but marched out of the room, head held high. He shrugged and smiled at the other two men and went after her.

They had almost completed the journey in silence when she spoke. 'Do you think it will happen tomorrow?'

Her voice was conciliatory and he smiled in the darkness of the coach. For all her defiance, she was a frightened girl and needed someone to lean on. Well, she could lean on him, that was why he was there, but only for as long as it took to get her, her father and his grandfather to safety. He was doing it because his mother had asked it of him and for no other reason.

'I don't know,' he said. 'But we must not be caught unprepared.'

'I will be ready,' she said quietly.

He almost regretted his defeat of her. He did not like to see her spirit broken, but it was necessary if they were to succeed. 'Good.'

The coach stopped, he jumped out and held out his hand to help her alight. She took his hand and stepped down. 'You wish to speak to Hortense, *monsieur?*'

He smiled. 'Do I need to?'

'No. I will tell her what you have said and Georges will make sure the horses are ready.'

'Then I will bid you goodnight.' He lifted her hand to his lips, then strode away.

Chapter Three

Lisette went indoors. The strain of the last few weeks and especially today had exhausted her. She trusted Sir John, and as Sir John trusted his grandson, she had no choice but to do so too. Jay Drymore was obviously a man used to command and today he had been especially cool and practical, but she wondered how good he was at dealing with the French people whose mood was volatile and bloodthirsty. If anything went wrong with the rescue attempt, his gaolers would not hesitate to kill Papa and the rescuers too. Did the Commodore realise that? *Louis d'or* would not save them.

She found Hortense anxiously waiting for her. 'Lissie, where have you been all day? I expected you home hours ago. It is not fair of you to worry me so. I do believe that Englishman has you in thrall.'

Lisette flung herself down on a sofa. 'That's nonsense. He has come to rescue Papa and it is natural that we need to talk. It is no more than that. Besides, I have not been with him all day. We parted before we reached the prison.'

'I'm glad he had the sense not to take you to that dreadful place with him, but where have you been?'

'I went to the market and bought food and listened to the gossip. The Assembly has taken away all the King's power and there is talk of putting him on trial.'

Hortense gasped. 'Surely they will never do such a wicked thing.'

'Who knows? And they say Marie Antoinette is plotting with the Austrians.'

'I would not put that past her. What else?'

'I heard Henri Canard is going to stand for the legislature at the next elections. His hatred of the nobility is spreading to everyone. I shall be glad to leave, but we have to free Papa first. I went to visit Sir John on the way home. Monsieur Drymore joined us after he had been to the prison. He said there is talk of Papa being moved to Paris for a trial. I think he has a plan to waylay the guards, but he would not tell me the details.'

'Why not?'

Lisette shrugged. 'I do not think he trusts me.'

'Then he is an arrogant fool.'

'No, Hortense, he may be arrogant, that is an Englishman's way, I think, but he is not a fool. He bade me be ready to move at a moment's notice. You may come too, if you wish it. I know it will be a great upheaval for you, so I will not insist.'

'Naturally I will come. Do you think I will let you go without me?'

'Thank you, Hortense. I am so tired, I am going to bed and you must do so too, but tomorrow morning, we must pack.' She rose and together they climbed the stairs where Hortense helped her mistress to bed and then went to her own chamber.

In spite of her tiredness Lisette could not sleep. She found herself going over and over everything she and the Commodore had said to each other, every nuance, every meaningful look, every curt response, every compliment he had paid her, every censure too. None of it helped her to understand him. She had to take him as she found him, a complex individual who was charming one minute and annoying the next. But none of that mattered if he saved her father.

Her thoughts strayed to visions of the rescue. She imagined the vehicle conveying her father to Paris being held up by Jay and his servant at gunpoint, of shots being fired, of people being wounded, perhaps the guards, perhaps the rescuers, perhaps her father. She saw them fighting their way to her coach and driving hell for leather to the coast, pursued on all sides. She saw the yacht rocking on the sea, out of reach, and their pursuers on their heels. And supposing they were all caught, what then? It did not bear thinking about. Surely there was another way.

She had fallen asleep at last, to wake in the morning bleary-eyed and with a bad headache. Hortense gave her a tisane and made her eat some breakfast, after which she felt well enough to pack a few clothes and toiletries in two portmanteaux, then Lisette found a velvet bag and scooped all her jewels into it: necklaces, ear drops, bracelets and tiaras, some she had inherited from her mother, some her father had bought for her. She knew the

French authorities would not take kindly to her taking them out of the country, so she hid them securely in the stuffing of one of the cushions in the carriage.

She had a little money in the house, most of it *assignats* which would be worthless in England, but there was money and stocks held at the bank in Honfleur and she needed those too. 'I'm going into Honfleur,' she told Hortense. 'I need to draw money out of the bank.'

'Do you think that is a good idea, Lissie? It will surely indicate that you are planning to flee and put the authorities on their guard.'

'Monsieur Gascon has been the family banker for years and years, he will not betray me.'

'You cannot be sure of that. Everyone is afraid to have secrets nowadays.'

'I shall say I wish to use the money to pay a lawyer to defend my father and he insists on being paid in cash.'

'If you must, but I am afraid it will not please the Englishman.'

'I think it will please him very much,' Lisette said stubbornly. 'It means I can pay him for his trouble and we will be able to live independently in England and not have to rely on charity.'

'Shall I ask Georges to put the horses to the carriage?'

'No. I have been told they must be kept fresh and ready to go at a moment's notice. I will walk. Besides, a walk will help to clear my head.'

'Then I shall come too.'

Lisette did not object to that and they set off, both wearing plain gowns, bright red shawls and red ribbons in their hair. It was difficult to tell who was servant and who mistress except that Hortense was carrying a shopping basket. The maid deplored the necessity, but if it was the only way to keep her darling safe, then it had to be. They met a few people on the road, but no one exchanged a greeting, nor even a smile.

At the bank, Hortense waited in the vestibule while Lisette went into the bank manager's inner sanctum to make her request.

'My dear *mademoiselle*,' he said. 'I cannot release your father's money to you. It is in his name and only he can withdraw it.'

'But he is in prison.'

'Yes, I had heard.'

'I need it for his defence and that could be costly. Lawyers seem to be able to charge whatever they like these days.'

'If you could visit the Comte and obtain written authorisation from him, then I would be happy to oblige you.'

'They will not let me see him.'

'Then I am sorry.'

'I thought you were my friend,' she said, disappointed and angry. 'You are as bad as all the others. You have done well out of Papa over the years, is that not worth something?'

He looked distressed, but could only repeat, 'I am sorry. I dare not.' He paused, then went on. 'You have a little money of your own your mother left you. You can certainly have that.'

'Then please let me have it in gold coin, *louis d'or* or *ecus,* not *assignat.*'

'I don't know...' He hesitated.

'Please, at least do this for me.'

'Very well.' He went to a safe and unlocked it, then counted out the equivalent of a thousand *livres* which he put into a pouch and handed to her. 'Let us hope you are not robbed of it before you can use it.'

She put it in the pocket of her skirt and tied the red scarf round her waist like a belt with its ends hanging down to disguise the bulk of the pouch, then she bade him good day and left.

'What now?' Hortense asked after she had told her what had happened. 'Home again?'

She did not answer because they had emerged on to the street just as a black carriage bowled past. 'That's Henri Canard back from Paris,' she said, catching a glimpse of the man sitting in it. 'Come on.' She started to hurry after it.

'Where are you going?' Hortense, being plumper and not so nimble as Lisette, was breathlessly trying to keep up with her.

'To speak to him. He might free Papa for a price.'

'You know he won't. He will have you in custody as soon as you blink and then what good will you be to your papa? Leave it to the Englishman.'

'No. I want to avoid bloodshed if I can and what Monsieur Drymore is planning could very well be violent.'

The carriage had gone out of sight, but Lisette knew where the lawyer lived and set off in that direction.

* * *

Canard's house was a substantial one in the middle of the town. The carriage had gone by the time they reached it, but Lisette did not doubt her quarry was inside. Pausing only to catch her breath, she strode up to the door and knocked.

Canard himself answered it. He had a sheaf of papers in his hand, as if he had been studying them. 'Well, well, well, Citoyenne Giradet. And what do you want?'

Lisette prepared to humble herself. 'Please, Monsieur Canard, will you not relent and set my father free? He has not harmed you or the Revolution. He is an old man content to live quietly on his estate, no trouble to anyone. Please let me have him back.'

She had said all this before and it moved him no more than it had the first time. His lip curled in a sneer. 'He is an enemy of the Revolution, plotting counter-revolution. His estate will be forfeit when he is sentenced.'

'But he is innocent.'

'That is for others to decide and you may be sure the verdict will be guilty.'

'Then what will happen to me? I have no other

home and cannot manage without him. I will give you money…'

He laughed. 'Oh, dear me, bribing an official is most certainly against the law.'

'I didn't mean it as a bribe.' She backtracked quickly. 'I meant to pay for his defence.'

'He has no defence. I suggest you find a husband among the good citizens of this town and settle down in humble domesticity. Your father is going to be taken to Paris for trial.'

'Paris?' She feigned surprise. 'Why?'

'His crimes are so great he is to have a public trial in the Palais de Justice.'

'When?' she asked.

'Soon.'

'But I must know when. I must be there to support him. I must find someone to defend him.'

'He will leave here tomorrow morning at dawn. And do not think about trying to set him free because he will be under armed escort.'

'I cannot do that, as you must know, Monsieur Canard, there is no one to help me. My servants have all deserted me.'

He laughed and shut the door in her face. She turned back to Hortense, who had been standing behind her quaking with fear all through the exchange, but far from being subdued there was a light of triumph in Lisette's eyes. 'Good, now we call on Sir John.'

Sir John, Jay and Sam were in conference, sitting over glasses of exceptionally good wine in Sir John's withdrawing room. Jay and his grandfather were dressed as the gentlemen they were, but Sam's appearance was repellent. He was wearing the short trousers of the proletariat, worn-down shoes, a cotton shirt and a bright red waistcoat, all filthy. His hair was a tangle and he was unshaven. He was also a little under the weather, having spent most of the night carousing.

'The guards confirmed that the Comte was to be moved,' he told them, leaving his wine untouched. 'But they did not know exactly when. They are waiting for the summons from Paris. Apparently Henri Canard was too impatient for it to come by the mail and went off to Paris to fetch it in person. He has not returned, at least he had not returned by the time I left about dawn.'

'Then we must watch out for him,' Jay said. 'Well done, Sam.'

'I will have hot water taken upstairs for you to wash and change out of that disgusting garb,' Sir John said. He rang a bell at his side and when a servant appeared, gave the necessary order.

'Oh, and another thing I learned,' Sam went on. 'Henri Canard has a grudge against the Comte. Bullard was unclear about the details, but it goes back generations. It has something to do with the Comte's grandfather and his own grandfather and he is bent on revenge.'

'Then the arrest of the Comte is not political,' Jay said thoughtfully. 'It is a vendetta. Have you any idea how it started, Grandfather?'

'No. I knew Gervais's father, but not his grand-father. He had died before I came to France. I do know that his grandfather had purchased the es-tate and the title. You can—or could—do that sort of thing in France. Perhaps the people resented that, though why Canard would be bothered about it, I do not know.'

The servant returned to say that Sam's bath was ready and that Mademoiselle Giradet had arrived.

All three rose as Lisette entered the room fol-lowed by Hortense. They bowed. Sam muttered,

'Excusez-moi, mademoiselle,' and hurried from the room.

'Lisette, please sit down,' Sir John said, indicating a sofa. 'Would you like some wine? Or coffee, perhaps?'

'You have coffee?' she asked in surprise, knowing the import of coffee and other luxuries from abroad had been banned.

'Jay brought it with him from England.'

'Then I would like a dish of coffee, please.' She sat down and Hortense found a chair by the window where she could look out on to the garden.

Jay studied Lisette while Sir John summoned the servant to order the beverage. The plain clothes she wore were far from chic, but she wore them with a certain elegance which could not disguise her aristocratic bearing. And today she seemed to glow with an inner fire. When he had left her the previous evening, she had been tired and dejected, but now there was a tautness about her, like a coiled spring ready to fly off. Something had happened to bring that about.

'What can I do for you?' Sir John asked her. 'I am afraid we have no more news.'

'But I have news for you,' she said. 'Henri Canard is back and my father is to be taken to Paris early tomorrow morning under armed escort.'

'Tomorrow!' Sir John echoed, indicating to his servant to put the coffee pot and dishes down on a table and leave them. 'We do not have much time.'

'How did you learn this?' Jay asked, as Sir John poured the coffee, which, for those who had been deprived of it, smelled delicious. 'It could be idle rumour.'

'It is not. I learned it from Henri Canard himself not half an hour since.' She paused to drink coffee, making Jay think she was deliberately trying his patience. 'I was in town when he returned and decided I had nothing to lose by asking him once again if he would have my father released, and in the course of the conversation he told me it was out of his hands and Papa was being sent to Paris tomorrow. He waved the papers in my face when he said it.'

Jay was filled with a mixture of annoyance and admiration. For the moment the annoyance won. 'You could have ruined everything,' he said. 'You could have put him on his guard.'

'I am sure I did not,' she retorted. 'He laughed

in my face, knowing how helpless I am. Hortense will vouch for that, won't you, Hortense?'

'Yes, to be sure, he was triumphant, the evil man.'

'Then we do not have a moment to lose,' Jay said, determined not to bend. 'I asked you to pack, *mademoiselle,* and have the carriage ready. I suggest you go home and do that.'

'I have packed two portmanteaux and they are already in the boot of the carriage and my jewels hidden in the cushions and I have been to the bank and drawn out all my money in gold coin. Monsieur Gascon would not let me have Papa's money without authorisation from him.'

'Good God, woman!' Jay exclaimed, really angry now. He wished she was a man; a man he could command, could punish if he was disobeyed, but a woman was another matter entirely. She was as headstrong as Marianne had been and probably as devious. 'Is there no end to your foolishness? Now half the town will know there is something afoot to rescue the Comte. It will make the task doubly difficult, even impossible.'

She had to defend herself. 'Why should anyone know? The bank manager will say nothing, he dare not. What he did was illegal. He is supposed to use all gold coin for the benefit of the state.'

'Jay, calm yourself,' Sir John said. 'We are in possession of information we did not have before, let us be thankful for that and make our plans accordingly.'

Sam entered the room dressed in a brown-frieze coat and breeches, his newly washed hair springing into dark curls. Jay turned to him, laughing. 'You look halfway decent now, my friend. Sit down while I tell you the latest news.' To Lisette he said, '*Mademoiselle,* I am sorry if I spoke harshly. You have done well. Go home now and bring your carriage here after dark tonight. We shall need two vehicles to carry out our plans, one to convey you, your maid and Sir John directly to the *Lady Amy* as soon as it is light enough to see, the other to bring me, Mr Roker and the Comte. Sam, you will go and make sure Lieutenant Sandford knows he has to have the ship's boat on the shore ready to push off the minute *mademoiselle* and Sir John arrive, then it is to come back for us. If we do not arrive within two hours, he is not to wait, but sail for England.'

'Without you and Papa?' Lisette queried, as Sam hurried off on his errand.

'Yes. If a bid to free your father fails, you will certainly not be safe in France.'

'But I cannot, will not, leave without him.'

'Lisette, Jay will bring him to you,' Sir John said. 'Please do not make difficulties.'

'You cannot be sure of that.'

'Nothing is sure,' Jay told her. 'But rest assured, if we do not come, then the chances are we have perished in the attempt.' He smiled to reassure her. 'And believe me, I have no plans to depart this life just yet.'

'What are you going to do?' she asked in a quiet voice.

'Free your father. When and how, I shall decide when Sam has returned from his errand.'

'I will have beds made up for you and your maid,' Sir John said. 'At least you will be able to have a few hours' rest before your journey.'

She finished her coffee and took her leave. Everything was in the hands of the Englishman now and she was not at all sure how she felt about that. She supposed his coolness was an asset in a sticky situation, but she wished he would show just a little warmth. At this moment, she would have given anything for a hug, someone's arms about her to make her feel loved and safe. Good heavens! Whatever was she thinking of?

Jay watched her go. He could not help feeling sorry for her. She must be worried to death and it had been unkind of him to be so brusque with her when all she wanted to do was help. He sincerely hoped that the visit to Henri Canard was the last of such efforts and that she would do exactly as he told her from now on.

He turned to his grandfather. 'You will look after her and make sure she does nothing foolish, won't you? Watching out for her at the same time as trying to deal with her father and the guards is more than I wish to contemplate.'

'Of course I will. She is like a granddaughter to me and if anything should happen to her father, I will be all she has.'

'She has a brother and relatives in England.'

'You can hardly count on them. Earl Wentworth banished her mother and, though he is long dead, I have no reason to think his heirs will welcome the daughter. As for Michel, he will share his monarch's fate, whatever that might be.'

'Are they alike, Michel and Lisette?'

'To look at, yes, like peas in a pod, but I am not sure if they are temperamentally. I do not know the boy as well as I do Lisette. He has not often been home to see his father and sister since he went to court and when he has, I have not always seen him.'

'The Comte is much older than I imagined he would be. There must have been a big age difference between him and his wife.'

'Yes, that was another reason why her family were so against the marriage. He was a bachelor nearer fifty than forty and she was young and lovely and could take her pick of the London eligibles.'

'There must have been a strong attraction between them for her to choose him above others. Were they happy together?'

'Indeed, yes. They adored each other. She kept him young, but the poor man aged suddenly when she died, as if half of him had died too. It is only Lisette who has kept him going for all these years.'

'He was in a sorry state when I saw him, filthy,

unshaven, very thin and weak. I did not say anything to Mademoiselle Giradet for fear of upsetting her, but I hope he is strong enough to transfer from one coach to another.'

'What do you have in mind?'

'I will tell you when Sam comes back. Have you finished putting your affairs in order?'

Sir John laughed. 'I have always been an exile, always hoping that I might return to England one day, and in over thirty years I have not put down strong roots. All I have of any worth—my family—is already in England. I have packed a few clothes and paid all the servants off—generously, I may add—and they will scatter after I have left. I have told the coachman he may keep the carriage and horses after I am safely aboard the yacht and he tells me he thinks he will use it to set up a hire business in another town.' He smiled. 'He will not wish to stay here for fear of being associated with our little adventure.'

'No, I can see he would not.'

'You cannot know how much this means to me, Jay. The prospect of going back to England, and not as a renegade but one of the family, fills me with happy anticipation.'

Jay smiled. 'We have a few hurdles to overcome before that happens. The next twenty-four hours are crucial.'

'I know, but I do not doubt you can do it.'

'I pray I may be worthy of your trust.' He stood up. 'I think I'll take a stroll round the town until Sam comes back. It might give me some ideas. If *mademoiselle* returns while I'm gone, try to reassure her.'

The town was quiet. The trade it had once done had faded to almost nothing and the people were suffering. It was strange that they did not seem to blame the new regime for this, but the King and his nobility. He did not doubt he was not the only smuggler; so far as he could tell there was a lively trade in forbidden goods in and out. The authorities did nothing about that, being more concerned with putting people like Comte Giradet in gaol.

He studied the layout of the town and watched its inhabitants. Most were in the garb of the Revolution, though some were a little better dressed. And there were a few blue-uniformed National Guard patrolling the streets on foot. Occasionally they searched someone's shopping basket, and arrested one old man because he had real tobacco in his pocket. Jay did not see the National Guard as a great threat to his plans—the *maréchaussée* were more of a problem. Employed to keep to law and order, they were mounted and armed, younger and stronger, and would probably provide the escort taking the Comte to Paris.

He left the town and walked along the road towards Rouen, which was almost certainly the route the prison vehicle would take. The wide estuary was on his left, farmland and orchards on his right, which provided little cover for an ambush. He turned and retraced his steps, deep in thought.

Lisette had been all over the château, into every one of its many rooms, touching the remaining furniture and ornaments, her head full of memories. This had been her mother's embroidery frame, that her father's desk, and here were her dolls in the nursery, waiting for the next generation to play with them. There would be no next generation, not here in this lovely home she was leaving for ever, probably not anywhere unless Michel survived to bring up a family. Her father's

valuable library, the important pictures and ornaments her parents had collected over the years, the
carpets and stylish furniture would have to be left
for the mob, who certainly would not appreciate
them. The hundreds of bottles of Calvados in the
cellar would be plundered and drunk by people
with no taste. It was heartbreaking and only the
thought of saving her beloved papa gave her the
strength to endure it.

She had hesitated about writing to Michel to say
goodbye but then decided against it. If the letter
were intercepted, all Jay's plans would be set at
nought and she did not want to tempt his wrath.
She would write to her brother once they were all
safely in England.

It was strange how she had begun to think of the
Englishman as Jay. She supposed it was because
Sir John always addressed him thus and she had
absorbed that. Perhaps once they were in England
and all danger passed, he might become more
human. Why she wanted that to be so, she did
not know, except it was hard to express gratitude
to someone so disdainful of her. Her gratitude
would have to take the form of gold or a piece or
two of jewellery. She pulled herself up; he had yet

to earn it. Tomorrow would be the testing time. God willing, tomorrow at this time, they would all be halfway across *La Manche*.

She fell on her knees in front of the icon in what had been her mother's boudoir and prayed as she had never prayed before. Then she rose and went in search of Hortense, who was talking earnestly to Georges in the kitchen. Lisette had already given the coachman some money and told him that, once she had finished with them, he could take the carriage and horses anywhere he pleased and sell them for what they would fetch. The population was not as equal as their rulers would have them believe; there were still people who rode in carriages, pretending their elevated position in the hierarchy demanded it, men like Henri Canard.

'Time to go,' she said.

They went round the house extinguishing the lamps and candles, made sure the doors and windows were all locked and then left it to its ghosts.

Sam was once again dressed in his filthy clothes and Jay was not looking much better. They had spent the whole evening wandering about the

town, studying its inhabitants and how they re-
acted to the National Guard and the *maréchaussée.*
'I want to avoid bloodshed if I can,' Jay said. 'Better to rescue the Comte by guile than by force
when people might be hurt.'

'You might not be able to avoid it.' Sam had
been on his feet all day and was longing for his
bed, especially as he would have to be up again
before dawn.

'True. But if we had uniforms, preferably
maréchaussée uniforms and horses, it would help.'

'How are we going to come by those?'

'Steal them.'

'Of course, steal them,' Sam said with heavy
irony.

'I noticed there are two of those fellows lodging at the Black Horse and they keep their mounts
in the stable behind the inn. Let us go and drink
some of that excruciating cider and weigh up the
possibilities. If I should be taken ill of a sudden
and have to leave the room, do not be surprised.'

'If you are thinking what I think you are, sir, it
is better I should be ill.'

'No, you have already proved you can tolerate
the drink, while I have done nothing but com-

plain of it. Wait half an hour, then pretend to be concerned and come looking for me. I will meet you in the stable yard.'

The two guards they had met before were in the inn's parlour and greeted them like long-lost friends. Jay did not doubt they expected to relieve them of a little more gold. They sat with them to drink and play cards. Jay hardly touched his cider, but the amount of liquid in his glass went down gradually, tipped on the floor under the table. Nevertheless he seemed to grow more and more intoxicated, until he suddenly dashed from the room retching and declaring he was about to be sick. The rest laughed, ordered more drink and invited another man to take up Jay's hand. The game continued. Sam thought it wise to pretend he did not know how to play properly and lost a great deal of the money the Commodore had given him for the purpose.

Half an hour later, he declared they had cleaned him out and he had better go and find out what had happened to his friend. 'He's no doubt sleeping it off somewhere,' he said, regretfully leaving the pot of *billets de confiance* and *assignat* in the middle of the table.

He found Jay in the yard, carrying a heap of clothing and leading two saddled horses. He handed one of the bundles and one set of reins to Sam and together they crept out on to the road and, once clear of the inn and out of earshot, mounted up and rode out of town.

'What happened to the fellows these belong to?' Sam asked.

'Securely gagged and tied up in their beds and the door locked.' He threw a key into some bushes as he spoke. 'I do not suppose anyone will disturb them before breakfast time, not even then if we are lucky. By that time we will be on our way.'

Sam chuckled. 'I did not realise thieving was one of your accomplishments, sir.'

'All's fair in love and war.'

'And which is this, love or war?'

Jay looked sharply at him and decided not to reprimand him. 'It feels like war. I hadn't realised until tonight how much I missed the excitement of it.' He paused to chuckle. 'Not that I ever had to steal a man's clothes before.'

'Do you think they'll fit?'

'Good God, man! Did you think I had time to pick and choose? They will have to do.'

'Where are we going?' Sam asked as they rode out of the town and took the road to Rouen.

'There's a barn just along here. I noticed it this afternoon. We'll lie up there. Tomorrow is going to be a busy day and if all goes well, we shall spend our next night at sea.'

'Amen to that,' Sam said fervently, following Jay into the barn and dismounting.

The next minute he had thrown himself down on a pile of straw and was soon snoring. Jay joined him on the straw, but lay wide awake, going over every move they would make the next day again and again, trying to foresee the pitfalls, deciding how to overcome them. If his grandfather and Lisette failed to reach the rendezvous with the boat, they could not leave; if Georges did not arrive at his allotted place and time with the Giradet carriage, they could be in trouble. They would have to take the prison van down to the shore and that would be cumbersome and slow and attract unwelcome attention. There were so many things that could go wrong and he had to rely on others doing their part.

In the navy he had known he could command obedience, but could you command obedience from coachmen like Georges, who owed him no allegiance and saw the Revolution as a way to set him free? Or from a young lady with strong views of her own and a reluctance to leave France's shores without her father?

Lisette was like no other woman he had ever met. She was a strange mixture of the *ingénue* and the worldly-wise, which was somehow penetrating the hedge he had grown around himself and he was not sure he wanted that to happen. It was far too disturbing.

He woke Sam before dawn and they donned the uniforms; his was too small and Sam's too large, but they would have to do. Then he sent Sam down the road to watch out for the prison van. He hoped Lisette had been right about the time and it would be along soon and that the papers he had stolen along with the uniforms would be enough to persuade the guard to hand the Comte over to him. This waiting about was the worst part. It was already daylight and he wondered if the prison authorities had changed their minds or found the two guards and put two and two together. He had been banking on the prison van setting out before that happened.

The sun rose high in the sky and still there was no sign of it. Had he been wrong and it was not on this road at all? He didn't fancy chasing after the van all the way to Paris. He didn't fancy going to Paris. Lisette and his grandfather should be on board the *Lady Amy* by now, waiting for him. He had given instructions that the boat was to wait no longer than two hours for him, not even that if there was trouble. It was going to be tight, very tight.

Chapter Four

The portmanteaux, those of Lisette and Hortense and another belonging to Sir John, together with the jewel-stuffed cushion, had been transferred from Sir John's carriage to the ship's boat and Lieutenant Sandford was waiting to help the passengers into it. Lisette was reluctant to comply. She stood on the beach looking inland, waiting for a glimpse of her carriage arriving with her father on board. There were one or two people on the road above the beach and a cart wending its way into town, but no sign of the carriage.

'*Mademoiselle,*' the lieutenant said, 'I must insist you allow me to help you into the boat now.'

'Let me wait a little longer.' It was not the first time she had said that; it had been repeated at intervals ever since they had arrived on the foreshore and each time her worry increased. What had happened? Had Monsieur Drymore failed? Had the plan backfired and everyone been taken back to the prison? Had they even left the prison? Or, God forbid, had they all been killed? She could not stand still and kept going back towards the road and then returning to the boat in increasing despair.

'I cannot,' the lieutenant said. 'The Commodore's orders are to come back for him and he will be mightily displeased if he arrives and I am still here with you. The boat is small, it cannot accommodate everyone in one trip.'

'Then take Sir John and Hortense and leave me here to wait.'

'I won't go without you,' Hortense said.

'Lisette, you will put the whole operation in jeopardy,' Sir John said. 'We must follow Jay's instructions to the letter or all will be lost. He will be in a great hurry, perhaps pursued by guards, and the boat must be waiting for him. If it is not, how is he to get your father to safety?'

His words went home. With a last despairing look towards the road, Lisette turned and allowed herself to be helped aboard, followed by Hortense and Sir John. The lieutenant did not need to tell the two oarsmen to cast off, they were already pulling away when he scrambled in behind them. Lisette continued to gaze towards the receding shore as they were rowed away from the land of her birth and from her beloved father. Tears were streaming down her face and she could not stop them. No one tried to comfort her. The men did not know how and Hortense was sobbing herself.

'They're on the way at last.' Sam came back into the barn where Jay was waiting with the horses. He had begun to think their plan had failed and they would have to return to Honfleur to find out what had happened and that meant the *Lady Amy* would sail without them. How, then, could they free the Comte and return to England? Never having been one to give up on an enterprise, it did not occur to him to abandon his mission and make for the shore and the safety of his yacht. 'They will be here in a couple of shakes.'

'How many?'

'A driver, two mounted National Guard and whoever is in the van.'

'Are they the guards we know?'

'I could not tell from the distance. We might have a fight on our hands if they are.'

'So be it. Are your pistols primed?'

'Aye, aye, sir.'

'Then let us go and meet them, but do not fire unless you have to. I want this done without bloodshed and without the guards knowing we are English.'

They trotted down the road and Jay held up his hand to stop the vehicle, which was no more than a lumbering old coach with its windows blacked out. 'You have taken your time,' he said, thankful the guards were strangers. 'We thought to meet you on the road long before this.'

'Why, what's amiss?'

'You have the *ci-devant* Comte Giradet there?'

'Yes. What do you want with him?'

'We have been sent from Paris to take him to the Palais de Justice.' He took a sheet of paper from his pocket and held it up, but did not offer it to the guards. 'Here are our orders.'

'We don't know anything about that,' the older of the two said. 'Take him to La Force prison, that's was what we were told. Nothing was said about being met.'

'I cannot help it if your superiors forget their instructions,' Jay said.

'It is hardly to be wondered at,' the second guard put in. 'The *maréchaussée* who should have been bringing him failed to turn up for duty. We were told to bring him at a moment's notice, not even given time to tell our wives.'

'You will be relieved not to have to go all the way to Paris, then,' Jay said, putting the paper back into his pocket. He was tempted to look into the coach, but decided against it in case the Comte recognised him and gave the game away. 'Who is in with the prisoner?'

'No one.'

'You were not afraid he might escape?'

They both laughed. 'He would not get very far,' the older one said. 'He is an old man and too feeble to run. You will be lucky if he does not expire before you reach Paris, then all this fuss will have been for nought.'

Jay risked a quick peep at the old man; it would be a terrible blunder to rescue the wrong man, but it was undoubtedly the Comte who was leaning back with his eyes shut. He hardly seemed to be aware that the coach had stopped; he certainly showed no interest in what was happening in the road. His condition had deteriorated since the few days since Jay had seen him in prison and that worried him. They had to move fast, because once the guard returned to Honfleur the cry would go up and they would be pursued. He hoped fervently the Comte could withstand the jolting.

'Off you go back to your wives,' Jay told the guards. 'No doubt they will be pleased to see you.'

They hesitated, but Jay's air of authority, their disinclination to go the distance to Paris and the thought of returning home to a hot dinner finally persuaded them. They turned back the way they had come.

Jay and Sam turned their horses to ride alongside the vehicle. 'On you go, driver,' he said to the coachman.

'Pity you didn't bring a driver too,' he grumbled as they set off at the pace of a snail. Jay knew he could not hurry; the guards were watching them go and, until they were out of sight, they must continue on the road to Rouen.

'Faster,' he told the driver when the old guards had disappeared from sight. 'We will be a month of Sundays getting to Paris at this rate.'

The driver cracked his whip over the horses' backs, but they were old and skinny and although they tried, the pace hardly increased. Jay hoped and prayed Georges and the Giradet carriage had waited. It was long past the time they had expected to make the rendezvous.

Thankfully the sea was calm and the yacht rode easily at anchor. The rowing boat which had brought Lisette on board had gone back to the shore to wait for the rest of the party. She could see it on the beach, rocking on the slight swell.

'Take this, miss.' Lieutenant Sandford offered his telescope. 'You will be able to see better.'

She put the glass to her eye. The two sailors in the boat were resting on their oars. A few people moved up and down the beach, picking up shells and seaweed. There was traffic on the road, horses, carts, an odd carriage or two, but not the longed-for carriage. 'How long will they wait?' she asked. She had been standing at the rail, refusing to go below, for what seemed hours.

'The Commodore said two hours after the appointed time, but it has already been longer than that. I shall have to recall the men soon, before they begin to attract unwanted attention. We cannot afford to lose two of our crew, quite apart from causing a diplomatic incident. In the present unsettled situation it could even lead to war between our two countries. At the moment we are supposed to be neutral.'

'I wish I had not allowed myself to be persuaded to come aboard. I feel as though I have abandoned my poor father. I shall be miserable not knowing what has become of him. It would be better to share his fate.'

'I understand, miss, but I have my orders.'

'But you would not leave without the Commodore, surely? How will he get home if you leave him?'

'No doubt he will find a way.'

She was reminded of his words: *if we do not come, then the chances are we have perished in the attempt.* It did not bear thinking about. 'Just five more minutes,' she said.

'The Commodore will skin me alive if I disobey him. I shall already be in trouble for waiting so long.' If he, too, thought of the dreadful possibility that they were all lost, he did not voice it. He beckoned to a sailor who was carrying a small flag. 'Call them back, Sadler.'

The man raised the flag.

'Wait!' she shouted, scanning the shore through the telescope. 'There is a carriage on the road. It looks like ours.'

The rowers had already taken a few strokes from the shore. She watched in dismay as the coach stopped, two people got down from it and lifted something from the interior. It looked like the Commodore and Mr Roker, but the bundle they were carrying? Surely that was not her father? Was he ill? Wounded?

They waded out to the boat, which had stopped and waited for them, just as two *maréchaussée* galloped up and began shooting. With her heart pumping, she watched as the two men with their burden tumbled into the boat with shots spattering all round them. Not until they were out of range did she let her breath go.

Slowly they approached until they bumped against the hull. By leaning over the rail she could see down into the boat. Surely the bundle at the bottom was not her father?

'Send the chair down.' Sam Roker was standing up, steadying himself by hanging on to the ship's ladder hanging over the side. 'The old man cannot climb and the Commodore is wounded.'

Lisette was politely ushered to one side as a chair was lowered from a hoist and slowly, inch by inch, it brought her father to the deck. It *was* her father. This emaciated man, with the snow-white hair and beard and hands like claws, was really Papa. She watched as the chair was set down on the deck and then ran to kneel at his feet, eyes streaming with tears. 'Papa. Oh, Papa! Thank God you are safe.'

The seamen were going to send the chair back for Jay, but before they could do so he appeared at the top of the rope ladder, pulling himself up with his right arm. The left hung uselessly at his side. The sleeve was ripped and covered in blood. 'Set sail before we lose wind and tide,' he commanded, though it was an effort to speak. 'I am going below. See to the Comte's comfort.' Helped by Sam, who had followed him on board, he staggered away, leaving Lisette to help her father.

'Michel?' he queried. 'Is he with us?'

'No, Papa, he is still with the King. I have seen him and he is well.'

'He is a good boy.'

'Yes.'

It was always Michel he thought of first, she mused as two sailors carried him down to a cabin set aside for him, not a word about how she had managed in his absence.

Only when he had been comfortably ensconced in his cabin, had been given a light repast, which she fed him spoonful by spoonful, and he had fallen asleep did she go in search of Jay. By that time the land had disappeared and they were sailing north east with a fair wind.

Sam let her into the cabin where Jay lay propped up in a bunk that seemed too short for him. The servant had stripped off his coat and shirt and bandaged his upper arm and shoulder. His broad chest was bare. '*Mademoiselle,* you should not be here,' he said as Sam disappeared. 'It is hardly proper. I am not dressed.'

She ignored this objection and, looking round, saw a stool which she pulled to the side of the cot. She realised as soon as she sat on it that it made her even nearer his bare chest. She had never been close to a man in that stage of undress before and became almost mesmerised by the narrow thatch of dark hair that started just below his throat and disappeared into the top of his breeches. It was having a strange effect on her breathing and making her feel hot. She forced herself to look up into his face to meet quizzical blue eyes.

'I had to come to thank you,' she said, making herself sound calm. 'There are no words to express my gratitude.'

'Then do not try.'

'I must. Without you, Papa would surely have died, if not at the hands of the court, then of neglect and starvation. I do not know how I shall ever repay you.'

'I want no payment, Miss Giradet. How is your father?'

'He is very weak and confused and I am not sure if he knows where he is, but your men have provided food and drink and I helped him to eat.'

'Good. We must build up his strength.'

'I am hopeful that with careful nursing and good food he will recover and be his old self.' She paused to look at him, though doing so brought the warmth back to her face and made her tremble. Beneath his tan, his face had a greyish look.

'But you have been hurt. I would not have had that happen for worlds. According to Monsieur Roker, if you had not been protecting Papa with your own body he would have been killed, which makes me doubly in your debt.'

'It is nothing but a scratch. Sam dug the ball out of me and I think I will live.' This last was said with a wry smile which turned to a grimace when he tried to move.

'Are you in great pain?'

'No, a little discomfort, that is all.'

She stood up to reach across him to make his pillow more comfortable and found her face inches from his. It would be so easy to put her lips to his in a kiss. The thought flitted across her brain and vanished, but she saw, by the look in his eyes, that he had read her mind and was amused by it. She sat down again quickly and tried to compose herself. Talk, she admonished herself, say something, distract him, distract yourself.

'If anything I have done has made matters worse for you, then I am truly sorry,' she said, averting her gaze from his. 'But tell me what happened. You were so late coming I was afraid everything had gone wrong and you had all perished.'

He told her about stealing the uniforms and the long wait and the confrontation with the guards and the Comte's struggle when they realised they would have to manhandle him from one coach to the other because he had grown too weak to walk. 'We were dressed as *maréchaussée* and he thought we were taking him out to kill him,' he said. 'Your coachman calmed him and he consented to being put in his own carriage. We set off for the rendezvous at a fierce lick and for once I hoped my orders had been disobeyed and the boat had waited.'

'It very nearly did not. I was in despair.' She had calmed herself enough to look at him again. The steely look seemed to have gone from his eyes. Perhaps it was difficult to maintain when you were in pain. But the pain had been there before the coldness, she realised with a sudden flash of insight. She wondered what had caused it and remembered it was not so long since he had lost his wife.

'We were pursued by the owners of the uniforms we were wearing,' he went on slowly. 'I had locked them in a room at the inn near the prison, but they must have managed to spit out their gags and raise the alarm. Once they had been let out they would soon have found spare clothes and set off in pursuit. I knew it would happen, but I thought we would have time to effect the rescue and be on our way before they could catch us, but everything took longer than I expected.' The long speech had been an effort and he stopped to catch his breath. 'But all's well that ends well.'

'But it is not at an end, is it?' she queried. 'France is still suffering, King Louis and his Queen are still being vilified and my brother is still in the thick of it.'

'I regret I cannot, for the moment, do anything about that.'

It was meant to be a joke and she dutifully laughed. Was this stiff Englishman capable of humour after all? 'I think it would take more than one or even two brave Englishmen to remedy the situation in France,' she said.

'No,' he said wryly. 'But perhaps three or four might do it.'

She stood up, still smiling at his little sallies and wishing she could make him see how very grateful she was. She wished she could heap all her jewels and money on him, but that would leave her and her father impoverished. Besides, she felt sure he would be affronted. 'I will leave you to rest now and go and see how my father is.'

His right hand lay on the cover of the bed very close to her hand. On an impulse she picked it up and pressed her lips to the palm. 'Thank you,' she said and fled.

He lay there, looking down at his hand as if it did not belong to him. What, in heaven's name, had prompted her to do that? He came to the conclusion she was simply overwrought, and who would not be, given the circumstances? She would be able to relax now the danger was past and look after her father. What would the pair of them do when they landed in England? How much money did they have? Could they maintain themselves? Did they have friends they could go to? Or would they throw themselves on the mercy of Earl Wentworth?

The Earl was not the one who had banished his daughter—he had long gone—but his son and presumably Lisette's uncle. Jay hoped that if Lisette appealed to him, he would be welcoming. Why was he bothered? He had fulfilled his task and brought them out of France—did they expect anything more? But the fact that she was related to the Wentworths could not be banished from his mind. Did wickedness run in families?

He was tired of lying idle, in danger of letting the past overwhelm him. He needed a distraction. He shouted for Sam, who appeared almost immediately. 'Yes, sir?'

'Get me a clean shirt and coat. I'm getting up.'

'Sir, I don't think—'

'I did not ask you what you thought, Sam, I bade you find me clothes.'

'Aye, aye, sir.' Suitably admonished, Sam did as he was bid.

Jay sat up and swung his legs over the side of the cot and looked at his crumpled nether garments. 'Breeches, too, I think. These have got blood on them.'

The breeches were changed for another pair in dark blue and a clean shirt, being loose, was easy to put on, but the coat was another matter. It was tailored to fit and it would not go over the bandage and trying to force it was a painful business.

'I knew you should not try to dress,' Sam said. 'Lieutenant Sandford is easily able to sail the ship.'

'Of course he is. It is what he is paid to do,' he said sharply. 'I do not mean to take over from him, but I do not like to be below decks when we are under sail. It feels wrong. The weather is warm, I will go without a coat. Pray tidy this cabin while I am away.'

'Aye, aye, sir.'

Jay went on deck and stood breathing in the salty air. It was like being back in the navy, except the ships he had commanded in the service were considerably bigger than the *Lady Amy*. His father was not normally extravagant, but in this instance he had been; though small, the yacht was luxuriously appointed for passengers. Lisette and Hortense would be comfortable in the main cabin and the Comte and his grandfather sharing a slightly smaller one.

He paced the deck, noting the crew were going about their duties cheerfully and efficiently. All sails were set and they were tacking into a wind on their starboard side. Lieutenant Sandford approached him. 'We should reach the Kent coast by dark, sir. Do you wish to put in at Dover? The tide should be with us at dawn.'

'I think not. Carry on round the coast to Lynn,

as long as the wind is fair. We will be home all the sooner.'

'I wondered if the passengers might wish to go to London.'

'The Comte is not fit to go anywhere with only his daughter to help him. If they want to go to the capital, then it will be after the Comte has recovered some of his strength at Highbeck.'

'Miss Giradet might not wish to be so far from London and her compatriots.'

That had not occurred to him; few people refused an invitation to Blackfen Manor. His mother's hospitality was legendary. 'I will speak to her about it.'

He returned to the lower deck and knocked on the door of the Comte's cabin, guessing she would be with her father.

Lisette, who had been sitting beside her father's bunk watching him sleep, rose and went to the door to find Jay standing there in breeches and a shirt. He wore no coat, cravat or headgear. His injured arm was strapped across his chest underneath the shirt, the empty sleeve of which hung at his side. He was a little more covered than he had been when she had visited him in his cabin, but he still brought the heat rushing to her cheeks at the memory of what she had done. Kissing his hand like that was the act of a wanton, as if she were throwing herself at him, when in truth it was simply that she could not find the words to express her gratitude.

After rushing from his cabin, she had shut herself in with her father to calm herself and decided she would have to try to avoid Jay Drymore until they landed and parted, but in the confines of a small ship that was going to be difficult unless she stayed in her cabin. Even that would not work, because he could come to her. Here he was, looking at her as if nothing had happened, making her heart beat too fast for comfort.

'Papa is sleeping,' she whispered.

'Then perhaps it is a convenient time to take a turn on deck.' He kept his voice low. 'I wish to speak to you.'

'Oh.' Was he going to mention it? Had he taken that kiss as an invitation and was here to claim his reward? Or was he going to tell her he was disgusted with her? 'I do not think I should leave Papa. He might wake…'

'I will ask my grandfather to bear him company and I will not keep you above a few minutes.'

There was no help for it. She stepped into the passage and closed the door gently behind her. He followed her up the companionway on to the deck where they found Sir John standing at the rail, looking for his first glimpse of England. He readily agreed to go down and sit with his friend.

'Now, shall we take a walk about the deck?' he said. 'The sea does not make you feel ill?'

'Not while it is calm.'

'You are comfortable in your cabin?'

'Yes. I had not realised a small vessel such as this could be so well equipped.'

'It was built to my father's design. Have you made many sea voyages?'

'I used to go with my parents when Papa went trading, but not for many years. My mother's death hit him hard and he would not leave Villarive.' The conversation was so normal, so unexceptional, an exchange of pleasantries, no more, but it was an effort on her part. She was waiting with trepidation for him to state the true reason for wanting to speak to her. It was not to discuss voyages and trade, she felt sure.

'I understand.'

'Yes, of course. You have suffered loss yourself.' Now she was becoming personal and that she had never intended. Since the advent of Jay Drymore in her life, she had started to speak and act without thinking and she did not seem able to cure herself. 'I am sorry. I did not mean to remind you.'

'Do not keep apologising, *mademoiselle,* or thanking me. There is no need for either.'

'Oh.' Now he *was* referring to that kiss. As a rebuff it could not have been more plain. She wished the deck would open up and cast her into the sea, she felt so mortified.

'I wish to know your intentions,' he said, apparently impervious to her discomfort. 'When we reach England, I mean.'

'Intentions?' Oh, this was dreadful. What did he expect her to say? Did he think she was asking him to…? Oh, no, she could not. Somehow she managed to regain her composure and stiffened her spine. 'My intentions are my own affair.'

'Of course.' He bowed stiffly. 'You do not have to tell me of them, but it has been pointed out to me that you might wish to go to London and in that case, we will need to put in to Dover, or alternately sail round the Kent coast and up the Thames. At least that way, your father would be saved an uncomfortable ride in a public coach, but it would take longer.' He paused while she wondered what was coming next. 'I have to tell you I am reluctant to do either because the Comte is so frail. He requires careful nursing and time to recuperate and I am sure my mother would welcome you both at Blackfen Manor. There is ample room and he will be able to regain his strength in the peaceful surroundings of Highbeck.'

Her whole body sagged. Why was this man constantly surprising her? He must have a disgust of her and yet he was so concerned for her father he would overlook that and continue to help them. If she accepted, she would be even more in his debt. And she would see even more of him. Did she want that, considering she was always embarrassing herself—and him?

'I do not live at Highbeck,' he said, as if he could read her thoughts, which disconcerted her even more. 'My estate is a few miles distant. You will not be bothered by me.'

'Bothered by you, sir? Why should you bother

me?' She spoke more sharply than she intended. 'I fear I am more of a bother to you. You have exceeded all that could have been expected of you to rescue Papa from almost certain death and been wounded in doing so. We are alive and free because of you.' She paused and gulped hard. 'If my father were well, I would say that was more than enough, but as you are right and he needs to recuperate, I will be pleased to accept your offer to go to Highbeck for a short while, always providing your parents will have us.'

'Good. I will give orders to Lieutenant Sandford to bypass Dover and sail round the coast to Lynn. The wind is favourable at the moment and we should make good time.' He bowed and left her.

She continued to stand at the rail, watching the sea glide past the hull. Behind her was France and the life she had known, where until recently she had lived in luxury, helping her father manage the estate, at peace with those around her. Before her was the land of her mother's birth, a land she had never visited and knew nothing about. Would they be made welcome? Her father would never approach her mother's family, she knew that. Could they make a new life for themselves? Where? That question had been occupying her ever since she came on board. They would have to husband their resources, because the gold and jewels she had brought out of France were all they had. Jay had taken that worry from her, at least for the time being.

She would write to her brother and tell him what had happened and maybe he could arrange to sell some of the artefacts in the château and smuggle some money out to them. Perhaps she might even persuade him to join them. It would be good for them to be together again as a family and Michel could find a way of earning enough money to support them. She could find work, too. With so many French *émigrés* coming to England there would surely be a need for translators and teachers of English. They could live independently and not have to rely on the charity of people like Jay Drymore and his parents. It was one thing to be grateful for a favour—a huge one, it was true—and another to be dependent on him.

She looked up to see the white cliffs of England on their port side and a harbour which must be Dover. There was more shipping in the straits than she had noticed before; it was a busy seaway being the only route, apart from going round the north of Scotland, to pass from the German Ocean to the Atlantic and places beyond. She watched as Lieutenant Sandford issued orders and the crew scrambled aloft to adjust the sails to take them past Dover and round the coast of Kent. She felt the turbulence under her feet as the helmsman altered course. The wind became much cooler and she shivered in her thin gown and wished she had thought to bring a shawl on deck.

Jay rejoined her. 'We shall soon be sailing northwards,' he said. 'And the air becomes cool as night approaches. Allow me to escort you back to your cabin.'

'Thank you.'

He preceded her down the companionway, then turned and held out his hand to steady her. Below decks it was considerably warmer, or was it simply his proximity that was making her feel hot? She rescued her hand from his. 'You will find England several degrees colder than France and will need warm clothing,' he said as they reached her cabin door.

'Yes, I guessed it would be. I have packed for it.'

'Good. It is almost supper time. It can be served

to you in your cabin if you wish, but I hope you will join us in the mess.'

It would have been churlish to refuse. 'Thank you. I think my father would prefer to stay where he is, but I will join you when I have made sure he is comfortable.'

He reached past her to open the door, then bowed and returned to the deck. She went into her cabin to find Hortense sorting clothes. 'The evening air is cool,' the maid said. 'You should have come down earlier.'

'I was talking to the Commodore. He has invited us to Blackfen Manor. He says his parents will welcome us and Papa can recover there. I have said we will go.'

'He is a true gentleman, even if he is a little dour, but that is not to be wondered at. Mr Roker tells me he lost his wife some three years ago and has been bringing up his children alone.'

'Yes, so he told me, but I think his parents help him. They are a very close family, I believe.'

'Not close enough if they can banish a good man like Sir John and never want anything more to do with him.'

'They are no worse than Mama's kin, are they?'

'It was her ladyship's choice and she did have your father and you children to console her. Sir John had no one.'

'True, but now the shoe is on the other foot. Sir John is going home and we are the ones to be exiled.'

'What are we going to do?'

'I do not know. Once Papa is well, we shall have to find somewhere to live and I think I must earn a living.'

'Earn a living!' the old lady gasped. 'What is the world coming to when ladies have to soil their hands with work?'

Lisette smiled. 'If I have to, I have to. Now I am going to join the Commodore, Sir John and Lieutenant Sandford for supper. I will wear the blue taffeta with the quilted stomacher and matching shawl.'

She stripped and washed and donned the blue taffeta, then Hortense combed the knots out of her hair and tied it back with blue ribbon.

'There,' she said, fastening a string of pearls about her neck. 'That will do. I feel civilised again. Will you make sure Papa has some supper?'

'Of course. I will have mine with him and stay

until he goes to sleep. You go and enjoy yourself. After what you have been through in the last two days, you deserve it.'

Lisette found her way to the mess, smiling to herself at the thought of enjoying herself. She was not going to some grand ball, but a simple supper with a man whose presence unsettled her.

He was already in the mess when she arrived, talking to Lieutenant Sandford and his grandfather. Sir John was dressed in a suit of amber-coloured silk and the lieutenant in dark blue, but although Jay had changed his shirt and breeches, he still wore no coat. They all turned to bow to her and Jay hurried forwards to show her to a seat at the refectory table. 'I regret I cannot yet get into a coat, Miss Giradet,' he said. 'I pray you to excuse me.'

'Of course.'

The mess steward came in, carrying tureens of food which looked and smelled delicious. Lisette suddenly realised how hungry she was and set to with a hearty appetite. But they could not eat in silence; it behoved her to begin a conversation.

'It is a lovely night,' she said. 'The stars are so

clear. I had no trouble picking out some of the constellations.'

'You know something of the stars, ma'am?' the lieutenant asked.

'A little. My father used to point them out to me when we went voyaging. I learned to recognise the Great Bear and Orion and the Pleiades. And of course the North Star.' She paused, watching Jay struggling to cut up his food. 'Let me help you,' she said, taking his knife and fork from him. She cut up the meat and potatoes and handed the implements back to him.

'Thank you,' he said.

She laughed. 'It makes a change for you to say that to me. Until now the gratitude has all been on one side. I hope you will call on me again if you need help.'

'His greatest need is to get into a coat,' Sir John said, chuckling. 'No one seems able to help him with that.'

'I shall be able to do so tomorrow,' Jay said stiffly. 'If Sam had not bound me up so tight, I might have been able to dress properly this evening.'

'I expect it was necessary,' Lisette said.

'Of course it was,' Sir John agreed. 'He was bleeding like a stuck pig.'

'Grandfather,' Jay admonished him. 'I do not think that is something the lady wants to hear. Shall we change the subject?'

'Tell me about Highbeck,' Lisette said quickly. She did not want to be the cause of dissension between the two men.

'Highbeck is a small village on the borders of Cambridgeshire and Norfolk,' Jay said. 'It is only a few miles from Downham Market and not far from the city of Ely, which has a fine cathedral. In the other direction is the port of Lynn, which is where we shall dock in two days' time, given fair weather.'

'And Blackfen Manor?'

'That is where my mother grew up and where she and my father have lived ever since their marriage. It is a substantial Tudor house with a moat and a drawbridge. The surrounding countryside is arable farmland and fen, hence its name. It is very lovely. I and my siblings grew up there and since we have had our own homes, visit often. I am sure you will like it.'

'It sounds idyllic. How far from there do you live?'

'Only five miles. I have a small estate and a house at Falsham. Until my wife died I was often at sea and it was managed by a steward, but since then I have stayed at home and looked after it myself. I felt the children needed me.'

'Do you miss the sea?'

'Sometimes I do. I come from a long line of sailors. My father was a sea captain before he married Mama and took to country living, and my grandfather was a vice-admiral. My younger brother is at present serving in the navy as a first lieutenant.'

'No doubt this short voyage has brought it all back. Our little escapade has perhaps been unsettling.'

'I shall soon settle down again.'

She smiled. 'From sailor to farmer.'

'Yes.' He had been perfectly open, but now his expression seemed to close up as if she had hit a nerve.

'I look forward to learning more of the country,' she said, then turned to Lieutenant Sandford. 'What about you, Lieutenant, do you come from a long line of seafarers?'

'No, Miss Giradet, I am the first.'

She had narrowly managed to avoid annoying

Jay again and the conversation became more general. At the end of the meal, she left them to their port and brandy and retired to her cabin. It had been an excessively long and tiring day, but all was well and tonight she thought she might sleep.

The men did not stay drinking for long. Though he was loathe to admit it, Jay was exhausted and his injured arm was giving him hell. He went to his cabin and to bed.

He could have done nothing else but invite the Count and his daughter to Highbeck. The old man was in no state to look after himself and though Lisette was bearing up well he knew she was feeling the strain of all that had happened in the last few weeks; he could not leave them to struggle on alone. His mother would be appalled at such callousness, even though she understood how the very name of Wentworth was burned in his brain. There was a wound there which would never heal. Thank goodness he could retire to Falsham, his duty done.

Chapter Five

Two days later they docked at Lynn, on the north coast of The Wash, and Lisette and her father set foot on English soil, Lisette for the first time, her father for the first time for many years. No one knew when they were arriving, so Jay arranged onward transport for them. Public coaches plied frequently between Lynn and Ely, but it was not a practical way when there were six of them and a fair amount of luggage. They could go post-chaise, but it would need two coaches to take them all. It was Sam who suggested going by river. Boats were as easily hired as coaches; it was the accepted means of transport in the fens. And so it was that Lisette and her father made their slow progress in a barge towed by a big black horse.

While the Comte and Sir John rested below deck, Lisette sat on the roof of the tiny cabin and watched the landscape glide past. It was flat and watery and there were a great many seabirds and waterfowl flying in and feeding on the marshy ground before taking off again in great clouds. As the vessel made its way upstream, the marshes gave way to pasture grazed by cattle.

'Until the draining of the fens over a hundred years ago, much of what you can see was frequently under water,' Jay said, coming to sit beside her. His arm was only lightly bandaged now and no longer in a sling. He could wear his coat. 'But now it is good fertile land.'

'It is so flat. You can see for miles and there is so much sky. I had not realised there could be so many colours in the clouds: blue, white, pink, mauve, fiery red and orange, and all shades of grey from pale dove to nearly black.'

'The black line is a rain cloud, but it is several miles away. The orange and red denote wind and that might very well blow the black cloud in this direction and we shall have squalls, but perhaps not before we arrive at the Manor.' He smiled. 'It is a landscape you either love or hate.'

'And you love it.'

'Yes, to me it is home. When I was away at sea, it was here I always dreamed of returning.'

'But some of that must have been due to your family being here.'

'Oh, undoubtedly.'

'It must be lovely to have a family,' she said a little wistfully. 'I have only Papa and Michel.'

'But you have an English family.'

'I do not count them. They never counted us.'

'So, you will not consider applying to them?'

'No. There is no need. Papa and I can manage. I only agreed to come here with you in order for him to regain his strength. You need not worry that we will be a burden to your parents any longer than we can help.'

'Nothing was further from my thoughts,' he said. 'Pray, do not be so touchy.'

'I am sorry. It is not your fault.' There she was, having to apologise to him again for the sharpness of her tongue. Whatever was the matter with her?

'I know you will be welcome, my mother said so before I left for France and my grandfather looks on you as a granddaughter, he told me so.' He gave her a wry smile. 'Does that make us cousins or something?'

'You are very forgiving.'

'There is nothing to forgive. You have been through a terrible time in the last few weeks and especially recently, it is a wonder you are as calm as you are. Some young ladies would have become gibbering idiots. I am full of admiration for your courage and resourcefulness.'

'Thank you. I could say the same of you.'

He chuckled. 'You are not going to start thanking me again, are you?'

Oh, dear, he had not forgotten that impulsive kiss. Would he go on reminding her of it as long as they lived? 'It goes without saying,' she said.

They fell silent for a few moments and when he spoke again it was to talk about England and the fens and to ask what she would like to do to pass the time while she was at Highbeck. 'There are riding horses and boats to use for exploring the countryside and fen,' he said. 'And you could go sightseeing in Ely. I am sure Sam would drive you in.'

It was then she remembered he had his own home a few miles distant and would not be at Highbeck to keep reminding her of her indiscretion. She should have been glad of that, but somehow the realisation left her feeling flat. 'Perhaps when Papa is better and can come too.'

The barge took them all the way to the staithe in Highbeck village, which was within easy walking distance of Blackfen Manor, but Jay sent Sam ahead to fetch the gig to convey the Comte who was still too weak to walk far. In that way those at the Manor were warned of their imminent arrival and Lord and Lady Drymore were waiting at the door as the little cavalcade crossed the drawbridge over the moat and into the enclosed courtyard.

Lisette helped her father from the gig and they stood to one side as Jay was embraced by Lady Drymore. 'Oh, I am so thankful you are safely back,' she said. 'We have been on tenterhooks the whole time and I was wishing I had never asked you to go, except of course, Papa is here now.' She turned to Sir John. 'You are welcome home, Papa,' she said, holding him at arm's length to look at him.

'And I am glad to be here. Home at last. And you do not look a year older.'

'Nonsense, I am over thirty years older.' She

laughed and turned towards the Comte and Lisette. 'Are you going to introduce us?'

'To be sure. Amy, my dear, this is my good friend Comte Gervais Giradet and his daughter, Lisette.'

Lady Drymore approached them, smiling. 'You are very welcome,' she said as the Comte bowed stiffly and Lisette dipped into a deep curtsy. 'I long to hear all your adventures, but not until you have been shown to your rooms and rested after your travels. You must be exhausted.'

There were shrieks of delight as two children ran from the house and hurled themselves into Jay's arms. 'Papa! Papa! You are back.'

He hugged them and put them from him. 'Now, be good, for I have someone I want you to meet.' He turned to his grandfather. 'This is your great-grandfather, your grandmama's father. Give him your best greeting.' They dutifully obeyed, Edward bowing and saying, 'How do you do', while Anne gave him a wobbly curtsy. 'And this is Comte Giradet and Miss Giradet.' Shyly they repeated their greeting and were sent back to their governess.

'Let us all go indoors,' Lord Drymore said as

the first few spots of rain pattered on the cobbles. He ushered them into a huge baronial hall lined with pictures, from which a wide staircase went up to a galleried landing. It was evidently the centre of the house, for doors led off in three directions. James preceded them into one and bade them be seated.

While they waited for refreshments to be brought, Lisette gazed about her. The room was large and furnished in a mixture of blackened old Tudor furniture and more up-to-date sofas, chairs and tables. There were pictures on the walls, some of the countryside, some portraits, and there were shelves displaying ornaments. It was so very different from what she had been used to at the château, with its carefully arranged rooms and tiled floors. Here the floors were of polished oak planks, as shiny and dark as the heavy oak settles and chests which stood on them. She suspected the thick walls and the presence of the moat which surrounded the house made it cold, even in summer, because a bright fire burned in the huge grate. It hissed a little as the rain came down the wide chimney on to the hot coals.

She became aware that Jay was telling his parents about the rescue, though he was carefully playing down the danger. 'I knew you would welcome the Comte and Miss Giradet,' he finished. 'At the moment they have not formulated any plans for the future.'

'Nor need they,' Amy said, then, turning to the Count, added, 'You have been through a terrible ordeal, sir, and need to regain your strength. I insist you stay here until you are fully recovered.'

'I thank you, my lady.' His voice was weak and even those few words, spoken in English with a strong French accent, seemed an effort to utter.

'I fear we are tiring you with our chatter,' Amy went on. 'If you prefer to go to your room and have supper brought to you there, it can soon be arranged.'

'Yes, I would, my lady,' he said. 'Perhaps tomorrow I will feel more the thing.'

A servant was delegated to help him, then Sir John said that he would like to retire too. 'I know we have a great deal of catching up to do,' he told his daughter. 'But there will be time enough for that tomorrow.'

'And the next day and the next.' Amy laughed.

'And all the days after that. Go to bed, Papa dear. It is good to have you under our roof again.'

'And in happier circumstances,' James added.

'We will not talk of that,' Amy admonished him. 'Not ever. It is a closed book.'

Sir John rose. He was not as fragile in health as the Count, but nevertheless was an old man and moved slowly. Another manservant was allocated to act as his valet and he was helped from the room, leaving Lisette alone to dine with Lord and Lady Drymore and Jay.

She rose and was shown to a bedchamber where Hortense was already unpacking and sorting out her clothes, grumbling that she had so few she might as well be a pauper. Nevertheless a greensack dress in a heavy taffeta with a laced stomacher and ruffled sleeves was found for her. Lisette washed off the grime of travel and was helped into it. Before returning downstairs she went to make sure her father was comfortable. He was already fast asleep. She crept from the room and joined Jay and his parents who had changed and were waiting for her in the salon.

'Tell us about France, Miss Giradet,' Lady Drymore said when they had taken their places at the table in the oak-panelled dining room and were being served with a substantial meal, which was surprising since the newcomers had not been expected. 'Is it very dreadful?'

'I do not know what it to become of the country,' Lisette answered. 'The population is divided among Revolutionaries and counter-Revolutionaries and there are daily riots and skirmishes. There is a man called Henri Canard in Honfleur who leads the Revolutionaries there. It was he who arrested my father. He was determined to have him tried and sentenced to death. If it had not been for your son, he would have succeeded. We are both in the Commodore's debt.'

'We will have no more of your constant gratitude,' Jay said. 'I was there to bring my grandfather out too, remember.'

'What was your father accused of?' Lord Drymore asked, handing round a dish of turbot in a white sauce.

'I don't know—they do not need much evidence, or indeed any at all, to throw a man in prison.'

'I did hear that Canard has a grudge against your family,' Jay said. 'Something to do with your great-grandfather and his grandfather. Do you know anything about that?'

'No, nothing. Who told you of it?'

'Sam heard it from the prison guards.'

'Rumour,' she said. 'Idle gossip. Until these troubles my father was universally liked and respected and he will be again when it is all over.'

'I pray you are right,' Lord Drymore said.

'Amen to that,' added his wife, then went on. 'Tell us about your family. You have a brother, I believe.'

'Yes. He is in the service of King Louis. There is some talk of putting the King on trial, although I do not see how they can do that, do you?'

'We did it,' Jay said drily. 'Over a century ago. The Parliamentarians beheaded Charles the First.'

'We won't go into that,' his mother said. 'Do go on, Miss Giradet.'

'Please, will you call me Lisette? I feel I know you so well already and just lately in France we have abolished titles. We are all calling each other *citoyen* and *citoyeness* now. It is hateful.'

'Lisette, a pretty name,' Amy said. 'What will happen to your brother if the King is put on trial?'

'I hope he will have the sense and opportunity

to leave the country. He could join us in England and we could make a new life together. I mean to write to him and suggest it.'

'I believe you have relations in England.'

'Yes, but we do not correspond. They did not approve of my mother marrying my father.'

'Why not?'

'Because Papa was so much older than Mama and only a French Comte, while Mama's father was an English Earl.'

'An Earl!' Amy said in surprise. 'But that means you are well connected. It could open doors for you.'

'I think not.'

'Mama,' Jay put in quietly, 'Miss Giradet's grandfather was the late Earl Wentworth.'

'But that's...' she began and stopped.

'Yes, Mama, but it is of no consequence. Pray, do not go on.'

Lisette looked from one to the other in puzzlement. Jay's face was stony, his eyes had become hard and she noticed his hand was gripping his fork so tightly, the knuckles were white. The name Wentworth meant something to him, something he did not want to talk about. It left her curious, but not daring to ask.

'I have a few jewels and a little gold in coin,' she said. 'They will last me a little while and then I could earn some money translating and teaching English. There must be French people wanting to learn.'

'Indeed there are,' Lord Drymore said. His wife was looking at Jay in consternation and Jay was pretending to concentrate on the fish on his plate. 'I am sure we can introduce you to some. Even out here in the countryside, there are *émigrés* and their families. The children in particular need to speak English if they are to live here.' He chuckled softly. 'And it would not do my grandchildren any harm to learn French. You have already met two of them and there are four more. Would you undertake that?'

'Gladly. It will help pay for my keep.'

'That is not why I suggested it.'

'No, but it is why I accept.'

'Sir,' Jay put in. 'My children have a governess who teaches them.'

'Miss Corton's French is atrocious,' his lordship said. 'Even I can do better than that. Let Miss...

Lisette teach them properly. You never know, Edward might want to enter the diplomatic service
when he is older, and as for Anne, knowledge of
French is always a good accomplishment for a
lady.'

'Edward will very likely go into the navy.'

'So he might and a facility in languages will
still be an advantage. I cannot think why you are
so against it, Jay. What would you have Lisette
think of her kind offer?'

'It does not matter,' Lisette put in quickly. 'I
will teach the other four, if their parents approve.'

'And have my two left out?' Jay said. 'They will
wonder why and feel hurt. Miss Giradet, I will
be pleased for you to teach my children French.
I will send them here to join their cousins for the
lessons when you have decided the day and time.'

'Then I will write to Amelia and Charlotte and
suggest it,' Lord Drymore said. Then to Lisette,
'Amelia lives in Downham Market and Charlotte
in Ely, neither of them very far away.' He turned
as servants came in to remove the first course
and bring the second. 'Ah, I smell roast chicken.'

His remark signalled the end of the discussion
and they moved on to more general observations.

Lisette watched Jay covertly. He seemed to have returned to his previous good humour, but she could not be sure. He had been manoeuvred by his father into a position he did not care for, but could not refuse without being uncivil, and she wondered why he found it so abhorrent. All she wanted to do was teach his children French. That would not corrupt them or mean that she would be any more often in his company; he had said he would send the children, not come himself.

As soon as the meal was finished, she pleaded tiredness and made her way to her room. Tomorrow she would sit with her father for a while, write her letter to Michel, prepare the French lessons and perhaps explore her surroundings. There would be plenty to keep her busy.

She woke to the sound of childish laughter. For a moment she wondered where she was, but then it all came flooding back: the escape and the voyage and the slow journey up the river when she had learned a little more about the enigmatic Jay Drymore. She had never been very curious about her English relations, perhaps because speaking of them distressed her mother while her father forbade the name mentioned, but now it had been aroused by a few words said at supper the previous evening. What connection did Earl Wentworth have with Jay Drymore? Why did his whole demeanour change at the sound of the name? It would seem her mother had not been the only one ill used by the man. But Jay had referred to him as the late Earl, so the man who had been her grandfather was dead. But what of his heirs? Did they even know of her existence?

The sound of squeals of laughter came to her again. Guessing it was Edward and his sister, she rose and padded over to the window. The rain had gone and below her the moat sparkled in the early morning sun. On the other side of it was a garden and an area of grass. Here the children were playing a game of tag. Edward was hugging a large ball made of stuffed hide and Anne was chasing him to take it from him. Lisette smiled as she watched them, two happy children without a care in the world. Jay had done a good job helping them over their grief at the loss of their mother.

Edward looked up and saw her. He stopped running and gave her a wave. She waved back and then Anne came and stood beside him and stared up at her. Lisette leaned out. *'Bonjour, mes en-fants,'* she called.

They conferred a moment as if translating what she had said, then Edward looked up again. *'Bon-jour, mademoiselle.'*

'Très bon.'

Hortense came into the room behind her carrying a bowl of hot water. 'You are awake at last. Will you dress?'

'Yes. Something plain and easy to walk in. That petticoat dress I wore yesterday will do.'

She washed and scrambled into her underclothes, while Hortense found the gown. 'Shall I ask for your breakfast to be brought up?'

'No, I will have it later downstairs. I'm going out into the garden.'

She left Hortense to tidy the room and ran lightly downstairs and out of the main door. To reach the children it was necessary to cross the drawbridge and walk round the outside of the moat. They were still there, but had abandoned the ball and were kneeling beside the moat, peering into the water.

'What can you see?' she asked, squatting down beside them.

'A fish,' Anne said.

'An eel,' Edward added.

'Une anguille,' Lisette said, then added when they looked mystified, 'That is French for eel. Where is it?'

'There, in the reeds.' Edward pointed.

'My goodness, it is a long one. Are they all as big as that in the fens?'

'Some are. The village men go out in boats and catch them in traps to send to London. Cook sometimes makes eel pie. Do you like eel pie, *mademoiselle?'*

'I have never tasted it.'

'You should,' said a voice behind them. 'It is a staple diet in these parts.'

All three twisted round to see Jay standing over them. Lisette scrambled to her feet. 'Good morning, *monsieur.'*

'Good morning, *mademoiselle.* Did you sleep well?'

'Exceedingly well. After all the upheaval of recent days, it was so quiet and peaceful, I fell asleep almost at once.'

'I am glad to hear it. Blackfen Manor has that effect on people. Have you breakfasted?'

'Not yet. The day was so lovely and I could hear the children so I thought to join them.'

'Can we take a boat out on the fen and show *mademoiselle* how eels are caught?' Edward said. 'An eel is *une anguille,* did you know?'

'I might have learned it a long time ago,' Jay said with a smile. 'But I had forgotten it.' He paused. 'Would you like Mademoiselle Giradet to teach you French with your cousins?'

'Does it mean we can stay here with Grandmama and Grandpapa?' Anne asked.

'Not all the time, but you will come back for the lessons.'

'Good,' the child said with satisfaction. 'I like it here.'

'Of course you do, everyone does, but you do have a home, you know, and I have work to do there.'

'What about going on the mere?' Edward persisted. 'I am sure *mademoiselle* wants to go, don't you?' He appealed to Lisette.

'I think that would be *très interessant,*' she said.

Jay laughed. 'It seems the lessons have already begun.'

'It is the best way to learn, as you go. It is better than sitting in a classroom, chanting verbs.'

'Would you like a little excursion on to the fen in a boat?'

'Very much.'

'Then let us go and have breakfast first. We will be back for dinner at three o'clock and afterwards I will take the children home and leave you and your father in peace.'

'The children do not disturb me,' she said, though she said nothing of the man himself who never failed to set her heart pounding. 'I love children, especially when they are so well behaved as these are.'

They began to walk back towards the drawbridge. 'Have you never thought of marrying and having children yourself, *mademoiselle?*' Jay asked.

'Alas, the right man has never come along. Perhaps I am too particular.' She laughed suddenly. 'Or perhaps the gentlemen are. I am too tall and thin, which is not at all fashionable. It has been said I could easily be mistaken for my brother.'

'Whoever said that must be blind,' he said.

She laughed. 'Thank you for that, kind sir.'

* * *

Lord Drymore had already breakfasted and gone about the business of the estate and her ladyship had her breakfast in her room, so Jay and Lisette had joined the children in the kitchen. After enjoying a hearty breakfast, they set off for the narrow tributary of the river which joined the moat to the fen. Here Jay, helped by Edward, pulled a boat out of a boathouse and tied it to a stake while they all they all climbed in. Jay untied the rope, jumped in and picked up the oars to row them into open water.

There was a long, narrow basket in the bottom of the boat which Edward explained was an eel trap. 'They go in this end after the bait,' he told Lisette, picking it up. 'But it is too narrow for them to turn round and they cannot swim backwards.'

'They are caught alive?'

'Oh, yes. They are sent to London in barrels so they arrive fresh. Mr Roker uses this one to catch eels for Cook.'

The expanse of water was edged with reeds and here and there a windmill was used to scoop water off the adjoining land and tip it into the mere. The only sound was the creaking of the water wheels, the cry of the water birds as they squabbled over the titbits Anne threw to them, and the croaking of frogs in the reeds. There were other boats on the water whose occupants were busy pulling baskets out of the water and examining them for captured eels. Others were shooting ducks and some were laden with reeds for thatch or willows for making the eel traps.

'The fen provides a livelihood for many of the village men,' Jay said, smiling at his son who explained all this to an attentive Lisette. 'Others are employed on the land.'

'I recall you said you had a farm on your estate.'

'So I do, that is why I must go home and deprive myself of your company.'

'But you will be bringing the children for their lessons, will you not?' she queried, conveniently forgetting that he had said he would send them.

'To be sure, when my work allows,' he said. 'I frequently visit my parents and they visit me. You should ask them to bring you. Falsham Hall is not as large or as old as Blackfen Manor, but it is set in gently rolling countryside, fertile land for the growing of crops and rearing cattle. There is even an orchard where we grow apples for cider.

It is perhaps not as fine as Normandy cider, but a very pleasant drink to quench a thirst. You must come and try some.'

She smiled. He was a different man here in the place he loved, with his children who undoubtedly meant the world to him. The man he had been in France, and for a brief moment at supper the previous evening, she had found difficult to like, but the man whose muscular arms pulled on the oars of the little boat was altogether more agreeable. 'I should like that,' she said.

They spent hours on the lake, watching the birds and the other boats or talking quietly, until it was time to return to the Manor. And later that day, Jay took the children home.

Their absence left her feeling strangely at odds with herself. It was the children she missed, she told herself, not the man, but she could not convince herself. Jay Drymore was such a powerful presence his absence left a void which she was determined to try to fill. There was a well-stocked book room at the Manor and she spent an hour or so browsing before selecting *Gulliver's Trav-*

els to read to her father. He was recovering well, but she knew he worried about Michel.

Five days later the house echoed once again to children's laughter, as both of Jay's sisters arrived—Lady Amelia Jepson with her two daughters, Matilda and Charlotte, and Mrs Charlotte Granger with her two, Sophie and Thomas, who was only three—then Jay arrived with Edward and Anne. Once everyone had been introduced, Lisette took all the children, including Thomas, out into the garden to begin French lessons, playing games and learning the names of the flowers.

They came twice a week after that. On other days Lisette was kept busy with translating work and teaching adult *émigrés* the rudiments of the English language, but they found it a struggle and some would never manage to do more than utter a few phrases. The children were so much easier to teach.

In early September Jay gathered in his harvest and invited the whole family over to celebrate it and naturally Lisette and the Comte were included in the invitation.

It was evidently an annual custom for the squire to host a feast to thank the labourers for their hard work and it was held in a barn on the farm. When they arrived, Jay was busy overseeing the preparations and, having greeted them politely and made sure they had refreshments, he left Edward and his mother to show Lisette and her father round the house.

It was a solidly built square building with large airy rooms furnished in the French style, which pleased the Comte. He eagerly pointed out pieces that were similar to those he had had at home and which he did not doubt had been looted now the château was uninhabited. Downstairs there were three reception rooms, a dining room and a library. They peeped in the kitchens, which were a hive of activity as the cook-housekeeper and her extra staff worked to provide the feast, but quickly withdrew for fear of getting in the way. On the next floor, there were six bedrooms and above them the servants' bedrooms, though they did not venture up there, but returned to the drawing room to take tea, supervised by Lady Drymore in the absence of a hostess. 'Jay could do with a wife,' Amy said. 'But he says he will never marry again. It is hardly to be wondered at, but I wish he would get over it.'

Lisette assumed she was speaking of the loss of Jay's wife, but decided not to comment.

By the time they had finished their tea, Jay returned. 'All is ready,' he said. 'Shall we go over?'

Everyone, including the children, trooped out behind him, across a lane to a barn in the yard of the Home Farm, which was already filling with people, young, old and every age between. The unthreshed wheat, with its unique scent of summer, was piled up almost to the ceiling at one end, but the rest of the floor had been cleared. A long table had been set up down the length of this space and groaned under the weight of the food it held. No one would go away hungry.

Jay showed them to their places, then left them again to make sure everyone was seated at the table. He made a short speech praising the workers, to which the lord of the harvest replied, calling for three cheers for the Commodore. The sound of the hurrahs rose to the rafters. Jay was undoubtedly a popular employer and landlord.

* * *

When every last scrap of food had been con-
sumed and the table cleared away, space was made
in the middle of the floor for dancing, the music
for which was provided by a fiddler and a flautist.

'I wonder what the grain is like in Villarive this
year,' Lisette mused aloud as she sat beside her
father on a bale of straw, watching the merriment.

'I hope it is better than last year,' he said. 'More
to the point, is there anyone to harvest it? And
what about the apples? It will soon be time to
pick those.'

'Are you very homesick, Papa?' He had regained
a little of his strength, but he was often to be
found deep in thought, tears filling his eyes. It
hurt her to see it.

'Of course I am. I wish we could go back.'

'So do I, but I don't think that is possible, Papa,
not at the moment. Later, perhaps when the troubles are at an end and France is peaceful again.'

'Why have we not heard from Michel? You did
write to him, did you not?'

'Yes, Papa, I did, more than once. I suggested
he should join us.'

'He will not do that while the King needs him

and Louis will not release him, even if he wanted to come.'

'I will write again. Perhaps he has not received my earlier letters. Now, we must not be miserable when Monsieur Drymore has been so good as to invite us to a celebration. They are all very good to us, do you not agree?'

'Yes. I have to admit that, as far as Englishmen go, Lord Drymore is a good man and his wife so charming, she could almost be French.'

Lisette laughed at this grudging praise. 'And the Commodore?'

'He is a brave man and I will always be in his debt.' He sighed. 'If only we could have brought Michel out with us.'

'You know that wasn't possible at the time, Papa.'

'I know.' It was said with a heavy sigh.

'Papa,' she said slowly. 'Tell me about Earl Wentworth.'

He had been watching the company with a faraway look in his eye, but turned sharply towards her at this. 'What do you want to know about him for?'

'Curiosity,' she said. 'What manner of man was he?'

'Rude, dictatorial, the sort of man to lose his temper violently when he could not have his own way. He had a husband lined up for your mother and would have had her marry him whether she willed it or no. She was in terror of him.'

'And the rest of the family?'

'Two sons, George, the present earl, and Gerald—both as bad as he was.' He paused. 'You are not contemplating making their acquaintance, are you?'

'No, but I believe Jay—' She stopped suddenly when she realised she had spoken his given name aloud and quickly corrected herself. 'The Commodore has been ill used by them or someone in the family. He cannot bear the name mentioned.'

'Neither can I, so we will not mention it.'

'Very well.'

They fell silent, watching the men and women and even the little children dancing. Lisette found her foot tapping to the music.

Jay had been busy making sure everyone was enjoying themselves and curbing the more riotous of the labourers who were taking advantage of the free ale to become drunk. 'This a family affair,' he told them. 'Your wives and children are present, do not embarrass them.' Only now did he find time to look about him. He saw Lisette and her father, sitting together, apparently in silence, and went over to them.

'I am sorry I have neglected you.'

'Indeed, you have not,' Lisette said quickly. 'We are enjoying the music, are we not, Papa?'

'To be sure. We have a celebration something like this in Villarive when the apples have been picked.'

'We have made you sad with our jollity,' Jay said. 'I am sorry. I had hoped to cheer you.'

'You have,' Lisette assured him. 'But Papa often thinks of home and what is happening there. There is so little news and what there is, is bad. Some of the *émigrés* I teach tell frightening stories of horror and cruelty, especially towards the nobility.'

'Perhaps they exaggerate. People do, you know, if they have a ready audience. And tales grow with the telling.'

'No doubt you are right.'

'Would you like to dance with me? The steps are easy to learn.' He held out his hand to her.

She took it and he led her into a country dance which was energetic to say the least. They laughed a great deal as she tripped over her own feet and stepped on his toes. 'I am clumsy,' she said. 'Papa always said I ought to have been another boy.'

'I am glad you are not,' he said and when she looked up into his eyes, added hastily, 'I should look a fool dancing with another man.'

He was paying compliments to a lady, something he had learned when courting Marianne; it was, he told himself, simple courtesy, nothing more. She had no doubt been teased all her life about her figure and likeness to her brother and it had obviously had a profound effect on her. Had she deliberately played up to that masculine image of herself as a kind of defence? Had no one ever told her anything different? Certainly her father had not. He suspected that having lost one son to his King, he was using Lisette as a substitute. She *was* tall and exceptionally slim, but that did not mean she was unfeminine and incapable of feminine wiles. He was, he told himself sternly, immune to feminine wiles.

The dance came to an end and he escorted her back to her seat. She was flushed and a little breathless and her pale hair had become unpinned in places; wisps of it hung about her face. He felt a sudden urge to pull out all the pins and see it cascade about her shoulders. No one would doubt her femininity then. He shook himself, bowed over her, made his excuses and went to break up a quarrel between two village children. He was becoming soft and softness led to hurt and hurt led to anger. He must not let that happen. He must not.

Soon after that, the party broke up and Lisette and the Comte returned with Lord and Lady Drymore to Blackfen Manor. Apart from a brief bow on his part and a curtsy on hers, Lisette had no more conversation with Jay, whose rather sudden departure from her side after the dance had puzzled her. He was once more the cool, aloof man she thought had been banished. Whatever troubled him it was not so easy to banish. She wondered why it mattered to her and realised with a jolt that his happiness was important to her. And gratitude had nothing to do with it. It was a monumental discovery and one she dare not voice, dare not think about.

It was, she decided, time to think of leaving Highbeck and finding somewhere else to live. They could not impose on the generosity of Lord and Lady Drymore much longer. The only reason she had done nothing about it before now was that she was waiting to hear from her brother, but there had been nothing, not a word. She considered going back to France to find out for herself what was happening, but was unable to think of a practical way of doing it. She was also aware that if anything happened to her, her father would have no one.

Lady Drymore was vehemently opposed to them leaving. 'Your father is not fit to be moved,' she said. 'Please stay. There are people here who can look after him and we have all come to love you. There is no need for you to go. Jay did not bring you to England to cast you out.'

'I know.' It was her growing feelings for Jay which were causing most of her unease. He remained the same as he always had been, chivalrous but distant. If she had not broken through his armour by now, she never would.

'Then we will not speak of it again.'

Slowly the days slipped by, one after another. Lisette gave her lessons, translated letters and legal documents and listened to the gossip of fellow *émigrés*. It was the more recent of these who brought news from her homeland, which was worrying if for no other reason than Michel might be involved. An armed Parisian mob had stormed the Tuileries, massacred the Swiss Guard and demanded the abolition of the monarchy. The royal family had fled through the gardens to the protection of the Legislative Assembly. What that body had done was to arrest the whole family and send them to the Temple, an old fortress on the right bank of the Seine, now being used as a prison. The *émigré* armies, who would have freed him if they could, were suffering from a lack of money and many had been disbanded. Their leaders had either been arrested and executed or driven abroad, including the man who had come to see her. 'The Legislative Assembly was dissolved and a new National Convention elected,' he told her.

'It sat for the first time in September and the following day abolished the monarchy and declared France a republic. France no longer has a King; it is ruled by a rabble.' He was in tears as he spoke.

'What has happened to his court?'

The man shrugged. 'One must assume that, unless they have fled, they are still in the Tuileries.'

The dreadful news was reinforced by an article in *The Times* which told of thousands of people being massacred in three days of violence. 'The streets of Paris, strewed with the carcasses of the mangled victims, are become so familiar to the sight, that they are passed by and trod on without any particular notice,' she read. 'The mob think no more of killing a fellow creature, who is not even an object of suspicion, than wanton boys would of killing a cat or a dog. We have it from a Gentleman who has been but too often an eye witness to the fact. In the massacre last week, every person who had the appearance of a gentleman, whether stranger or not, was run through the body with a pike. He was, of course, an aristocrat and that was a sufficient crime. A ring, a watch chain, a handsome pair of buckles, a new coat, or a good pair of boots—in a word, every-

thing which marked the appearance of a gentleman, and which the mob fancied, was sure to cost
the owner his life.'

She dare not tell her father. It would undoubtedly halt his recovery, but the longer they went
without news of Michel, the more sorrowful he
became, lost in a kind of reverie which hurt her
to see. Sometimes he was so confused he thought
himself back at Villarive and began issuing orders to the servants, which puzzled them. Sometimes he even addressed her as Michel. He was
too fragile to be told. She wrote to Michel again,
not knowing if her letter would ever reach him.

Autumn began to take hold, the trees in the
copse beside the house were losing their leaves
and a keen wind ruffled the waters of the mere
when a newly arrived *émigré* sought Lisette out
at Blackfen Manor, bringing with him the first
positive tidings of her brother: a letter from him,
smuggled out of the Tuileries. Overjoyed to have
news at last, she thanked the messenger, but did
not immediately break the seal, waiting instead
until he had left. On the way to take it to her fa-

ther, she changed her mind and went into the library where she sat in the window seat to read it.

'My dearest sister,' Michel had written. 'I cannot come to you. I am virtually a prisoner, guarded night and day. I am stopped whenever I try to leave the palace and my letters are intercepted. I fear I will be the next to go to the Temple. There is nothing you can do for me. Give my fondest regards to our father and pray for my soul.'

It was plain that Michel did not expect to survive and this was a farewell letter. Coming as it did on top of the dreadful stories she had heard and read of what was happening in France, it left her desolate. She sat with the letter in her hands, remembering the happy brother who had shared her childhood, and she thought her heart would break.

Chapter Six

Jay had brought the children for their lesson, but Lisette was not in the morning room where they usually gathered. He had left the children with their cousins to go in search of her. 'She had a visitor earlier,' his mother told him when he found her taking tea with his sisters in the morning room. 'It was a Frenchman, an *émigré,* I imagined, who had come to ask about lessons. I saw him leave a few minutes ago. Where she went after that I do not know. To her bedchamber, perhaps.'

Lisette was not in her room. Hortense was there, busy sponging a gown that Lisette had worn when playing with the children which had become soiled. She had not seen her mistress since breakfast. On the way past the open door of the book room he heard the sound of weeping.

'Lisette, whatever is the matter?' he asked, hurrying to sit beside her. 'Please tell me.'

As she continued to sob, he put his arm about her shoulders and gave her his handkerchief and waited until she calmed herself. It did not occur to him that it was unseemly to hold an unmarried lady in that way. He did what instinct demanded. 'My mother said there was a Frenchman here. Did he bring bad news?'

She did not answer, but handed him the letter.

'Oh, dear, this is not good,' he said, after he had scanned it. 'But cheer up. It does not say he has been arrested, only that he is fearful he might be.'

She lifted her head to look at him with eyes blotched by tears. She had endured so much and to have this extra burden was, to his mind, unfair. He was filled with a pity bordering on tenderness, something he had not felt for a woman for a very long time. 'Have you told your father?'

'No, I dare not. It might kill him. I must go back to France...'

'You will do no such thing.'

'But I must save Michel.'

'How?'

'I do not know. I'll think of something.'

'And if you die in the attempt, your father will have no one. Be sensible, Lisette.'

Her annoyance at being told to be sensible overcame her pleasure at being addressed as Lisette. She pulled herself away from him, realising as she did so, how stupid she had been to throw herself into his arms like that. That most definitely was not sensible. 'I am being sensible. Sons are more important than daughters and if Papa gains his son at the expense of his daughter, so be it.'

'Rubbish. I am prepared to wager if you were to tell your father what you propose, he would forbid it.'

'Then I shall not tell him.'

'I cannot allow this, Lisette.'

'Who are you to allow or not to allow, Jay Drymore? You are not my keeper.'

'No,' he said thoughtfully. 'But I do have an interest in your welfare.'

'Because you saved me and Papa from a French prison and, like some medieval knight, you think that makes you responsible for my life for ever more. I have said I am grateful. Must I go on saying it to the end of my days?'

He smiled; her attempt to be angry with him

failed in view of her blotched cheeks and tear-filled eyes. 'No, I have told you before I want no thanks. I fetched you out with my grandfather. It was as easy to bring out three as one.'

'And that is not true. Your grandfather was a free man, he did not have to be rescued from prison.'

'But he did want to come home.'

'Not the same.'

He smiled and lifted her chin with his finger so that he could look into her face and then he surprised himself by adding, 'I will go back and bring your brother to you.'

He watched her tears miraculously dry up and a smile come to her face. 'How?' she asked.

'I do not know. I'll think of something.'

It was a moment or two before she realised that he had repeated her own words and managed a weak smile. 'You can't do that, Jay. You are a wanted man in France.'

'James Smith is wanted, not Jay Drymore.'

'What difference does that make if you are recognised?'

'I might be recognised in Honfleur, but not Paris. Michel is in Paris, is he not?'

'You would go openly as yourself?'

'Why not? Englishmen may not be popular, but England is neutral.'

'Why would you do that for me?'

'Oh, I don't know,' he said vaguely, wondering himself. 'Because you need help and I am here and able to give it, I suppose. Any man worth his salt would do the same.' He told himself that he would come to the aid of anyone in similar circumstances and the fact that he had held her in his arms and liked the way it felt had nothing to do with it. 'I will consult my father about the best way to go about it.'

'Thank you, oh, thank you.'

He smiled when she seized his hand, but thought better of it and let it go again as if it were a hot coal. 'Now, let there be no more tears. You must stay cheerful for your father's sake.'

'I will try.'

'Good. Now, go and give the children their lesson, they are waiting for you.' He rose, put her hand to his lips and strode away, leaving her rubbing the back of her hand pensively.

'I wondered if I might go on official business,' Jay told his father after he had explained what he intended to do. They were sitting together in the library where he had found him working on estate ledgers which were spread out on his desk. 'If I could have access to the palace, I could smuggle Giradet out without having to resort to violence.'

'But you know we have recalled our ambassador to France in protest at the dreadful massacres?'

'No. What happened?'

'There were rumours that the Prussians had taken Verdun and were at the gates of Paris and intended to restore Louis to the throne and release all the political prisoners. Every able-bodied man was called to defend the city, but instead they decided to massacre the prisoners in the most horrible and bloodthirsty way.'

'Are the Prussians at the gates of Paris?'

'I think not. It was a rumour, but who knows what the mob will do next? Lord Gower has been recalled and is even now presenting his report to the government.'

'All the more reason for me to try to fetch Monsieur Giradet out,' he said. 'There must be some people left at the embassy, if only to maintain it until things settle down.'

'At the moment, yes, but there is talk of end-ing the neutrality and declaring war on France. If that happened while you were there, you would be an enemy alien and subject to imprisonment, if nothing worse.'

Jay had not realised matters were as bad as that, but having given his word to Lisette, he could not go back on it; it had become a matter of honour. 'It would not happen without notice, would it? Warnings would surely arrive from London and give me time to leave the country. It is to be hoped with Michel Giradet.'

'And you wish me to arrange something for you?'

'Could you?'

'Possibly. But are you sure you want to do this, Jay?'

'Yes. I promised Miss Giradet and I cannot go back on that.'

'Very well, I will see what I can do, although what we will tell your mother, I do not know.'

'A diplomatic posting—nothing out of the ordinary about that, is there?'

His father smiled at him. 'I am thinking there is something out of the ordinary about your feelings for Miss Giradet, Jay.'

'Nonsense. I feel sorry for her, that's all. She was all for going herself and I could not let her do that, could I?'

'No, certainly not. I will go to London tomorrow and speak to Pitt personally. It will be quicker than writing. Will you take Sam again?'

'If you can spare him and if he will come.'

James chuckled. 'Oh. I think he will. He becomes bored when too long away from adventure.'

Jay thanked him and went in search of Sam to ask him if he would accompany him, to which that worthy instantly agreed. Then he went to the schoolroom.

Lisette was just drawing her lesson to a close. He watched her for a minute or two, admiring the way she dealt with six unruly children, firmly but with gentleness and humour. She would make an admirable mother. His sisters came and took their offspring home and he sent Edward and Anne to amuse his grandfather while he spoke to Lisette.

'My father is going to arrange for me to go to France as a diplomat with a special mission, all open and above board, no danger at all,' he told her. 'Once there, I shall find a way of reaching your brother. I hope he will not need persuading to come with me. Perhaps you could write him a letter for me to take to him telling him he may trust me.'

'I will do that, but are you sure you want to do this?'

'Of course, I said I would, didn't I? I won't go back on my word—besides, it is all very straight-forward.'

'When do you go?'

'When my father comes back from London with my assignment and the documents. He is leaving tomorrow morning. With luck he will be back the next evening or if not, the day after that.'

'Will you go in the *Lady Amy?*'

'Yes. Sam will go ahead to alert Lieutenant Sandford to make her ready for sea.'

'Will it be safe?'

'Safe! My dear *mademoiselle,* it is the safest and most seaworthy private yacht afloat.'

'I did not mean that,' she said, noting he had re-verted to using her title and not her name. 'I meant it was seen by those *maréchaussée* who fired at you on the beach. They will have the name of it.'

'I am going to Calais, not Honfleur, but you are right. It would be a wise precaution to change her name temporarily. I will ask my father if he minds me doing that. Now I must take the children home. I will bring them back tomorrow to stay here while I am gone. They will keep you company and help to take your mind off Michel until we are safely back again.'

He gathered up the children whom he had brought on horseback and together they rode home.

The next twenty-four hours were spent making arrangements for his steward to take over the business of the estate while he was gone. Luckily the threshing was all done, the stacks made and the fields were being ploughed. The apples had been picked and most sent to market in London, but the rest would need making into cider, but it was something that happened every year and Tom Goodyear had been his steward all through his absences at sea and really did not need telling what to do.

Lisette went about her self-allotted duties— preparing lessons for the children, translating a French pamphlet into English to be distributed to sympathisers among the British aristocracy, reading to her father, calling on the village poor with Lady Drymore—but all the time part of her mind was on what Jay was preparing to do. In spite of what he had said and his cheerful attitude, she knew how risky it was and did not doubt he knew it, too.

If his real mission became known, there would be no saving him. He would die and she would have to live the rest of her life knowing she had sent him to his death. It was unbearable. She must tell him not to go, and when he had gone back to Falsham Hall, she would go to France herself and persuade Michel to return to England with her.

'I cannot let you risk your life on so foolhardy a mission,' she told him when he returned to Black-fen Manor to await the return of his father. Everything was ready: his bags were packed, the *Lady Amy* was ready for sea, its gunwale repainted with the name *Lady Anne,* a name that could easily be wiped off for the original to emerge when they returned, and his children had been told of his impending departure. She found him in the library looking up the times of the tides around The Wash. 'I could not live with myself if you were to die and your children left orphans as a consequence.'

'My dear Miss Giradet, I am not going to die. I will be going as a British envoy and as such will be protected by our government. Not even the French Assembly would dare lift a finger against me.' He paused. 'Did you write the letter I asked for?'

'Yes, but I still do not think you should go. I am very sorry I burdened you with my problems; I wish I had never spoken of them.'

'But you did and it is my pleasure and privilege to do all in my power to help you. If a simple little voyage across the channel and a few days in Paris can do that, then I will do it. I beg you, think no more of it. I shall probably be back within the week.'

'Then let me come, too.'

'Certainly not. I will not hear of it.'

'But I could be useful.'

'You could also be an encumbrance. Now, unless you wish to make me angry, you will say no more.'

She turned and left him, annoyed with him and with herself for not being able to persuade him. She climbed the stairs to her bedchamber and flung herself down on the bed. In her mind's eye she saw him boarding the yacht and setting sail, saw him arriving in France and travelling to Paris. He would have to go by diligence or hire a carriage and, once in Paris, he would have to find lodgings. With no one to help him over the language and customs and the new laws being enacted all the time, he might well find himself in trouble. If she could save him from that, she ought to do so, whether he wanted her to or not. But how?

She rose and began throwing clothes in a bag, picking those she could manage herself because Hortense would be left behind and whatever she took she would have to carry. And she would need help to get her to Lynn. Whom could she trust not to betray her?

Lord Drymore had returned very late that night after the household had retired and it was only at breakfast the next morning that he and Jay were able to talk over the final arrangements. 'Pitt has agreed you are to go to Paris as a special envoy on a peace mission,' James said. 'It will mean talking to Robespierre, Danton and their minions in the Jacobin party, who have just ousted the Girondists from power—in truth, it is difficult to keep up with all the changes—and making diplomatic noises which will be meaningless, but he said if he sanctioned your visit to Paris, then you had better have something useful to do while you are there. He wants you to find out how the war with Austria is going, what the Prussians intend and if there is any likelihood of France surrendering. We do not want to become involved if we do not have to.'

'Spy, you mean?'

'Intelligence gathering. I have your official appointment which you will take with you and the other orders which you are to destroy when you have read them.' He paused before going on. 'He did emphasise that if you were arrested, the British government would have to deny all knowledge of what you were doing.'

'I understand.'

'If you don't want to do it, we can cancel the whole thing. God knows, I would rather you did.'

'I can't do that. Lisette is relying on me. I must leave within the hour if I am to catch the tide. I have to say goodbye to the children and Mama, and Mademoiselle Giradet, though if she starts to argue again I shall turn my back on her and leave her.'

'She did not come down to breakfast. Her maid said she was unwell and would remain in bed today.'

'It is nothing serious, I hope.'

'No. The headache. The servant said it was probably the worry of it all. I should slip away quietly.'

Before he left, he wrote a note to Lisette, wishing her a speedy recovery from her headache and telling her to try not to worry. He would be back with her brother in no time. He gave it to a worried-looking Hortense. Sam bade farewell to his wife and they left with his mother and father and children waving goodbye from the courtyard.

Lord Drymore's carriage was a strong one used by his lordship to ply between Norfolk and London and they fairly rattled along. They spent the time talking about the voyage and what they might expect when they arrived in France, but Jay could not banish the sight of Lisette's tear-filled eyes from his memory, nor the feel of her soft body in his arms and the smell of lavender in her hair. It had shaken him to the core to find he wanted her. Jay Drymore, who had eschewed the company of women and had sworn never to become entangled with one again, desired this French spinster who was, moreover, the niece of Gerald Wentworth. It was as well he was going away for a few days; it might cool his ardour.

The *Lady Anne,* with its newly painted name, was at anchor on the quay, but she was ready to sail as soon as Jay and Sam were aboard and wind and tide were favourable. The breeze was from the north-west, which would aid them when they were out of The Wash, but until then they were obliged to tack slowly out to sea. Once in the German Ocean, they turned to sail along the Norfolk coast before catching a strong north-easterly and the vessel fairly skimmed along.

'At this rate we should make Calais in three days,' Jay said to Sam on their second day at sea, as they stood at the rail watching the wake they left behind them. 'Two, three days to Paris and then—'

They heard a cry and a scuffle behind them and turned to see Lieutenant Sandford ushering Lisette towards them. 'Found her hiding in the ship's boat,' he said.

Jay surveyed the dishevelled woman. 'I might have known,' he said, shocked and angry with himself for not having foreseen what she would do. What a fool he had been to assume that because he said no, she would meekly accept it. She had already shown she could be wilful and determined and she had said she wanted to come, too; it ought to have alerted to him, especially when she did not appear for breakfast. 'How did you manage to get on board ahead of us?'

'I rode across country and before you say anything, the stable boy rode alongside me and took the horse back...'

'I'll have his guts...'

'You will not. I had the devil of a job to persuade him, but the threat that I would abandon a valuable horse finally overcame his reluctance. Do not blame him.'

'We will have to put ashore.'

'Why?'

'To take you back, of course.'

'I won't go back. You cannot spare the time. Michel could be thrown into prison, even executed, any day, and unless I miss my guess, the errand you have been given by the British Government won't allow you to loiter.'

'You are the most infuriating woman I have ever met,' Jay said, furious with her, even as he admired her courage. 'Very well, you may stay on board. And I do mean stay on board.' He turned to Lieutenant Sandford, who had been listening to the exchange with curiosity and no little amusement. 'Have my cabin prepared for Miss Giradet, if you please, and put my things in the second one.'

'Thank you.' She gave him a winning smile, which threatened to disarm him completely. 'I am prodigiously hungry. I have only had a piece of bread and cheese since I left.'

'And food,' Jay called after the lieutenant, who was disappearing down the companionway.

'You are not angry with me, are you?' she asked as Sam, who could not stifle his grin, took himself off to the other side of the yacht and they were alone.

'Very angry,' he said.

'I am sorry for that. But it was a risk I had to take, surely you understand that?'

'I could understand it of a man, but a gently brought up young lady is not expected to be so hoydenish.'

'I fear it was the way I was raised,' she said, re-membering Maurice Chasseur had made the same comment. It was a kind of stigma she had lived with for years and to have this man, whom she revered, say the same thing hurt dreadfully. 'Michel and I were always into mischief and where he went, I went. I did whatever he did, I would not be left behind.'

'Then it is no wonder your father thinks of you as a second son.'

'Yes, Michel had his heart. When he went away to court, I tried to take his place.'

'Impossible!' He laughed.

'I know that.' It was said with a sigh. 'It is why I must do what I can to restore Michel to him now.'

That she chose to interpret his comment in a way he had not intended, he let pass. 'That is why I am going to France. There was no necessity for you to come, too.'

'You are going to need me.'

'Oh, you think so, do you?'

'Yes.'

'No, because you will stay on board and not set foot in France. That is my last word on the subject.'

Lisette did not think there was anything to be gained by pursuing the argument. She was a good sailor and might as well enjoy the voyage and try not to think of what lay ahead. As the seaman who was also the cook came to tell them there was a meal prepared in the captain's day cabin, they repaired there and afterwards took a turn round the deck. The crew, many of whom had known Jay for years and had never known him bested by a woman, watched and awaited developments with covert amusement.

The wind, though decidedly cool, was fair for France and all sail was set to take advantage of it. She was determined to be pleasant and unargumentative in order to dispel his annoyance with her and asked questions about the yacht and how it was navigated. When that subject seemed exhausted, she asked him about his life at sea, which had begun when he was ten years old as a cabin boy. He had progressed to midshipman, then lieutenant, then captain and lastly commodore, he told her.

'Do you miss the sea?' she asked.

'Sometimes, but I am content at home with my children.'

'They must miss their mother.'

'They did at first. She was a little like you—too adventurous for her own good.'

'How did she die?'

'In a riding accident. She tried to jump a hedge, not realising there was a ditch on the other side of it. The horse fell on top of her.' It was said flatly, like something learned by rote and repeated whenever occasion demanded. She could not help feeling there was more to it than he was prepared to tell her.

'I am so sorry. I should not have asked. Please forgive me.'

'You are forgiven.'

They were silent for several minutes, looking out over the rail, each with their own thoughts. Then he spotted something on the horizon and beckoned to Lieutenant Sandford to give him his telescope. 'A Dutch East Indiaman,' he said, handing the glass to Lisette. 'See over there.' He leaned close to her to point the vessel out. 'It will not bother us.'

She felt his warm breath on her ear and a tingle coursed right through her body, which she suddenly recognised as desire. Her hand was shaking as she handed back the instrument. He must not see how he affected her, he must not. He thought she was a hoyden, almost mannish, but at that moment she never felt more feminine. 'I think I would like to go to my cabin and rest,' she said abruptly.

'Of course.' He chuckled. 'You could not have slept very well in the ship's boat last night.'

'No, I was too cold and hungry and the floor was hard.'

'Serves you right.' But he was smiling. Was he enjoying a joke at her expense? Did he know the effect he had on her? She had better take care in the future to remain aloof.

He escorted her down, opened her cabin door and bowed her in before returning to the deck where Sam joined him.

'What now, Commodore?' he asked.

'Nothing. Miss Giradet will be left on board

when we drop anchor at Calais. I can't have her muddying the waters.'

'She might be right, you know. You might need someone who knows her way about France and can help with the language and customs.'

'My French is more than adequate for a British diplomat. And how could I explain the presence of a single woman at my side? Do I travel with a mistress?' He laughed suddenly. 'Unless you fancy taking her on.'

'Not on your life.' Sam was indignant. 'I am a happily married man, have been this last thirty-eight years. Susan would slay me alive. Anyway, Miss Giradet would not agree.'

'I am sure she would not. We will say no more on the subject. Go and put out my clothes for this evening.'

'Aye, aye, sir.'

Jay paced the deck. He had laughed as if making a joke when he suggested Sam should take Lisette as a mistress, but the feelings that had raised were horribly akin to jealousy and that made him annoyed with himself. His emotions were in turmoil. His head told him the last thing he wanted was entanglement with a woman, any woman, but his heart was contradicting that. In order to still it, he kept telling himself she was Wentworth's niece and none of that family could be trusted.

They dropped anchor outside Calais in the afternoon three days later, there to await permission to enter the busy harbour. It was late when they docked and Jay decided to stay on board until the morning, when he intended to hire a coach to take him and Sam to Paris.

'I'm coming too,' Lisette told him as they ate breakfast together next morning. Sam had gone ashore to acquire a carriage.

'You, madam, are staying on board.'

'Jay, please let me come. I cannot bear to stay here doing nothing when I could be a help. I'll be good, I promise.'

'I doubt it.'

'I need to see and talk to Michel.'

'You may do that when we return with him.'

'Supposing he doesn't want to come and wishes to stay by the King? I will have to persuade him for Papa's sake. Please, Jay. I will not ask another thing of you, if you grant this request.'

'You have no chaperon.'

'Pah to that! We are too far from England for it to matter there, and the ordinary women of France don't bother with chaperons.'

'Let her come, sir.' Sam had returned from his errand unheard by either of them. 'After all, if you let her out of your sight, God knows what mischief she will get up to.'

Jay laughed. 'There is that. Oh, very well, madam, you may come, but I have a feeling I am going to regret it.'

Lisette scrambled to her feet and raced down to her cabin to fetch the bag containing her spare clothes before he could change his mind.

Sam had not hired a driver, preferring to drive the carriage himself. 'Can't have too many people knowing our business, can we, sir?' he explained.

Thus it was that Jay and Lisette travelled in the coach without the benefit of a third person. Determined not to be contentious, they talked intermittently about safe subjects, like their childhood, their likes and dislikes, and when they ran out of things to say and ask, sat side by side in companionable silence.

The first sign that the journey would not be

easy was their failure to find replacement horses. They were obliged to continue with the animals they had, which slowed them to a walking pace with frequent stops to rest. It gave the travellers the opportunity to observe the countryside. Everywhere was run down: plaster was falling off the buildings, window frames needed painting and often the glass was missing. The fields were overgrown and the cattle skinny. Most of the men they saw wore cut-off trousers, striped waistcoats and threadbare coats, earning them the name of *sans culottes,* and the women were in skirts and ragged shawls. Almost all wore the red caps of the Revolution. There were some more prosperous, who rode horses or travelled in carriages, whipping up their horses to pass the slow-moving coach, spattering it with mud.

Sam drove past several inns where they could have stopped for the night, saying they were hovels and he would find somewhere better. Jay, who would happily have stopped had he been alone, agreed to go on for Lisette's sake. She had long since ceased to chatter and was asleep with her head lolling on his shoulder. She needed a bed, not a flea pit.

* * *

It was very late when Sam drew up in the yard of what had once been a substantial posting inn in Amiens and jumped down to open the door for them. 'I'm afraid this will have to do,' he said. 'The horses are done for and we cannot keep going all night. I'll go in and bespeak beds.'

Jay roused Lisette. 'Wake up, Lisette. We have stopped.'

She opened her eyes, mortified to realise that she was in Jay's arms again. So much for aloofness; it was impossible with this man. She sat up. 'Where are we?'

'Amiens, still over a hundred kilometres from Paris. We need food and drink and somewhere to sleep.'

Sam returned followed by the innkeeper. He was enormously fat, the first fat man they had seen since leaving Calais. *'Bonsoir, monsieur, madame,'* he said, rubbing his hands in his sacking apron while endeavouring to bow to them. 'We have a room all ready for you. Your servant will have to share with others, I am afraid.'

'But…' Jay began, then stopped. How could he explain that Lisette was not his wife without compromising her? His conversation with Sam about mistresses came back to him. Lisette was not mistress material. How he wished he had not agreed to bring her, but he had and now he had to deal with the consequences. 'Thank you,' he said, leaving the coach and turning to help Lisette down. She was still drowsy and had not heard the conversation. 'Come, my dear, you will soon be comfortable,' he said in French and then murmured in English, 'Trust me.'

They were escorted indoors and up to a bedchamber with much bowing and scraping and a promise that food and drink and washing water would be brought up to them. Sam took their portmanteaux and put them on a table at the foot of the big four-poster bed and went to leave them. 'I will meet you downstairs in the parlour in ten minutes,' Jay told him.

'Aye, aye, sir.'

As soon as he had gone Jay turned to Lisette. She was sitting on the bed, her hands in her lap. 'They have brought your bag in here,' she said dully.

'Yes. I am sorry, Lisette, there has been a misunderstanding.'

'There certainly has. When I begged to come with you, I did not mean this. And if you think...'

'I don't. Nothing was further from my thoughts. The innkeeper misunderstood.'

'You were quick enough to take advantage.'

'Only of the room, madam, not of you.'

'Oh.'

'I am going downstairs. I suggest you go to bed.'

He left her to go in search of Sam, who was enjoying a bowl of onion soup in the deserted dining room. 'What did you tell the innkeeper about us?'

'Only that we required rooms. You know my French. He must have jumped to the wrong conclusion.'

'And left me in a fix. I shall have to explain she is not my wife and ask for another room...'

'There isn't one. I'm sharing with four others. Do you want to make a sixth?'

'So you expect me to share a room with Miss Giradet, do you?'

Sam grinned. 'Why not? What you do with it is your affair.'

'Anyone but you would have been knocked down for his impertinence,' Jay said. 'Be thankful I need you to drive the carriage or you would be on your way back.'

'Aside from that,' Sam said, suddenly serious, 'when we get to Paris, you will not be able to keep her presence a secret without locking her up and I doubt she'd stand for it.'

Jay admitted the truth of that. 'So?'

'Diplomats usually have wives. If you do not want to claim her as a mistress, then she could be Mrs Drymore.'

'Impossible. I have no intention of marrying again.'

'I was not suggesting you go through a marriage ceremony, but in Paris, who's to know you have not? And it will be easier to protect her—no one would dare molest the wife of a British envoy.'

Jay was thoughtful; Sam did have a point and he wondered why he had not thought of it himself. Lisette Giradet seemed to drive rational thought from him, but it was time he took command of the situation again. The innkeeper went to pass them with a heavily loaded tray. 'Is that for us?' he asked, nodding at it.

'Oui, monsieur.'

'I'll take it.' He stood up and relieved the man

of the tray. 'Sam, we will make an early start in the morning,' he said, and took the tray up to the bedchamber he was to share with Lisette.

Lisette had used the warm water that had been brought to her to wash off the grime of travel and undressed for bed. She was sitting up against the pillows when there was a knock at the door. Thinking it was a waiter, she pulled the curtains about the bed and bade him come in. 'Leave it on the table,' she said.

She heard him put the tray down and go to the door. Opening the curtains, intending to go to the table and eat something, she was shocked to find Jay, who had simply gone to shut and lock the door, taking off his coat.

'What are you doing?'

'I am going to have supper. It smells good.' He hung his coat over the back of a chair and pulled another out for her. 'Come, you must be hungry.'

'You can't stay in here.'

'I've nowhere else to go. You would not turn me out, would you?'

'But it is unseemly.'

'You should have thought of that before you

stowed away. The whole adventure is unseemly, as you must have known.'

'Yes, but I did not think...'

'That is your trouble, Miss Giradet, you do not think. I recall you promised to be good if I brought you.'

'Good, yes, wanton, no.'

'Touche!' He laughed. 'Come and eat. You may trust me not to pounce on you.'

She eyed the tray with its gently steaming dishes, smelled the delicious aroma coming from them and hunger won. She wrapped one of the blankets about her and padded in bare feet to join him at the table.

'This innkeeper seems able to keep a good table in hard times,' she said. 'The food at the places we had meals before were most unappetising.'

'No doubt he has a hidden source of supplies and we will be charged accordingly. Let us be thankful for it and eat our fill.' He ladled food on to a plate for her and then helped himself. 'We have a long day ahead of us again tomorrow.'

'Tomorrow,' she repeated. Before tomorrow came they had to spend the night in this room. Could she trust him to keep his promise? She had been in scrapes before, but nothing like this. If he did pounce on her, as he so inelegantly put it, would she fight him off? Did she even want to? If he loved her, she might welcome his advances, but to him she was an encumbrance, a hoyden, he had told her so. He still mourned a dead wife and was true to his vow not to marry again. But that did not mean he would not take a mistress, did it? Oh, she had no one but herself to blame for the pickle she was in.

'Now let us have done with this cat-and-mouse bickering and make some serious decisions,' he said when they had eaten and drunk their fill. 'It is clear the innkeeper thinks you are my wife.'

'You could have told him I was not.'

'I could, but then he would have drawn his own conclusions to your detriment. Besides, I could see the advantages...'

'I'll wager you could.'

'Do not be so waspish. Let me finish. If we pretend to be man and wife, you will, as a British citizen by way of marriage, be safe from arrest, even if it is discovered who you really are—or were before you married me. You will be able to go out and about openly. Otherwise you will have to stay in hiding. You may not care for your reputation, but I certainly care for mine.'

'I see.' She paused. 'But we don't really marry.'

'No, of course not. It is only a pretence for the duration of our stay.'

She could have wept. Torn between the disappointment of his rejection and thankfulness that he was thinking of her good name did not help her confusion. 'So what happens tonight?' she asked.

'If you let me have one of your blankets, I will be quite comfortable on the floor.'

She took off the blanket she was wearing and gave it to him before retiring behind the bed curtain.

She could not sleep. He was fidgeting about on the other side of the curtain, trying to make himself comfortable, and it was a cold night; one blanket would not keep him warm. She lay there, wrestling with her conscience. He was uncomfortable because of her; he could be at home in his own bed on a soft mattress with as many blankets as he needed, if he had not offered to help her. And even if he had come to France alone, he could have had this bed to himself.

'Jay,' she called softly. 'Are you awake?'

'Yes.'

'Come here. There is plenty of room in this bed for two.' She opened the curtains. A shaft of moonlight from the uncurtained window showed him sitting on the floor leaning against the wall, only partially covered by the blanket. He had not undressed beyond taking off his coat, waistcoat, neckcloth and shoes. 'Come and get warm.'

'Do you mean it?'

'I would not have said it otherwise.'

He came to the bed, bringing his blanket with him. If he thought he was going to sleep next to her, she disabused him of that idea by putting a bolster down the bed between them. Thus, suitably separated, with three blankets covering them, they settled down for what was left of the night.

'No one would ever believe this,' he murmured as he fell asleep.

Lisette watched him, knowing she had irredeemably condemned herself in his eyes. The worst of it was, she knew he did not want her, was not even tempted, and that was how it was going to be the whole time they were in France.

She leaned over and gently kissed his cheek. 'No, they wouldn't,' she whispered, then lay back with a sigh and closed her eyes.

Chapter Seven

The journey continued, each day the same as the one before. Day by day they looked out of the carriage windows on a landscape from which all crops, if there had ever been any, had been gathered, where the people shuffled rather than walked and often spat on the carriage as it passed, shouting, '*À bas les aristos!*'

Now and again they were able to find fresh horses and at the end of each day they ate in the dining room of whatever inn could accommodate them, sleeping in the same room, sometimes in the same bed, though more often Jay chose a chair and a footstool and woke with a stiff neck. It seemed to Lisette that this journey would never end, that they were destined to plod through France for ever, so close and yet so far apart. Superficially they had come to know each other well, but on a deeper level he was as much of an enigma as ever.

The coach was prone to breaking down and it took all Sam's ingenuity to find tools and materials to repair it, but repair it he did, and on they went. By now Jay and Lisette had little to say to each other—both were weary and disinclined to put into words what they expected, what they hoped, would happen at the end of the journey. Pontoise had been their last night stop before entering Paris and they set off next morning knowing that for good or ill their adventure was reaching another stage.

They knew they had arrived in Paris when they were stopped by a long queue at a barrier. Rather than make another stop so near their destination, they had elected to drive through the night and were tired and grubby. Lisette longed for a bath and a comfortable bed, one in which she was not haunted by the sound of Jay fidgeting a few feet away, but here they waited while everyone was questioned and searched by armed men in makeshift uniforms. Some were let through, others taken off screaming because contraband had been found in their possession. Gradually Sam drew the coach to a stop at the pole which had been placed across the road to prevent them advancing.

Jay had his papers ready. 'Commodore John Drymore and Mrs Drymore,' he said. 'British Envoy to the National Convention.' He had been saying it all along their route and had become so used to it, the lie slipped easily from his tongue.

His papers were inspected and puzzled over for several minutes before the guard decided it would be prudent to let him through. The barrier was lifted and Sam drove the tired horses into the city. They arrived in the middle of a riot.

It was some time since Jay had been in the city and he was appalled by the change which had taken place. Once-grand mansions and palaces, standing cheek by jowl with tumbledown hovels, had been deserted by their noble occupants and were already showing signs of neglect. The streets were filthy and kennels running down their middles ran slowly with their load of detritus. Paris, which had once been beautiful, the centre of fashion and manners, had been changed into a melting pot, a noisome stew of discontent.

Crowds of people of both sexes and all ages rushed through the streets, brandishing whatever weapons they could find: stolen muskets and picks, lumps of wood and stones torn up from the cobbles. They were breaking into food stores and helping themselves to whatever they could find. A contingent of National Guard was helpless against them and did not even try. Carts containing produce for the market were overturned and their contents looted. Sam used his whip freely to left and right to force a way through as the carriage was rocked by the press of bodies. Lisette, thoroughly frightened, clung to Jay, who put his arm protectively round her.

They made their way through at last and made for what had been the residence of the British Ambassador. There was no one to greet them but a housekeeper by the name of Madame Gilbert, who told them she could also cook for them, and an oddjob man called Albert Mouchon. The wages of both were being paid by the British Government and, as they were generous, the pair had chosen to stay where they felt safe. Jay took possession and sent Sam out with *madame* to buy provisions and ordered the man to light fires in the salon, the dining room and three bedrooms. Outside they could still hear the tumult, but it was far enough away not to bother them.

'The population are blaming the food shortages on hoarders and shopkeepers keeping goods back for those who can afford to pay exorbitant prices,' Sam said when he returned and all three, washed and changed into clean clothes, were sitting at the dining table eating a hastily prepared meal which, though frugal, had cost Sam hundreds of their *assignats*. 'The women are furious over the food shortages and are blaming hoarders. They are far more vociferous than the men. Thousands of men are being conscripted for the army and that's another grievance they have. Without their menfolk they have lost their breadwinners.'

'It will die down by tomorrow,' Jay said. 'We do not need to go out any more today. I for one could sleep the clock round.'

'Me, too,' Sam said, making Lisette realise she had had the better of their journey because Jay had always made sure she slept in a bed and she could doze in the carriage if she could ignore the jolting over the uneven roads, while he had perforce to stay alert against possible attack by the mob who saw a carriage as a sign of wealth. As for Sam, he had had the task of driving them and it could not have been easy, and where he had slept each night she did not know. The crowded hotels often crammed half-a-dozen sleepers into one room, sometimes into one bed.

'Tomorrow I will visit the Assembly and speak to Monsieur Pierre Martin,' Jay told them. 'He is to be my go-between with the French government.'

'What about Michel?' Lisette put in.

Jay turned to her. 'I need to find out how things stand officially with members of the court, whether they are under arrest or able to move about freely. And I must at least appear to be doing our Government's business.'

'Is that all? Every day we delay could be crucial to Michel's safety, surely you realise that after what we have witnessed today.'

'It will do no good making a nuisance of ourselves. As soon as I know how the land lies we can plan a course of action.'

'What do you want me to do?'

'Nothing.'

'Nothing! You would have me sit here all day with nothing to do but worry.'

'Lisette,' he said patiently, while Sam decided to make himself scarce by clearing away the dishes, 'I did not ask you to come with me. I would much rather you had stayed at home, or at least remained on board the yacht. Now you are here, will you please do as I say?'

'Like the dutiful wife I am supposed to be,' she said waspishly.

'Yes.'

'But I am not your wife.'

'No.' It was said quietly.

Sam had come back with a bottle of Calvados and some glasses, which he put on the table in front of Jay. Lisette stood up. 'I will leave you to your brandy, Commodore.'

The look on Jay's face when he had said that one word, 'No', had told her it would not be a comfortable evening if she stayed. She toiled up to her room and sat on a chair by the window. It was an effort not to think about Jay and what he thought of her, but they had come to France with a definite goal and she would be better employed contemplating that rather than eating her heart out for a man who considered her nothing but a nuisance. Michel must come first.

He was surely still at the Tuileries Palace and all they had to do was go there and find him. If he was being watched as he had written he was, then they must find some subterfuge for smuggling him out of the palace, out of the city and out of the country. Jay knew that, knew how worried and impatient she was, so why was he prevaricating? Was he more interested in his errand for the British Government than his promise to her? It was up to her to do something to expedite matters. Nothing could be done that day, while the streets were still seething with angry humanity and, besides, she was too tired to think clearly. She took off all her clothes and climbed into bed. It was soft and warm and she was soon asleep and did, indeed, almost sleep the clock round.

When she rose next morning, Jay had already left the house and her breakfast was served to her by Madame Gilbert. Where Sam was she did not know, but assumed he was with Jay. It meant they trusted her not to go out. More fool them.

As soon as she had finished eating she put a

warm burnous over the green skirt and laced bodice she wore and set off on foot for the Tuileries. The riots had died down, but there were overturned carts still littering the streets and broken glass from shop windows. And there were bodies swinging from some of the lamp posts, strung up there by the pulleys the lamplighters used. She shuddered and passed on.

The Tuileries, as she expected, was guarded and she was stopped and asked her business. 'I carry a petition to the National Convention from my home village,' she said.

'And where might that be?' The man was not unfriendly. Petitions were a daily occurrence and the petitioners usually allowed to pass.

'Villarive. We need our menfolk for the cider making and they are all being conscripted.'

The man laughed and waved her on. 'You had better join the queue, then.'

She went in the direction he had indicated towards the Salle du Manage, which was on the north side of the Tuileries Gardens. It had been home to the royal equestrian academy and because it was the largest indoor space in the city, it was where the Convention did its business. Here were lines of people waiting to be heard. Lisette attached herself to the end of one line, but as soon as the guard had turned his attention elsewhere, she pulled her shawl over her head and set off for the Palace and Michel's rooms.

He was not there. Her disappointment was profound; why she had expected to find him there, she did not know. The King was in prison, so where was Michel? Had they come too late and he had joined his monarch in the Temple? She stood undecided, wondering whether to make her way to that forbidding fortress with its huge, impenetrable walls, when she saw Auguste hurrying along the corridor. She dashed after him.

'Auguste, wait.'

He turned at the sound of his name. 'Mademoiselle Giradet, what are you doing here?' He was thin as a rake, hollow-eyed and badly dressed, nothing like the immaculate man she had known. 'I heard you were safe in England.'

'I came back for Michel. Where is he?'

'You are too late. He was arrested two days ago.'

'Oh, no. Why? On what charge?'

'Do they need a charge?' the man said. 'It is enough that he served the King. You must leave.

You are wanted yourself for breaking your father out of prison and so is your brother for aiding and abetting.'

'Michel had nothing to do with that. He was here in Paris. You can testify to it.'

'Me? Oh, no! I do not fancy losing my head to that awful contraption. It is waiting for you, too, if you stay here. You should never have come back. Henri Canard is after your blood. And your brother's. He went to Villarive after the King was arrested, expecting to live quietly at home, but Canard was there, lording it in the château as if he owned it. They fought, but Canard has many friends, and your brother had to flee for his life. He came back here and was immediately arrested.'

'Where is he being held?'

Auguste shrugged. 'I do not know. I am preparing to leave myself while I can. If I were you, I would make all haste to return to England. You cannot do anything for your brother.'

She turned and left him and made her way back the way she had come, all five senses at fever pitch in case she was recognised. Being so like her brother had its disadvantages. People were coming and going along the corridors, all going about their business and trying to make themselves as inconspicuous as possible. She could smell fear all around her. Her thoughts turned to Jay, who was doing his best to help her and who had trusted her not to do anything foolish while he was out; he would be furious with her for this. That is if she managed to return to the Embassy without being arrested herself. In that event he would never know what had happened to her. No doubt he would wash his hands of her and go home, and who could blame him? She pulled up the hood of her cloak and kept her head down.

Glad to be out in the fresh air again, she took a deep breath and made for the main gate. The same guard was there. 'You did not take long,' he said, recognising her. 'How did you manage it?'

'The queue was too long. I decided to try again another day.'

'It will not be any shorter tomorrow.'

'Perhaps. If so, I may not bother.'

'Very wise.' He waved her on.

She was out in the street again, safely merging with the populace. Where next? She turned and walked along the river bank to the Rue du Temple and made her way along it to the Temple and stood outside, wondering if Michel were inside with the Royal family. There were two distinct buildings: a palace and a tower, a forbidding square edifice, surrounded by four round turrets which the King had once used to imprison those who had offended him. Now he was the one to be incarcerated. Plucking up her courage, she took a step forwards, only to have her arm seized.

'Oh, no, you don't.'

She squirmed round, but she already knew who held her. Jay was looking very annoyed and very determined. 'I was only going to ask if Michel is there,' she told him.

'He is not. Louis is not allowed to have any of his old retainers with him.' He turned her round to walk back the way she had come. She did not resist.

'He has been arrested, his valet told me so.'

'So that was what you were doing at the Palace.'

Mr Roker must have followed her, or Albert Mouchon, ordered to do so by Jay, who did not trust her, after all. 'I wonder you did not think of enquiring there yourself.'

'Oh, but I did. Michel was arrested for assaulting a Deputy, one by the name of Henri Canard, and for assisting in the escape of the *ci-devant* Comte Giradet. He is in La Force.' La Force, situated in the Rue du Roi Sicile, was one of the many prisons in Paris.

'Who told you that? Auguste said he did not know where he was.'

'I have ways of learning these things,' he said. 'It is a pity you cannot trust me.'

She did not know what to say to that and was silent as they made their way through the crowded streets to the Embassy. No one challenged them, though she was on tenterhooks that they might. Once someone pushed past her, nearly knocking her over. Jay grabbed her and from then on kept her arm firmly in his.

'What else did you learn?' she asked, glad of his strength, though she would not admit it.

'About your brother?'

'Yes. I care nothing for politics.'

'It is politics and politicians that have brought France to this pass. They cannot agree among themselves about what is to be done, but if Marat has his way, every nobleman in France will lose his head. It is to be hoped that less bloodthirsty factions will restrain him.'

She glanced up at one of the bodies swinging gently from a lamp post. 'They don't seem to be having much success.'

'No, which is why we must proceed with caution.'

'So, what are you going to do?'

'Tonight, you and I are going to dine with Maximilien Robespierre. He is a committed Republican, so mind what you say.'

'I do not wish to go. He is one of the chief oppressors.'

'Whether you wish it or not, you will, as my wife, accompany me.'

'According to Auguste I am wanted for aiding my father's escape. If Monsieur Robespierre learns of that, not even you will be able to save me.'

'I am aware of that. It is why you are here as my wife, to give you some degree of protection.' He ushered her into the house. 'I must go and change and you should, too. Nothing too elaborate, we do not want to embarrass our host.'

'I do not have anything elaborate. I brought only what I could carry in a portmanteau. I have clothes in plenty at Villarive which I was obliged to leave behind. No doubt Henri Canard's wife is enjoying them. According to Auguste he has taken over the château and is living like a lord.' She gave a short, humourless laugh. 'Is it not strange that those who advocate equality and want to do away with the nobles are the first to ape them when the opportunity arises?'

'It is human nature. Now go and change. Come down to the salon when you are ready. We must give you a new history, an English one.'

They parted on the landing to go to their separate rooms. Lisette turned her clothes out on the bed. There were only two gowns to choose from: a dark blue cambric and a rose-coloured taffeta with a plain quilted stomacher. She chose the latter as being more suitable for an evening occasion. It had no false hips or cage, neither of which could be accommodated in her luggage. With no one to dress her hair, she simply brushed it out and tied it back with a ribbon. Then she made her way downstairs.

Jay was already in the salon. Dressed in a plain suit of dark blue cloth with a dove-grey waistcoat and white shirt, he was standing with his back to the fire. He moved away when she entered and came forwards to take her hand and lead her to a sofa.

'We have half an hour before we need to leave,' he said, sitting down beside her and retaining her hand in his. 'And we must decide who you are and how we came to meet and marry. I think it will be safer if you are English with no French antecedents.'

'Very well. I could use my mother's maiden name of Wentworth.'

'Not that,' he said sharply.

'You do not like it?'

'It will not serve.'

'Will you tell me why?'

'It is too well known and too easily checked.'

Curiosity got the better of her. 'Is that the only reason? I noticed your reaction on a previous occasion when the name was mentioned. There is, I think, some enmity there.'

'It is nothing that need concern you.'

'But I, as your wife——'

'But you are not, and my life before we met has no relevance to our present situation.'

'I meant if I am to play your wife,' she amended.

'I should know something of your past. Is it so painful to speak of it?'

'Yes.'

'You do not trust me.'

He laughed. 'Trust is a two-way affair, Lisette. Perhaps one day I will tell you, but not now. Let us go back to your name and history. I think we could use my mother's maiden name of Challon. If asked, we will say your father was her brother. If anyone takes the trouble to query it, my parents will vouch for you.'

'Does your mother have a brother?'

'No, we will invent one. William Challon, that will do. Long deceased, of course. So is your mother. You grew up at Blackfen Manor with my parents.'

'It will make us cousins.'

'All the better. We have known each other all our lives.'

'Yes, and when your wife died, I was there to comfort you and we fell in love.'

'Must you bring love into it?'

'Of course. We must be convincing.'

This pretend story was playing havoc with her emotions. The story might be fiction, but her love was real enough. Why could they not talk about it? A man should not mourn his wife for ever and be blind to new affection.

'Very well, the story is yours. You will probably not need to tell it anyway. What about a Christian name? Lisette is a little too French. Shall you be Elizabeth?'

'Elizabeth Challon,' she mused. 'Newly wed. Could this visit to France be our honeymoon, do you think?'

'It is a strange place to come for a wedding trip,' he said with a laugh. 'We are likely to lose our heads if we are not careful.'

'Is that not why you are here at the behest of the British Government, to prevent more bloodshed?'

'Yes, hence the need to be pleasant to Robespierre and his like. I have asked Sam to bring the carriage round at half past six.'

She looked up at the clock on the mantel. 'It is nearly that now.'

'Yes. He will come and tell us when he is ready.'

'What has he been doing all day?'

'Making enquiries for me. You would be surprised at what he manages to achieve, given a free hand. It would not surprise me to learn he knows the layout of La Force prison in perfect detail.'

'Oh, Jay,' she said. 'You have been thinking of me, after all.'

'Of course. You are forever in my thoughts, you and that brother of yours who seems to be able to command your utmost love and loyalty.'

'Why not?' she said, puzzled by the tone of his voice. 'Blood is thicker than water and he is my twin, which makes us extra close. Do you not feel like that about your sisters?'

'Naturally I do.'

'There you are, then.'

Sam arrived to tell them the carriage was at the door and if they did not want it purloined, they had best make haste and get into it.

The house in Rue St Honore where Robespierre lodged was the home of Maurice Duplay and it was he who greeted them and ushered them into the salon where his other guests had already arrived. Lisette was introduced to Maximilien Robespierre, an elegant little man with perfect manners, Georges Danton, the Minister of Justice, who was fat and not at all attractive, and

Philippe Le Bas, another Deputy who was married to their host's elder daughter, Elisabeth, who was there with her husband. The party was completed by Madame Duplay, her younger daughter, Eleanore, and Pierre Martin who, unlike the others who were Jacobins, served on the National Convention as an independent.

Lisette did not curtsy—such courtesies went out with the Revolution—but she inclined her head slightly and greeted each of them politely, calling them *monsieur, madame* or *mademoiselle,* though they referred to each other as *citoyen* or *citoyenne.*

Supper was served almost as soon as they arrived and the conversation at the table was entirely about politics and the war with Austria. Lisette took no part, preferring to listen. Jay, she noted, was circumspect in what he said, neither agreeing nor disagreeing with their fellow diners, even when what they said seemed outrageous.

'Is this your first visit to Paris, Mrs Drymore?' Lisette had not been paying attention and was startled to be addressed in English by Robespierre. She glanced up at Jay, who was looking closely at her, as if telling her to be careful how she answered.

'Yes, it is,' she said, also in English. 'I had heard so much about what a beautiful city it is and indeed that is true, there are some very grand buildings, but it has been spoilt by the dreadful violence. I was very frightened when we arrived in the middle of a riot and would have fainted if my dear husband had not shielded me.'

'Just lately the populace have been up in arms about the shortages of food and the conscription,' he explained. 'Hard as it is, we need men to fight the war.'

'Can you not control them?'

'The people are free to express their displeasure,' Danton put in. 'That is what the Revolution is all about.'

'But they are so bloodthirsty.'

'Unfortunately that is the inevitable consequence of revolution,' Robespierre told her. 'We cannot detain the whole population, but the ringleaders will be arrested and tried and will suffer the consequences. We can only control them with fear of reprisals.'

She refrained from saying what was in her mind when she saw Jay surreptitiously shaking his head. 'I am afraid I did not understand,' she said. 'What little French I learned in the school-room was quickly forgotten.'

Jay appeared to be choking and covered it by drinking from his wine glass. No one else seemed to think this statement anything but the truth and Robespierre was apologetic. 'I am sorry, madam, it is discourteous of us to converse in a language you cannot understand. I have been explaining to your husband that the French are a peaceful nation at heart and only go to war when there is no alternative.'

'Please carry on with your discussion,' she said. 'I am sure you must prefer to speak French. Do not mind me.'

'Thank you, *madame*. Citizen Danton has little English and it is important we all understand the discussion. Commodore Drymore's French is excellent.'

She smiled and continued to eat, listening to their talk about their peaceful intentions, though the Frenchmen deprecated the refuge Britain was giving to fleeing nobles and refactory priests, who had been ordered to return. 'If that were not bad enough,' Danton said, 'there are Englishmen in this country actively aiding nobles and priests to escape.'

'If there are, they are acting on their own account,' Jay said smoothly. 'They do not have the support of my government.'

'It would help to convince us of good intent if the British Government forbade such a thing,' Robespierre put in.

'Do you know who they are?' Jay asked.

'Unfortunately no, except for one who calls himself James Smith. He abducted the *ci-devant* Comte Giradet and smuggled him out of the country when he was on his way to his trial. But there have been others. I am told they call themselves the Piccadilly Gentlemen. If they could be brought to book, it would certainly help diplomatic relations between your country and ours.'

'I will put the problem to my government,' James said. 'But I am sure they will say no English law has been broken and it is up to the French government to find them and arrest them.'

'We would if we had their names...'

'I am afraid I cannot help you there.'

It was an effort on Lisette's part not to appear too interested in this, but it looked very much as though the success of the negotiations would be dependent on Jay supplying details of anyone helping the *émigrés*. And that included himself.

The meal ended and she retired with the ladies to take tea, which Jay had had the forethought to bring from England and present to their hostess. Still pretending she did not understand French, they spent an hilarious hour trying to communicate in sign language and the odd word of each other's language. When the gentlemen joined them, the whole charade was replayed for their benefit.

They were still laughing when the evening came to an end and Jay took her back to the Embassy. 'They want names,' she said, suddenly serious, as Sam drove them through the streets, quieter now after the tumult of the day before. 'You can't give them names, can you?'

'No, of course not. I shall have to hedge and say enquiries to identify the men could take some time.'

'How long will it be before they put two and

two together and realise James Smith is John Dry-more?'

'Not before we are safely on our way, I hope.'

'Then it is becoming urgent to find Michel and make our escape.'

'Not so urgent we make foolish mistakes. I know how impatient you are, Lisette, and I can understand that, but whatever I do must be fool-proof.' He paused before going on. 'Why did you pretend you could not understand French?'

'It seemed a good idea. People might talk in front of me and say things I am not supposed to hear. They might not have spoken about the *émigrés* and what they expected of the Brit-ish Government if they thought I could under-stand. Besides, if I have to adopt the disguise of a Frenchwoman, no one will suspect it is me, the foolish wife of a British envoy.'

'What makes you think you might have to adopt a disguise?'

'Well, you never know, do you?'

'Oh, yes, I do. You will take no part in the res-cue.'

'You might need me.'

'Never!'

That one word silenced her. The pleasure went out of the evening. She had been rejected yet again.

The carriage came to a stop outside the Embassy and Sam jumped down to open the door for them. Lisette preceded them into the house, made her excuses and went straight up to her room.

'What's the matter with madam?' Sam asked, fetching the half-empty bottle of Calvados and a couple of glasses from the cupboard in the salon. 'Did the evening not go well?'

'It went as well as can be expected. Robespierre assures me that the French government has no plans to declare war on England, though we are in bad cess with them over our willingness to shelter *émigrés*. He would like us to force them to return, but I told him we could not do that. England is a free country, they are welcome to stay as long as they abide by our laws. They want the names of anyone helping them out of France.'

'Lord Portman and Nathaniel Kingslake, for instance,' Sam said. 'And you and me.'

'Yes. James Smith is the only name they have.'

'Is that a sticking point?'

'I do not think so. They are fully committed to

war in Europe, they cannot afford to go to war with us. They haven't the men or the money.'

'What about Giradet?'

'Ah, Giradet. What did you find out about La Force?'

'It was once the residence of the Duc de la Force, but was converted into a prison twelve years ago. It is a warren of rooms and corridors, all secure and well guarded. Which one houses Monsieur Giradet, I have not yet been able to ascertain. If we are going to get him out of there, it will have to be by subterfuge—we'd need an army to fetch him out by force.'

'My thoughts exactly. We could try the same method we used to free his father.'

'You mean pretend to be guards conveying him to his trial? Do you know when it will be?'

'Not yet.'

'I suppose you can't ask Monsieur Martin to find out.'

'No. I have to keep my government business and the rescue of Giradet as far apart as possible. Unfortunately, Miss Giradet cannot understand that.'

'Oh, I see. She is sulking.'

'No, I do not think she is sulking, she is simply angry with me.'

Sam laughed again. 'I am thinking that it is as well you are not married to the lady—your life together would be tempestuous.'

'Oh, I don't know. She is frustrated. It might help if I could give her something to do that will not involve her in danger.'

'Buy her some knitting.'

Jay laughed. He could not imagine Lisette sitting still long enough to knit. But it left him wondering just how well he knew the lady. Did she sew and embroider? Did she read? Did she like shopping for clothes? What was there to buy in Paris?

He put the suggestion to her the next morning. She seemed to have forgotten their disagreement and was anxious to please him. He was not sure if that boded well or ill. 'We may be here longer than I thought,' he said. 'Two gowns and a skirt and blouse are hardly enough.'

'It is more than some women have,' she said, surprised that he knew the contents of her meagre wardrobe.

'True, but you are not some women. If we are asked to another function, you cannot appear in the same dress. I will give you *assignats* to go shopping, but make sure you take Madame Gilbert with you.'

'And what will you be doing while I am gone?'

'What I came to France to do.'

'Making peace with the monsters?'

'Yes, but also trying to free your brother.'

'You have a plan?' she asked eagerly.

'Not yet. I need to find out everything I can, whereabouts in the prison he is being held and the routine of the guards, when and where he will be tried and on what charge. Then I need to appoint a defence lawyer whom we can trust to help us.'

'You mean to try and defend him in a court of law? You know the result of that is a foregone conclusion. He will be sentenced to death.'

'I hope and pray it will not come to that.'

As soon as they finished their breakfast, he left to go about his business and Lisette and Madame Gilbert set off to look for clothes. Many of the shops had been looted, even those selling ladies' finery. Lisette had seen several women in bedraggled gowns that had once been fashionable, the material of which was too fine to last in the hurly-burly life of a Parisian peasant. They were already so faded and grubby it was difficult to tell the colour they had originally been. She was not looking for finery and eventually they found a bolt of blue silk and a mantua maker to make it into a gown. Stays were another matter. There were none to be had except second-hand ones and she would not buy those. The dressmaker was instructed to make a simple round gown with a bodice that closed at the front. That done, Lisette went in search of masculine garments.

'What do you want those for?' Madame Gilbert demanded.

'For my brother. He will be joining us shortly.' She did not explain how or why; it was no business of the *concierge*.

They completed their shopping by buying food at exorbitant prices; the bread alone cost more than twice what it had when she was last in France and the *assignat* had been devalued by at least half. The country was close to bankruptcy which was why everything looked so run-down.

They set off back to the Embassy, making a detour along Rue St Antoine in order to look at La Force prison. It was situated in an alley, rising tall and grim above the buildings that surrounded it. There was a courtyard in front of it where two guards were marching back and forth before a heavy wooden door. Lisette stopped to look up at its many barred windows, wondering where Michel was and if he could see her if he were to look out. As they watched, a tumbril was driven into the courtyard and came to a stop. The door of the prison was thrown open and several men and two women were prodded out by armed guards. The women were crying and clinging together and had to be forcibly lifted into the tumbril. The men climbed in and stood stoically waiting for it to move off.

The *concierge* shuddered and crossed herself as the tumbril passed them, escorted by armed guards and accompanied by a crowd on foot, jeering at its occupants. 'God have mercy on them,' she said. 'Let us go, *madame,* before we are made to join them.'

Lisette turned to leave. 'Where are they being taken?'

'To Madame Guillotine. It is the fate of everyone who leaves that place.'

'Is no one found innocent and set free?'

The woman shrugged. 'I have never heard of such a thing.'

Jay was not back when they returned to the Embassy and had not returned by supper time. Lisette ate a lonely meal and went to bed. She could not sleep. The sight of that tumbril and its white-faced, weeping occupants haunted her. If the mob had emptied the prisons in that dreadful massacre the previous month, they had soon been filled again. Did Jay have any intention of risking life and limb to get Michel out? He had never met Michel, so why would he? It was up to her. But how? Would the prison warders allow her to speak to her brother? Could she change places with him? If she did, how could she get out herself? Was she prepared to die in his place? In the quiet of the early hours, when the house was silent and even the noise in the street had quieted, it was easy to contemplate doing it. But in the light of a new dawn, would she feel so brave? Was there any other way?

Chapter Eight

Jay was at breakfast when Lisette went down-stairs the following morning. He looked tired and was reading some official-looking papers while he ate. He laid them aside to greet her. 'Lisette, good morning. Did you sleep well?'

'Yes, thank you.' She sat down and poured her-self a cup of coffee which, like the tea, had been brought from England. 'What are you going to do today?'

'I am going to attend a court session to see how the justice system works. You may come with me if you wish, but only if you promise to remain si-lent.'

Wanting to know what it would be like if Michel were brought before a court of law, she decided to ignore his hint that she could not hold her tongue and go with him.

* * *

The court sat in the great hall of the Conciergerie on the Île de la Cité. It housed the Palais de Justice as well as the oldest prison in Paris. If the accused were not already held there, they were transferred there in the days before their trial and brought up from the dungeons to attend it. It would not be an easy place to effect a breakout, Lisette decided as they made their way to the courtroom.

There was ample room for hundreds of spectators. Most of the prisoners were political, but not all. There were also thieves, arsonists, blackmailers and prostitutes. These were dealt with swiftly and fairly, but it was those accused of plotting against the Revolution who fared worst. Neither judge nor jury was inclined to leniency—certainly the vociferous public were not. Time after time the judge had to call loudly for order. Witnesses were called, but they came in fear and trepidation.

'She has been bullied into it,' Lisette whispered to Jay as one housekeeper gave evidence against her employer, who was accused of writing pamphlets against the Revolution. Another was arraigned for allowing a refractory priest to say mass in his home and his own tearful daughter was required to give evidence against him. Lisette was reminded that her father had done the same thing. Thank goodness he was safe in England.

They had seen and heard enough long before the day's business was done and left to go back to the Embassy. 'Michel will have to be freed before he is brought here,' she said. 'We could not take him from here with all those people around.'

'Yes, I agree,' he said, then stopped as they came face-to-face with a tall, broad-shouldered man who might once have been handsome, but whose features had become flabby with good living. Instead of moving to one side to allow them to pass, he stood, feet apart, in front of Jay and laughed. 'Well, well, if it isn't John Drymore,' he said in English. 'You are a long way from home, Drymore. Feeling brave, were you? Did you think you were safe from me in Paris?'

Jay's face was stony. 'Out of the way, Wentworth, and let us pass.'

'Wentworth,' Lisette gasped.

'That is my name,' the stranger said. 'Gerald Wentworth *à votre service, madame.*' To Jay he said, 'Are you not going to present me to your friend?'

Jay, who had been staring at the man with loathing, turned to Lisette. 'Elizabeth, this is—'

'I think I know who he is,' she said. 'But does he know me?'

'I am afraid I do not have that honour,' he said.

She turned to Jay. 'Tell him.'

'My wife, Mrs Drymore. Elizabeth, Mr Gerald Wentworth,' Jay said tersely. 'Now will you allow us to pass?'

'Your wife, eh? Well, I never.' He stepped to one side, removed his tall hat and gave Lisette an elaborate bow. 'Good day to you, Mrs Drymore. No doubt we will meet again ere long.' He went off, chuckling to himself.

'Why did you not tell him the truth?' Lisette said when she and Jay were out of earshot.

'Because you are in Paris using a pseudonym and it is as well to maintain it to everyone. You never know who might be listening.'

'But if my guess is right, he is my uncle.'

'I was under the impression you had no love for your English relatives.'

'Nor have I. I was curious to know what his re-action might be on learning my identity.'

'No doubt he would find it comical.'

'You dislike him, don't you?'

'Yes.'

'You once said you would tell me why one day. I think that day has come, don't you?'

'Perhaps, but I cannot speak of it in the street and I have arranged to meet Pierre Martin later. We will talk this evening.'

At last, she was going to find out what made Jay Drymore the serious, uncompromising man he was, and perhaps she would be able to soften him. She tucked her hand under his elbow as any wife might, half-expecting him to move away, but instead she felt a slight squeeze. That was a good sign, surely?

They were almost at the entrance to the Embassy when they were accosted by a miserable-looking beggar dressed in dirty rags. Old and bent, his hair was unkempt and his face filthy. The only bright thing about him was his red cap. When he grinned at them he showed blackened teeth. Lisette shuddered at the sight of him, especially when he caught hold of Jay's coat. 'A sou for a drink, citizen,' he whined. 'I've had not a sup all day.'

Jay reached into his pocket and handed over a small coin. The man bit into it and began to laugh. It was such a curiously joyful sound for one in such dire straits that Lisette found herself staring at him in puzzlement. 'The devil it is to get you to part with money, my friend,' he said to Jay in perfect English. 'I shall keep it as a souvenir.'

'Harry! You devil!' Jay's eyes lit with pleasure. 'Where did you spring from?'

'I have just arrived from Calais. Speaking of that drink…'

Jay looked about him. There was no one in the street. He ushered Lisette and then Harry into the Embassy and shut the door. The bent old beggar stood upright; he was even taller than Jay. He was not old either, being in his early fifties, and his eyes, which had seemed dull, gleamed with intelligence and humour.

'Lisette, this is Lord Portman,' Jay said. 'I am sure you have heard my father mention his name. Harry, meet Miss Giradet, though for the moment she is known as Mrs Drymore.'

'How do you do, Mrs Drymore.' He executed a flourishing bow, which was so incongruous set against his rags that she burst out laughing. 'You like my disguise?' he queried.

'It is very convincing,' she said. 'How do you do it?'

'I once trod the boards with Jay's grandmother when I was a mere stripling and played many roles, even old men. Alas, I am no longer a stripling, but I can still play a part.'

Sam came into the hall from the back of the house. 'I thought I heard voices...' He stopped suddenly. 'Lord Portman. Well, I'll be damned.'

'I did not deceive you then, Sam?'

'I have seen you in too many guises, my lord, to be taken in.'

'Show his lordship up to one of the spare rooms and take some hot water up for him to wash that dreadful stuff off his face and teeth,' Jay told Sam. 'And find him some decent clothes.'

Harry followed Sam up the stairs while Lisette went into the kitchen to tell Madame Gilbert there would be a guest for dinner and they would like some refreshment to stave off the hunger pangs until then.

* * *

It was over tea and some unappetising cakes that they sat down to talk. Harry had changed into some of Jay's clothes and though he was able to wear Jay's stockings, his shoes were too small. 'I trust you will excuse me, coming into your presence in stockinged feet, Mrs Drymore,' he said, maintaining the pretence in case the *concierge* was listening. 'And in this suit. Truly, Jay is not the most fashionably dressed of men. It comes with being a sailor and then a farmer, I think.'

'It is not a good idea to be too well dressed in Paris now,' Jay said. 'Your usual flamboyant garb would have you hanging from the nearest lamp post at the blink of an eye.'

'I am aware of that.'

'Do you also know you are a wanted man?'

'I guessed that might be so.'

'Then why, in heaven's name, risk coming back?'

'I heard from your father what was afoot and decided you might be glad of a little help, so here I am. I came with Nat Kingslake and Joe Potton. I left them playing cards with mine host at the tavern where we are lodging. They will no doubt have lost their money by the time I return, but it is good to keep in with the local population, especially one as helpful as Monsieur Barnard has been.' Nat was Nathaniel Kingslake, brother-in-law of Lord Cadogan, who, as Sir Ashley Saunders, was another prominent member of the Society, and Joe had been rescued by James from poverty and a life of crime in Ely when he was ten years old and been given an education and a job, but he had never lost the ability to live on his wits.

'I am obliged to you,' Jay said. 'Five heads are better than two.'

'Better than three,' Lisette corrected him. 'Now we are six.'

'You, madam, will stay out of it,' Jay said.

'Oh, dear, do I detect a little dissension?' Harry queried.

'Lisette is not here at my behest,' Jay told him. 'She smuggled herself aboard the yacht and I am stuck with her.'

'How *ungallant* you are, my friend. I wonder she bothers with you.'

'We are stuck with each other,' Lisette said, not to be outdone. 'The Commodore is being very difficult. I am sure I can help, but he will not tell me what his plans are.'

'Jay was always one to play his cards close to his chest, Mrs Drymore. It is why he won so many battles at sea and earned his promotion. You may safely trust him.'

'I would if he would only confide in me, but he tells me nothing. I don't think he knows what to do and he will not listen to my ideas.'

'What ideas?' Harry asked. 'I am listening.'

'I could dress up as Michel and change places with him. We are very alike and when we were children often used to dress in each other's clothes and pretend to be each other. It was a game we played with our friends.'

'And what do you hope to achieve?' Jay demanded. 'Have you thought how you will escape when the prison guards find out they have been duped? Do you imagine they will simply let you go?'

'Probably not.'

'Now can you see why I will not let her become involved?' Jay asked Harry. 'Her ideas are madness.'

'Jay has a point, madam,' Harry said. 'If you

took your brother's place, you would be signing your own death warrant. We cannot allow that.' Then, to Jay, 'What have you done so far?'

'I discovered Michel is being held in La Force, but where exactly we do not yet know. Prisoners are taken from there to the Conciergerie a day or two before their trial and held there after sentencing until the tumbril comes to take them to the guillotine. They are, of course, guarded closely at all times.'

'What is he being charged with?'

'I have not heard the formal arraignment, but Sam heard that he is accused of planning counter-revolution, aiding and abetting the escape of the *ci-devant* Comte Giradet from prison, and assaulting a member of a provincial assembly on his lawful business.'

'That is surely enough to hang any man.'

'None of it is true,' Lisette said. 'He had nothing to do with Papa's escape, as Jay perfectly knows, and as for assaulting Henri Canard—can you blame him when the man is squatting in our home as if he owned it?'

'When is the trial to be?'

'We don't know,' Jay said. 'I don't think the

date has been fixed. Perhaps they do not have a strong enough case to condemn him and are looking for more evidence. Until we can discover exactly where Giradet is being held and can gain access to him, Lisette and I must continue to play our part as a British envoy and his wife.'

'Aah.'

Madame Gilbert knocked and entered and said their dinner was on the table and they repaired to the dining room to eat boiled mutton and some tarts, which were more turnips than meat. It was followed by stewed apple, making a real peasant meal for which the housekeeper made no apology. They were joined by Sam at Jay's behest.

'Can you do anything to help us, my lord?' Lisette asked when the *concierge* left them to serve themselves.

'It needs some thought and careful preparation.'

'That is exactly what I have been saying,' Jay said. 'We cannot go at it with guns half-cocked.'

'It is best not to use guns, either cocked or half-cocked,' Harry said.

Jay laughed. 'You know what I mean.'

'Yes.' Harry turned to Lisette. 'Jay is right, you know. Until the date of your brother's trial has been fixed, he will come to no harm where he is. In truth, he is better off, for out on the streets he could well become the victim of the mob. I must caution you to be patient.'

'I know, but it is difficult. If only I could see Michel and talk to him, to let him know we are working on his behalf, I would feel so much easier in my mind.'

'If you are as much like your brother as you say you are, I would not recommend you go anywhere near La Force,' Jay said.

'Lord Portman will show me how to disguise myself.'

'Oh, will I?' Harry said. 'I have no wish to fall out with your husband.'

'He is not my husband.'

'While you are in Paris, I am,' Jay said. 'And a most inconvenient spouse you are to boot. When we go back to England is another matter.' He paused and changed tack. 'Tell me, Harry, have you been to Highbeck recently?'

'I was there last week. They are all well, though your mother is worried about you. There are such gruesome tales being told in the newspapers, she is half-convinced she will never see you again and she is inclined to blame your father for aiding and abetting you to go.'

'I have never known them quarrel.'

'Oh, they are not quarrelling. Like all good wives, she is suffering in silence. I only found out from one of your sisters.'

'See,' Jay said to Lisette. 'Even Harry thinks good wives should keep their own counsel and do not defy their lords.'

'Then it is as well our state of matrimony is only temporary,' she said with some asperity.

Jay changed the subject and turned back to Harry. 'Did you see Edward and Anne?'

'To be sure I did. I was taken to see an enormous eel in the moat which they told me no one was allowed to catch because they wanted to see how long it would grow. They did not believe me when I said it would swim away to find a mate and make more little eels. When I told them I should shortly see you, they sent their respectful regards and hoped you would both be home soon. I think they like you, Mrs Drymore.'

'And I am very fond of them. Was my father well?'

'Yes, but pining for you and for his son. He told

me he was very vexed with you for going off as you did and putting yourself in danger, but I was to tell you he forgave you and prayed for your safe return. I assured him I would add my weight to Jay's to bring matters to a successful outcome.'

'Thank you,' she said. The advent of Lord Portman with his cheerful optimism had made her feel much better, and even Jay seemed to have regained some of his good humour. They finished their meal in pleasant conversation, in which Harry told of some of his adventures, making light of dangerous situations, and Jay countered with stories of his days at sea.

When the repast was finished, Harry laid down his cutlery and stood up. 'Thank you, madam, for an entertaining meal. I can hardly be truthful and call it delicious. When we are all back in England, you and Jay, and your brother too, shall be my guests. Rosamund will welcome you, I know. Now I must go back to Nat and Joe or they will wonder what has become of me.' He went off to put on his down-at-heel shoes and picked up his bundle of rags. 'I shall need these again, no doubt.

I will return your clothes next time we meet.' He bowed to Lisette. 'Good day, madam.'

'I am going out myself,' Jay said, retrieving his hat and outdoor coat from a cupboard in the vestibule. 'I will accompany you as far as the corner.' To Lisette, he said, 'I do not know when I shall be back. Do not wait supper for me.'

He followed Harry out of the house, leaving Lisette to spend the evening alone.

'You are taking a very great risk,' Jay said as they walked. 'Mama said you were nearly caught the last time you were here and had decided not to come again.'

'But I could not let you struggle on alone when it is within my power to help. I did not say anything in front of Miss Giradet, but her father is very weak and confused. Your mother has employed a nurse to look after him. Let us hope the safe arrival of both his children will effect a cure.'

'I hope so too.'

'Whose idea was it for Miss Giradet to be your wife?'

'Mine. It was after she insisted on coming with

me. As a respectable British diplomat, I could hardly arrive with a mistress.'

'Mistress?' Harry queried, one eyebrow raised.

'No, of course not, but that is how it would be viewed.'

'And she agreed?'

'I think she would have agreed to anything to be allowed to stay with me.'

'Aah.'

'I wish you would not say "Aah" in that knowing fashion, Harry. It is the second time you have done so today. There is nothing between Miss Giradet and me, nor will there be. We have naught in common.'

'Except pig-headedness.' Harry laughed. 'Tell me, has she made you a good wife?'

'In so far as she accompanied me to a supper party at Robespierre's and managed not to embarrass me.' He chuckled suddenly. 'She told them she could not speak French and enjoyed herself no end when the ladies retired and they spent a whole hour trying to understand each other.'

'She has a sense of humour, then.'

'Yes. When she is not being argumentative, she

can be good company. And don't you dare "Aah" me again.'

'Then I will refrain. But have a care, Jay, you might find yourself falling in love.'

'I don't think so.'

'It is not something you can control and I tell you this from experience. I was determined not to fall in love with my wife, but I did. I promise you I have never regretted it.'

'Then you were lucky.'

'Oh, no doubt of it. You could be too.'

'Shall we speak of other things?' Jay said to stop him enlarging on this theme which made him feel decidedly uncomfortable. 'How to rescue the lady's brother, for instance. You brought the Comte and Comtesse d'Estrange safely to England. How did you manage that?'

'I took over the tumbril that was to take them to the guillotine. We were surrounded by a mob, baying for blood, but I used it to my advantage. I appealed to the *maréchaussée* that if they did not whisk the prisoners away, Madame Guillotine would be deprived of two of her victims before they even reached her. They forced a way through so that we could drive down a side alley. While they were busy holding off the crowd at the head of the alley, we made our escape. We went to the tavern where I am staying now and changed our clothes. I had a coach and fast horses waiting nearby and forged passes. It was planned down to the last minute.'

'But you did have a narrow escape.'

'Yes, the *maréchaussée* were soon on our tail, but we managed to outwit them.'

'When I was with Robespierre, he asked for the names of the Piccadilly Gentlemen who have been helping the *émigrés* and he expects me to provide them. How he found out about them I have no idea. He must have spies everywhere. It was hinted that peace between our countries might depend upon them being brought to book. Now you are here, it makes it doubly awkward.' He paused. 'There is another difficulty I had not envisaged. Gerald Wentworth is in Paris.'

'The devil he is! What is he doing here?'

'I do not know, but it can't be good.'

'Have you met?'

'We were accosted by him on the way out of the Conciergerie earlier today.'

'We?'

'Lisette was with me. Fortunately he has never met her and I introduced her as my wife. He seemed to think that was cause for merriment.'

'Does Miss Giradet know about Marianne?'

'Only that she died in a riding accident. I did not see that it would help to tell her any more than that. Did you know she is Wentworth's niece?'

Harry whistled. 'No, I had no idea.'

'Lisette's mother was his sister. She became estranged from the family when she married the Comte and Lisette had never met any of them until today. Unfortunately she is curious.'

'She deserves the truth, Jay. After all, you have done nothing to be ashamed of—quite the opposite.'

'I know, but I have been putting it off. I try not to think about it at all because it makes me angry and having to drag it up again and explain myself is going to be hard. I have enough to contend with without that.'

'Does Wentworth know who the Piccadilly Gentlemen are?'

'I don't know, but I doubt it. You have not been active of late and my father has been talking of winding up the Association. You are all past the first bloom of youth.'

'You do have a way of making a fellow feel good, Jay. I'll have you know I'm as fit as a man half my age.'

Jay laughed. 'And twice as wily.'

'You may be thankful for that, ere long, my friend.'

'I meant it as a compliment.'

They had arrived at the corner of the street where they stopped. 'I have to meet Pierre Martin,' Jay said. 'He is my go-between with the National Convention. I think he is going to suggest I appease Robespierre by promising him at least some of the names he asked for. I'll have to prevaricate. There is nothing would make me betray you.'

'That goes without saying, Jay. Come and see me when you are done. I will be at the Cross Keys. It's in the Rue St Antoine. Bring Sam. We can talk business.'

'It might be late.'

'No matter. Any time before midnight.'

Jay watched Harry walk away. He seemed perfectly at ease, but Jay was worried. Harry's was one of the names Robespierre wanted and his presence in Paris put him in great danger. He would have to persuade him his help was not needed and he and the others should go home. It was a great pity because he could be a great asset. He would meet them later and glean as much advice as possible before they left. It meant he would not have that talk with Lisette as planned, but that was just as well. The truth might easily sully their relationship, tenuous as it was; she might even go off to meet Wentworth. Even thinking about such a possibility had him clenching his fists.

Lisette roamed about the house all evening, poking into rooms she had not entered before, reading the titles on the books in the library, even going so far as to pull one out, but she could not settle to read. There was too much going on in her head. Did Jay go out on purpose to avoid talking to her about her uncle? Early on she had been convinced there was antipathy between the two men, but now she realised it was downright enmity. What had happened between them? Who was in the right and who in the wrong? Would it make a difference about how she felt about Jay?

Did she really want to know? What she had seen of her uncle, she had not liked. There seemed to be a threat in every word he had said. Perhaps it was better to remain in ignorance.

There was a desk in the library and some pens and ink on it. She found some paper and began making a list of things in her brother's favour and things against his release. When she had finished, she put the pen down with a heavy sigh.

There was so little in the positive column, except a tenuous defence which the prosecuting counsel would easily demolish. She had added Lord Portman to that side as well as Jay's earlier success at freeing her father. On the opposite side the list was much longer. Michel was in a secure prison, closely guarded and not allowed visitors. The Revolutionaries were intent on doing away with the nobility, especially anyone who was loyal to the King. Michel had been with Louis when he tried to flee and had stayed at his post even after his Majesty had been sent to the Temple. He had fought with Henri Canard and Henri Canard was not one to let the matter drop. Lastly, no one could be found to defend him in court.

It made her so miserable, she screwed the paper

into a ball and threw it in the fire. If only Jay would come home. She needed him. Even if they were quarrelling, it was better than sitting alone dwelling on what seemed insurmountable problems. One of the biggest was that Jay did not love her. What his motives were for offering help, she did not know, but it was certainly not love.

She picked at a frugal supper, then went to bed, where she lay awake, trying to think of ways of freeing her brother without Jay Drymore's help. The only way she could think of was to throw herself on the mercy of Robespierre or Danton, but how could she do that without telling them her real name and betraying Jay?

She heard low voices in the corridor outside her bedroom and then the sound of something being dropped with a thud, followed by an oath. She crept to the door and flung it open. Jay was in the act of bending to pick up the shoe he had dropped and Sam was creeping past, his shoes in his hand. Both were dressed very shabbily in black suits going green with age and the red cap of the Revolution. Their faces were dirty, their hair matted. She burst into laughter.

'You find us comical, no doubt,' Jay said, as Sam continued on his way and disappeared into his own room.

'What have you been doing?'

'Learning to live like a *citoyen* of Paris.'

'With Lord Portman?'

'Yes. Please go back to bed. You are not decent.'

He was unsmiling and brusque. She retreated and banged the door shut. It wasn't fair of him to make her love him so, when there was no hope of a happy conclusion. She was just as unmarriageable as she had always been and this pretence of theirs only heightened that.

Jay went on to his own room and stripped off the filthy clothes. Harry might take easily to being one of the *sans culottes,* but he was not comfortable in the garb. But if it helped to get Michel out of gaol and all of them safely back to England he would have to heed Harry's lessons, because the sooner that happened the better for all concerned. How convincing could he make himself? Not very, if Lisette's reaction was any measure; she had laughed at him.

Had she realised that the nightrail she was wearing was almost transparent? He had been given a tantalising glimpse of womanly curves and firm breasts which had roused him as nothing else had done since he had last shared a bed with Marianne. And his wife had been deceiving him even then. How she must have been laughing at him. And now Lisette laughed. It was for a different reason, it was true, but it had been enough to bring it all back. If only he had not drunk so much of that rough wine...

He was woken next morning when Sam brought water for him to wash and shave. 'You are awake at last,' he said. 'Seems to me late nights do not suit you, if you cannot rouse yourself before noon.'

'Don't be ridiculous. I've stood many a night watch as you well know. It was that rotgut wine they serve at the Cross Keys.'

'You have me there. I was feeling decidedly queasy myself when I woke. A glass of Calvados soon cured it. Shall I fetch you some?'

'If you please. Where is Miss Giradet? Has she had her breakfast?'

'Hours ago, Commodore. Then she went out.'

'Out? Where?'

'Shopping, so she said.'

'With Madame Gilbert?'

'No. Madame is cooking your breakfast.'

'Fetch my clothes, Sam, and be quick about it. Heaven knows what mischief the woman will get up to out on her own.'

He flung himself into his clothes and left the house without having anything to eat or drink except a hastily swallowed glass of brandy.

Lisette was standing outside Monsieur Duplay's house, wondering if she dare knock on the door. Her hesitation was not fear for herself, but the knowledge that if she took the next step she would be betraying Jay. He was an exasperating man, so cool-headed, so convinced he was always right, so blind to her feelings, that she ought not to hesitate. If he did not care for her and thought of her as an encumbrance, then he had no one to blame but himself if she took steps to free her brother herself.

The morning was cold—frost clung to the bare branches of the trees and on the bodies that still swung from the lamp posts—but it was not the weather that was making her shake, it was the

thought of what she was contemplating. Unable
to bring herself to do it, she turned, intending to
walk away, when the door opened and Gerald
Wentworth came out. He evidently did not think
it necessary to hide his rank; he was immacu-
lately dressed in a silk coat with silver buttons
and striped breeches with ribbons at the knees.

'Mrs Drymore,' he called, doffing his hat. 'Good
morning to you.'

She could not ignore him. 'Good morning, sir.'

'You are out and about early.'

'Yes, I felt like a walk.'

'But you have been standing outside this house
for the last ten minutes, I saw you from that window.' He waved his cane at an upper window. 'Is
there someone there you wish to speak to? Monsieur Robespierre, perhaps?'

She had to think quickly. 'My husband and I
dined with him two nights ago and it is the custom to call on one's host and thank him for his
hospitality, but I realised it was too early in the
day and no doubt he was at his breakfast.'

'I believe his repast is done, I have just left the
gentleman. Would you like me to escort you inside? I am sure he will see you.'

'No, I do not think I shall trouble him, after all.'
She began to walk away.

'Come now, you are not afraid of him, are you?'
he asked, falling into step beside her.

'Why should I be afraid? He is a man like any
other.'

'Not like any other, Mrs Drymore. He is one of
the most powerful men in France, he can command the life and death of thousands with a flick
of his fingers. He is the most admired and the
most feared of all men.'

'I am aware of that.'

'You were—are—agitated. He is also, I believe,
very fond of the ladies, so could it be you had
an assignation and were having second thoughts
about the wisdom of it?'

She stopped and turned angrily towards him.
'How dare you, sir? How dare you? My husband
could call you out for that.'

He laughed. 'It would not be the first time.'

Curiosity got the better of her. 'What do you
mean?'

'Ah, I see he has not confided in you. I am not
surprised; it is not something he can boast of and

especially he would not want a new wife to know about his unsavoury past.'

'Unsavoury,' she echoed. She ought to turn and walk away from him, she ought not to listen to him, but if Jay would not tell her why he hated this man, then he could not blame her if someone else chose to do so and she listened.

'Oh, yes. He was responsible for the death of his first wife.'

'How can you say that? He loved her and mourned her passing.'

'That is what he would like the world to think, but in reality the case is very different. He treated her abominably. She stuck it as long as she could for the sake of her children, but in the end his cruelty became too much to bear and she fled on horseback and came to me because she knew I was aware of what he was like and had promised to protect her. He chased after her and in her desperation she tried to jump a hedge that was too high. She was thrown and landed in a ditch with the horse on top of her. The horse struggled up, but by that time she had been badly trodden on. I found her and took her home and cared for her, but sadly she died next day.' He gave a soft chuckle. 'Drymore had the effrontery to challenge me over it.'

'You fought?' She ought not to heed him, but he was very sure of himself and she did not seem able to help herself.

'Yes. I overcame him, but I decided to spare his life. He has never recovered from the humiliation.'

'Why are you telling me this?'

'I think it is something you ought to know. After all, how can you be sure the same fate will not befall you? He is a violent and ill-tempered man—I would advise you to take care.'

'Rubbish!'

'Is it?' He paused. 'Does he know you are out and about alone?'

'I do not have to ask his permission to leave the house, Mr Wentworth.'

'Ah, so he does not. But if it was not an assignation, what was so urgent about visiting Monsieur Robespierre that you had to creep out early before you were missed?'

'I did not creep out. I can come and go as I please.'

He laughed. 'You know, you are extraordinarily like Marianne, both of you headstrong and independent. It does not bode well for your continued existence.'

'I have heard enough of this, Mr Wentworth. Pray do not speak to me on the subject again.'

'I do not need to. You have the facts—what you do about them is your affair.'

She began to walk very fast, but he was not ready to leave her yet. 'Tell me, what were you going to see Monsieur Robespierre about? It wasn't just to thank him for giving you supper, was it?'

'It is not important.'

'Anything that upsets you is important to me, Mrs Drymore. Pray, confide in me, I might be able to help.'

She hesitated, but then she thought of Michel, her beloved brother, incarcerated in prison and likely to be executed, and the effect that would have on their father, and took a deep breath, deciding to tell him the story that she had concocted for Robespierre. 'There is a French Comte and his daughter staying with Lord and Lady Drymore at Blackfen Manor and when the young lady heard that I was to accompany Commodore Drymore to Paris, she begged me to use my best endeavours to see her brother and persuade him to return to England with us. Unfortunately I have discovered he has been arrested and I am at a loss to know how to fulfil the promise I made to her. I thought Monsieur Robespierre might help.'

'What has the young man been accused of?'

'Nothing that I know of, except that he was in the King's service.'

'I see,' he said thoughtfully. 'And your husband was not to know of your visit to Monsieur Robespierre?'

'My husband is in Paris on a diplomatic mission, Mr Wentworth, he cannot compromise himself or Britain by involving himself with one prisoner in the hands of French justice.'

'I am glad you told me, Mrs Drymore. If you tell me the name of the young man, I might be able to help. I have the ear of Robespierre and Danton, too.'

'Thank you,' she said, not questioning how he came to know those gentlemen so well or why he should choose to help her. 'His name is Michel Giradet and he is being held in La Force.'

'Giradet,' he repeated. 'How strange. I have heard that name.'

Of course he would know the name, his sister had married her father! 'Perhaps you read it in the London newspapers,' she said, thinking quickly. 'The Comte's arrival in England was hailed as a triumph.'

'Yes, that must be it. If my memory serves me, he was taken out of France by two Englishmen.'

Only then did she realise the damage she had done. It would not be difficult for him to fill in the whole story with what she had told him, James Smith's real name, the names of Lord Portman and his friends, not to mention her own and the fact that she and Jay were not married. If he hated Jay as much as Jay hated him, there could be terrible repercussions. 'You do not need to tell Monsieur Robespierre about that, do you? It would be an ungrateful way to repay those concerned for saving the Comte and his daughter from almost certain death.'

He smiled. 'You may trust me to do what I can, Mrs Drymore.'

'And please, do not say anything to my husband.'

He laughed. 'My dear, you may depend on that. I have no wish to converse with that gentleman.'

'Thank you.' She looked up to see Jay striding towards them, his coat open and flapping out behind him. She turned to bid her companion good day, but he had disappeared down a side road leading to the Tuileries Gardens.

Chapter Nine

'Lisette, was that Gerald Wentworth?' Jay asked when he reached her.

'Yes, we met quite by chance and passed the time of day.'

He turned to walk beside her. 'Speaking of time of day, what are you doing out so early and without an escort? Don't you know how risky that is?'

'Why is it risky? I am an Englishwoman, a stranger to France, who speaks no French. Who would be interested in me?'

'Wentworth, perhaps? Did you tell him who you really were?'

'Certainly not. That would be madness.'

'I am glad you realise it. Did you have breakfast before you left?'

'No.'

'Then let us go back to the Embassy and have it

together.' He took her hand and tucked it beneath his elbow. 'I need to talk to you.'

'About your wife? About Marianne?'

'No, why did you say that?' he asked in surprise. 'What has Wentworth been telling you?'

'He told me you had driven your wife away with your cruelty and that she fled to him and died falling from her horse.'

'I told you how she died myself.'

'So you did, but you did not tell me about Mr Wentworth.'

'It is not something I wish to talk about or even remember. I beg you to refrain from bringing up the subject, we have more important things to discuss if you wish to free your brother.'

He had become once again the ice-cold man she had met in Honfleur. 'You know I do.'

'Then let us concentrate on that.'

She gave up. He was not going to tell her his side of the story, but perhaps that meant there was some truth in what Mr Wentworth had told her and he was ashamed. She looked sideways at him, wondering if she ought to be afraid of him, but found she was not. He might belay her with words, but he had never once threatened her person. Apart from taking her hand now and again, he had never even touched her. Sometimes, during that long journey from Calais to Paris she had wanted him to take her in his arms, to make her feel that she meant something to him, but he never had, not even when they had shared a bed. Ought she to feel glad of that? Why, oh, why were her emotions so confused?

They entered the ambassador's residence and Sam joined them for breakfast. He was dressed in the dreadful garb of the night before. 'I am going to La Force,' he told them while eating the unappetising grey bread, butter and plum conserve which was all Madame Gilbert said she could obtain. She had put the food on the table together with a pot of coffee and gone off to do her housework, grumbling that she only had one pair of hands and could do with some help. Jay had promised to see what he could do.

'Are you going to try to see Michel?' Lisette asked Sam. Her early morning jaunt had made her hungry and she was obliged to overcome her distaste of the food to eat.

'If I can.'

'Tell him I am thinking of him and am doing my utmost to have him released.'

'I will if we can speak without being overheard.'

'What are you going to do, Commodore?' she asked.

'I am to meet Lord Portman. We are going exploring. I need to learn the geography of Paris.'

'May I come?'

'No. We will be going into some unsavoury quarters and your presence would cause curiosity and suspicion.'

'Why am I always to be excluded?'

He sighed. 'Do I need to explain that all over again, Lisette? You are here under sufferance and this is not work for ladies. When the time comes I will tell you how we plan to effect your brother's release, but until then I beg you to contain yourself in patience.'

'Very well, but I hope it will be soon.'

When the meal was finished, Sam left the house and Jay changed into the shabby clothes he had worn the night before and went out again. If he had ever imagined that rescuing Michel Giradet from prison and carrying him in triumph to

England under the noses of the Revolutionaries would be an adventure to be savoured, he thought it no more. It was fraught with difficulty and danger, made worse by the presence of Lisette. He worried that her independent spirit and penchant for going out on her own could lead her into trouble. Her meeting with Wentworth, however innocent, was worrying, too. If her true identity were discovered, they would all be in trouble.

She had denied giving it to Wentworth and, whatever else she was, she was honest, so that was something to be thankful for. But had the man guessed? Had he waylaid her in order to confirm his suspicions? How did he know where she would be and at what time? What did the man know about how Comte Giradet had arrived in England? What was his game? He might trust Lisette, but he definitely did not trust her uncle and the more she knew of the escape plans, the more vulnerable she was. He had to hold her at arm's length and try to keep her in check for her own good, though it was the last thing he wanted to do.

Harry, Nat and Joe were waiting for him at the Cross Keys. None seemed any the worse for the previous night's carousal. They were all dressed in the rough garb prevalent in Paris at that time. They had glasses of wine on the table in front of them and were studying a map of Paris. 'I don't know how accurate this is,' Harry said when Jay joined them. 'We will have to test it out. Our escape route must be planned, every inch of road, every corner, every alley.'

'We have to get the man out of gaol first.'

'What is the good of that if we don't know what to do with him when we have him? No, my friend, we have to work backwards.'

Jay conceded the wisdom of that. 'Sam has gone to reconnoitre the prison. If he is allowed to see Giradet, he might learn more and can tell him to be ready.'

'Good,' Harry said. 'We will need your carriage and some good horses. Nat will find us all suitable disguises and Joe will ride ahead and bespoke fresh horses along our route and safe houses where we might rest a while.'

'The fly in the ointment is Gerald Wentworth,' Jay said. 'He and Lisette met this morning and though she says it was by accident and they only passed the time of day, it is worrying. He is sly enough to wheedle information from her without her even knowing he had.'

'Why would he want to?' Nat asked.

'That I do not know. Lisette met him in the Rue St Honore not far from Robespierre's lodgings. I am wondering if he has some contact with that gentleman.'

'Are you worried enough to think we should cancel our project?'

'No, I must go through with it for Lisette's sake, but if you think the risk is too great, then I beg you all not to hesitate, but return to England at once.'

'Certainly not,' Harry said. 'But Wentworth will bear watching. He knows us too well, Jay, so perhaps Nat can keep an eye on him.'

'I will do that,' Nat said, then to Jay, 'Do you know where he is lodging?'

'No, but start in the Rue St Honore,' Jay said. 'You cannot miss him in the street, he dresses like the English aristocrat in frills and flounces and high heels. He is even more flamboyant than you are, Harry, though no one would think it to look at you now.'

Harry was used to being teased about his dress

and, laughing, stood up. 'Come, let us go on our perambulation. We will start from the barrier on the road to Pontoise and work our way back to La Force, taking careful note of side alleys, unoccupied houses and the presence of troops. Joe and Nat, off you go. Take as much gold coin as you think you will need, but beware of robbers. We will meet here again at five o'clock this evening.'

All four left the tavern.

Lisette decided to go back to the court and listen to more trials. Contrary to what Madame Gilbert had said, not all the accused were condemned. She wanted to make a note of the successful defences; such knowledge might be useful if Michel ever came to trial. After listening to a dozen trials, which for the most part only lasted a few minutes, she came to the conclusion that they were not based on logic or jurisprudence so much as the mood of the jury and she felt many had been bribed. That might have to be their way forwards.

She went back to the Embassy to wait for Jay to return. She had hardly taken off her hat and coat when Madame Gilbert came to announce a visitor. 'Shall I show him in?' she asked.

It was the visitor himself who answered. 'No need,' he said. 'I am already in.'

Lisette sprang to her feet. 'Mr Wentworth!'

'Mr Wentworth is too formal, don't you think?' he said pleasantly as the *concierge* withdrew. 'Why not call me Uncle?'

'Uncle,' she repeated, her heart thumping.

'Yes, Lisette, I am your uncle, but I am sure you knew that, didn't you?'

'If I did, what does it signify? You turned your back on my mother, cut her out of the family, so why should I acknowledge you?'

'Not I, Lisette, that was my father. I was only a young man at the time and had no hand in the decision. On the contrary, I was very fond of Louise.'

'But you did nothing to keep in touch with her, you never visited, you never wrote to her.'

'I believed that was her wish. We did not turn our backs on her, she turned her back on us.' He looked about him. 'Are you not going to invite me to be seated?'

She was in a quandary. If Jay came back now,

there would be an unholy row and she dreaded the consequences, but she could not send the man away, not because he was her uncle, but because he might have news of Michel. She indicated a chair. 'Please be seated.'

He flung up his coat and sat down. 'That is better. Now that we have established our relationship, we can talk of your brother.'

'Is that how you found out who I was?'

He chuckled. 'I had to go and see the young man after you told me his name. He is my nephew, after all. As soon as I saw him, I knew. You are as like as two peas in a pod.'

'He is my twin. What did he say?'

'Naturally he begged me to help him.'

'And can you?'

'I am prepared to try, but you know he was very surprised to learn you had married Commodore Drymore. Why did you do that, Lisette?'

'Why does one usually marry? We fell in love.'

'After he had liberated your father from gaol and sailed away with you.'

'Whatever gave you that idea?'

'It did not take a genius at mathematics to work it out.'

'Oh.' The worst had happened. The danger had increased a thousandfold and it was all her fault. She wished herself anywhere but where she was. She longed for Jay to come home at the same time as she dreaded it.

He smiled. 'You see, my dear, I am in possession of information that could send you both to Madame Guillotine.' He paused to watch her face, while she tried not to show her dismay. 'However, I may not make use of it.'

'You want something from me.' It was said with a heavy heart.

'Let us say you could provide some names which I can exchange for your brother's release.'

'Names?'

'Of those Englishmen who have become a thorn in the side of the Revolutionary government.'

'I do not know what you mean.'

'Come now, I think you do. Jay Drymore is one, that I know, and so, I believe, do you.'

'I know nothing of the kind,' she retorted, pretending anger. 'My husband is an envoy for the British Government. I told you before that he would not jeopardise his position for the sake of one prisoner and that still holds good.'

'Not even when that prisoner is his brother-in-law?' he queried with a twisted smile. 'I know you are anxious to set your brother free and I cannot believe a man would turn a deaf ear to the entreaties of the woman he professes to love.'

'He is a man of strong principles.'

He laughed. 'What about your principles, Lisette? Where do they lie? You are a Frenchwoman, your loyalties should lie with France, not with someone who will abandon you as soon as your presence becomes inconvenient. For your brother's sake I urge you to consider what I have said. His fate is in your hands. I know for a fact that his trial has only been delayed because the court is waiting for Henri Canard to come to Paris to give evidence. He is bringing the two gaolers with him who were guarding your father. They, of course, are eager to save their own skins.'

With every word he uttered her heart sank further. He had her in a vise from which she could see no way out. Betray Jay and save her brother or remain silent and see Michel go to the guillotine. 'And what do you hope to gain by this, Mr Wentworth?' she asked, desperate to turn the tables on him. 'You are an Englishman and yet you consort with Revolutionaries and lecture me on patriotism.'

He laughed. 'France is not at war with England, only with those who interfere in her internal affairs, people like your husband.'

'If you know so much, why do you need me?'

'Because there are others besides Drymore at work. Not only will they not stop at saving a few *aristo* heads, but even more importantly they will be taking thousands of gold coin and precious jewels out of the country, wealth it can ill afford to lose. There is a strong belief in the Department of Justice that these men mean to free Louis and the rest of the royal family. Evidence has been uncovered, letters found in a chest hidden behind panelling in the royal apartments in the Tuileries Palace, which point to counter-revolution and an attempt to regain the throne. If they are published there will be a hue and cry among the populace that will outdo any previous riots and massacres. Thousands will die. The French Government is naturally anxious to avoid that.'

'What is that to do with you?'

'Any involvement of British subjects in the conspiracy is bound to have diplomatic consequences.

It might mean war. I, as a loyal subject of King George, wish to prevent that at all costs and if it means the sacrifice of a few English lives, then it will be worth it.'

He sounded so convincing she found herself wondering how much truth there was in what he was saying. If it were true, it made the rescue of Michel insignificant compared to the wider issues. Did Jay know this? Did Lord Portman? Was that why his lordship had come to Paris, nothing to do with Michel?

'I do not see what this has to do with me or my husband,' she said, trying hard to sound cool, though she was shaking and wished fervently her visitor would go away and allow her to think.

'It has everything to do with him. Why do you think the British Government has sent an envoy to Paris so soon after the Ambassador left, if not to oversee a conspiracy to undermine the elected government of France, something the Ambassador could not condone?' He stood up suddenly. 'I will leave you to think about it, but do not take too long. I will meet you in the foyer of the Palais de Justice tomorrow at noon. Bring me the names Monsieur Robespierre wants and your brother could be free by tomorrow evening. If not, Henri Canard will have his way.'

He bowed, replaced his hat on his head and left her. She heard him speak to Madame Gilbert and then the front door slamming. Only then did her taut muscles relax and she sank forwards on the sofa with her head in her hands. She was being torn apart—Jay or Michel? Michel or Jay? If Mr Wentworth had been right about the conspiracy to stage a counter-revolution, then the sacrifice of two or three lives might be considered justifiable compared to the saving of thousands. But if the two or three were people she knew and respected and, in the case of Jay, had learned to love, what then? It was like a refrain going round and round in her head, driving her insane.

It was late when at last Jay and Sam came back. She heard Jay bid Sam goodnight and then he joined her. It was immediately obvious he was stiff with cold and suffering from sore feet. He hobbled to a chair and flung himself into it. 'I have never walked so far in my life,' he said. 'Harry must have legs of steel. I do not think there is a corner of Paris we have not explored and some of it extremely noisome.'

She had been waiting to have the whole matter out with him, to demand answers, to be told the truth, not only about his mission to France and how it affected Michel, but what Lord Portman's presence really meant, and most of all, the exact nature of his enmity with Gerald Wentworth. It was not fear of his temper that made her hold back, but an overwhelming feeling of tenderness towards him. He had been wounded freeing her father; she and Papa owed their lives to him, she ought not to forget that. And even now, he suffered on her behalf. How could she betray him? How could she tell him about the blackmail, for blackmail it was, and give him something else to worry about?

She bent to pull off his shoes. They were old ones in keeping with the lowly garb he wore and the soles had worn right through. No wonder he had sore feet.

'Lisette, you should not be doing that,' he murmured. 'I will go up to my room by and by and make myself respectable.'

'No, stay there.'

She went to the kitchen to fetch a bowl of warm water, a towel and, after a search of the kitchen cupboards, some salve and soft muslin to make a bandage. When she came back he had fallen asleep. Gently she knelt and removed his ragged stockings and put his feet into the water. He did not stir. She looked up into his face; his eyes were shut as if asleep. Carefully she bathed and dried his feet, then applied some of the ointment and bandaged them. She could not put his stockings back on, they were full of holes and covered in blood and mud. Still on the floor, she sat back and surveyed him.

In repose the stern look had left him. He was more like the man she had come to know at Highbeck, the man who loved his home and his children, the man who had a keen sense of humour and was the epitome of genteel behaviour, the man respected, even loved, by his tenants and servants, the man she had come to love. How could she even think of betraying him? But what of Michel? What of her father waiting patiently at Highbeck for her to return with her brother? There had to be a way, there had to be, even if it meant sacrificing her own life.

He stirred and opened his eyes. 'Lisette.' His voice was husky and full of sleep. 'What are you doing down there?'

'I, as a good wife, have been tending your wounds.'

'Wounds? I am not wounded.'

She indicated the pink water in the bowl. 'Your feet were a mess.'

'You did not need to do that. I could have done it myself.'

'It was my privilege. You must have found walking very painful.'

'Sailors, unlike soldiers, do not learn to march long distances and I have grown soft.' He leant forwards to take her hand. 'Thank you, my dear. They feel better already.'

The feel of his hand covering hers, his gratitude, his blue eyes looking into hers with such trust and tenderness was too much to bear after the turbulent day she had had. Her eyes filled with tears.

'Crying, Lisette?' He reached out and touched her cheek, catching a tear as it fell from her bottom lid. 'What is the matter? Has something happened today?'

He was altogether too perspicacious. 'No, nothing,' she said quickly, blinking hard. 'I'm tired and you must be too.'

'I shall be right as ninepence in the morning.'

She pulled herself together. 'Have you had anything to eat? Shall I fetch something for you?'

'I ate with Lord Portman at the Cross Keys. All I want now is to find my bed.'

'Then, if you will excuse me, I shall go to my room.' She attempted to get to her feet, but sitting on the floor with her legs under her had made them go numb. She stumbled and fell into his lap.

He caught her and held her. 'Oh, Lisette,' he said. 'You do try a man, don't you?' And then he kissed her.

His lips were warm on hers, not demanding, not hot with passion, not tentative either—nothing Jay did was tentative—but it was enough to set her body trembling as the warmth spread right through her. No one had ever kissed her like that before, no one had stirred all her senses in the same chaotic way. She put her arms about his neck and allowed it to go on, then found herself responding, clinging to him, wanting more. She was, for that brief moment in time, deliriously happy, and when he would have drawn away, she pulled his face down to hers again.

He came to his senses before she did. 'Go to bed, temptress, before I forget myself entirely,' he said, gently pushing her from him.

She scrambled to her feet. 'I…' She stopped, lost for words.

He looked up at her. Her hair had come loose, her clothing was in disarray and her eyes were dark with passion. With an effort of will, he resisted the temptation to pull her back on to his knee. 'Go to bed, Lisette.' His voice was flat.

She fled, leaving him to dispose of the bowl of pink water and his ruined stockings. He took them to the kitchen, musing on the almost-forgotten sensation of kissing a beautiful woman. She had been so pliable, so receptive, naïve and yet knowledgeable in that instinctive way all women seemed to have when it came to men. In the heat of the moment he had forgotten his avowed intention to keep his distance. She was a danger to his peace of mind, always had been, ever since he had first met her, and, he suspected, always would be. Whatever he was doing, she filled his thoughts when they were apart and all his senses when they were together; she made him feel both protective and exasperated. And, yes, he loved her. How that had come about he did not know, nor did he know what to do about it.

Madame Gilbert was dozing by the fire in the kitchen, but roused herself to get up and take the bowl from him. 'Your wife had a visitor this afternoon,' she told him.

'I do not deny my wife visitors, *madame.*'

'This was a gentleman, an Englishman, dressed very fine. *Madame* did not refuse to see him.'

'Why should she?' he said evenly. 'He is her uncle. Goodnight, Madame Gilbert.'

He climbed the stairs to bed, deep in thought. The *concierge's* revelation, coming on top of Sam's earlier news—that he had seen a gentleman emerge from La Force who was undoubtedly an Englishman and one he had seen somewhere before, though he could not remember where or when—ruined the euphoria of those last few minutes with Lisette. Passing her room, he was tempted to go in and demand to know what was going on, but refrained. Tackling her when he felt hurt and betrayed would not help.

That it was Wentworth he was certain and

Wentworth undoubtedly knew who she was, but what he was unsure of was the man's motive. Was he hand in glove with the Revolutionary government, inflaming passions against Britain, or was it personal? From what Lisette had told him, it was probably the latter and he felt he could deal with that, if only she would confide in him. But in honesty he had to admit he had not confided in her. Had he been afraid to?

He flung himself on his bed and fell asleep, only to have the recurring dream that had plagued him ever since Marianne died. Someone had come to tell him there had been an accident and he was riding hell for leather to Wentworth Castle. It wasn't an old building, not medieval at any rate, but it was huge and ostentatious. It was also shabby and the garden overgrown. Why he noticed that in the heat of the moment he did not know, but the image was etched on his mind as if put there with a branding iron. He flung himself off his lathered horse and rapped on the door with his riding crop.

A footman in livery admitted him and asked him to wait in the great hall, with its threadbare tapestries, blackened furniture and cantilever staircase, while he went to find his master. The servant was gone a long time and he was about to go in search of someone when the Countess came down the stairs.

'Commodore, you are too late,' she said. 'She is dead.'

'Dead?' The sound of that word echoed in his sleeping brain. 'When? How?'

'She was thrown from her horse while jumping a ditch. The horse fell on top of her. She was alive when she was brought here, but in spite of our best endeavours, died an hour ago.'

'I want to see her.'

'Naturally you do. I suggest you make arrangements to take her body home. We do not want it here.'

Gerald and his brother, the Earl, came downstairs to join them. Gerald was white-faced, his brother cold and unbending. 'Take her away,' the latter said. 'It was bad enough having a live whore here, a dead one is too much.'

Whatever Marianne had done, he had to defend her from that. 'She was never a whore.'

'Oh, no,' Gerald said with a sneer. 'Then you did not know your wife very well, Drymore.'

'I hold you responsible for her death, Wentworth. I should have ended your miserable existence when I had the chance.'

'This discussion is pointless,' the Earl said. 'I must ask you to leave, Commodore, and make arrangements for your wife to be removed. I am sure you will find a suitable conveyance for hire in the village.'

He turned and left. The scene changed abruptly, as dreams often do, and he was back with a covered cart drawn by two horses. A footman conducted him to the room where Marianne lay. 'Do you want help carrying her?' he asked in a whisper.

'No, I can manage.' He bent over the corpse, expecting to see the face of the wife he had married seven years before, and recoiled in horror. The dead face was that of Lisette Giradet.

The shock of it was enough to wake him. He lay bathed in sweat, trying to make sense of it. He had relived that time in his disturbed sleep many times, but the woman he picked up and carried down the stairs to the waiting cart had always been Marianne, beautiful and still in death. The image of a dead Lisette set him trembling. Did that mean she was so like Marianne she would suffer the same fate? Would she, too, betray him?

When morning came, he decided to say nothing, but give her the opportunity to tell him of her visitor without being asked.

He dressed in clothes befitting a gentleman and stooped to remove the bandages on his feet, smiling a little at the memory of them being put on. Then he put on fresh stockings and his own shoes and went downstairs. Lisette was already in the breakfast room and Madame Gilbert was dispensing coffee. He waved her away and sat down next to Lisette. 'Good morning, my dear.' It was said cheerfully.

'Good morning.' She looked heavy-eyed, as if she had not slept, but managed a smile. 'How are your feet?'

'Oh, they are as good as new, thanks to you.'

'Do you have any more walking to do today?'

'No, a gentle stroll perhaps.'

'Has anything been decided?'

'What about?'

'Don't tease, Jay. About freeing Michel from prison, of course.'

'I'll tell you after I have seen Robespierre again.'

'Are you going to appeal to him to let Michel go?'

'I doubt that would serve, Lisette. The less he knows about our real errand, the better, don't you think? Our government would not condone any interference with the way France dispenses justice.'

'You call it justice!'

'No, but the revolutionary French do.'

She sighed. 'I suppose you are right, but does that mean you are going to have to get Michel out without official help?'

'It does indeed.'

'Then why go back to Robespierre? Why not simply leave?'

It was obvious from the hunch of her shoulders, the way she held her head and gripped her hands in her lap, that she was tense, like a coiled spring ready to fly off goodness knew where, and he needed her calm and doing as she was told. 'I must conclude our discussions on my official errand,' he went on patiently, taking her hand. 'I cannot disappear without doing that; Robespierre must believe I am simply an envoy return-

ing home and I also need a permit to get us safely
through the barriers. His signature will ensure it.'

'And is that going to be soon?'

'Very soon, my dear, if you can curb your im-
patience just a little longer.'

'How much longer?'

'Until this evening. Be ready to leave at a moment's notice.'

'You said you would tell me what you were
planning to do when the time came.'

'So I did. Suffice it for you to know that Commodore Drymore and his lady will leave Paris
this evening at six of the clock to go home after
his fruitful discussions with the Revolutionary
Government, all legal and above board with all
the necessary papers. That is important if we are
to stay ahead of anyone trying to follow us.'

'And Michel? Will he be with us?'

'It is to be hoped so.'

'How are you going to effect his release?'

He hesitated. Dare he tell her everything? He
decided it would be prudent to hold back on the
finer details. 'Harry and the others will do that
and bring him to us.'

'But we cannot all squeeze into one carriage.'

'No, of course not. Until we have safely nego-
tiated the barricade there can only be two people
in the carriage. Michel will be with you, posing
as me.'

'But what about you?' she asked. 'How will you
get out? You surely don't intend to be left behind? Oh, Jay, I could not bear that. The risk is
too great.'

'Nothing can be achieved without a degree of
risk,' he said, surprised by her vehemence. Did it
mean she cared what became of him, apart from
what he could do for her and her brother? 'But if
everyone plays their part, the risk will be mini-
mal. The rest of us will acquire mounts and make
our own way out of the city. Once safely past the
barricades and out into the country we will all
meet up and proceed together.'

'What if Lord Portman fails? If he is caught—
if you are all caught—what then?'

'He will not fail, Lisette. I trust him implicitly.
If I did not, I would not have agreed to let him
help us. The only thing that can stop us now is if
we are betrayed. I do not altogether trust the *concierge,* nor that uncle of yours.'

He watched her carefully, giving her the opportunity to tell him about the man's visit, but was thrown into despair when all she said was, 'Madame Gilbert knows only what we have told her and I shall be extra careful if, by chance, I should encounter Mr Wentworth again.' She paused and seemed to take a deep breath before going on. 'Jay, what of King Louis?'

'What of him?'

'I heard rumours about a chest of correspondence being found in the King's quarters in the palace which prove there is a conspiracy afoot to free him and set him back on the throne. It is said Englishmen are involved.'

'Where did you hear that?'

She could not tell him the truth without explaining Wentworth's demands. 'I heard people talking at the Palais de Justice. I went there to listen to more cases.'

'Why are you worrying about the King?'

'I wondered about Lord Portman...'

Someone, and he did not need to look far to realise who it was, had been feeding her information intended to undermine her confidence in him and their whole enterprise. 'Oh, I see. No, Lisette, we have nothing to do with any such conspiracy.

It would be tantamount to a declaration of war if we were to become involved in that. You may tell Mr Wentworth that if you should see him again.'

She gasped. 'Mr Wentworth?'

'He was your informer, was he not? You do not have to answer that, I should hate you to have to lie, but I must warn you that if you have any more *accidental* meetings with that gentleman, you will put your brother's freedom at risk.' He was so angry he could hardly contain himself; angry not so much that she had seen and spoken to Wentworth, but that she was intent on deceiving him. He had given her an opportunity to explain what had happened and she had refused to take advantage of it. He abandoned his breakfast and left her before he lost patience with her completely. The sooner this whole escapade was brought to an end and they were safely back in England, the better.

Lisette heard the door bang, heard him run up the stairs, calling for Sam as he did so. She wanted to run after him, to tell him about her uncle's visit and what the man was asking of her, to put her whole dilemma on his shoulders, which were so much broader than hers. She might have done so if he had not been so furious. His face had been white, his jaw rigid. The man who had kissed her so tenderly had gone and with him any hope of understanding. He was angry and yet he was still going ahead with the plans he had made. She ought to be grateful for that. But how could she be easy about it when she knew the risk was even greater than he realised? And all on account of her uncle.

Jay's mission for the British Government had been completed, whether successfully or not she did not know, but there was now nothing to keep him in France except Michel. If she told him about her uncle's demands, would that make a difference? Would he abandon Michel and force her to go back to England without her brother? She could not let that happen; it would kill her father. Oh, how she hated to be out of sorts with Jay. At a time like this, she needed his strong arms about her, his strength to give her courage, his tenderness to bolster her weakness. But he had gone, goodness knew where, leaving her to her misery.

It would soon be noon and she had to decide what to do about Mr Wentworth. Her uncle knew who she was, had already guessed that it was Jay, posing as James Smith, who had rescued her father; he could denounce them both whenever he chose. He would certainly do so if she did not meet him as arranged. He would become suspicious and, if he had told Robespierre he expected to be given the names and was not able to produce them, she would not be the only one in trouble. If she were the only one, she told herself, she could bear it, but the others did not deserve to die because of her foolhardiness. But what to do? The whole enterprise was in jeopardy because of her and it was up to her to do something about it.

A little before half past eleven, she left the house.

Chapter Ten

It was cold, in keeping with her mood; the last of the leaves had been stripped from the trees by a raw east wind which made her cloak flap about her legs and threatened to take her hat from her head. She held it on with one gloved hand and walked steadfastly forwards until she was once more approaching the Palais de Justice.

It was another day of trials—the Revolutionary government was determined to eradicate all dissent—and crowds of people were pushing their way into the courtroom, eager to witness the humiliation and terror of the latest batch of defendants, to cheer or hiss as the fancy took them. Lisette took a deep breath and let the tide carry her forwards but once inside she allowed everyone else to continue into the courtroom while she stepped behind a pillar to wait for the arrival of Gerald Wentworth.

It was not yet noon and she had a few minutes to wait if he were punctual, longer if he decided to be late. She wished she had not come so early, this waiting about was making her resolve crumble. Then she gasped and put her hand to her mouth in horror. Her uncle was on the other side of the vestibule in earnest conversation with Henri Canard. It was definitely Henri, but he had discarded his shabby black suit and was dressed in a frock coat of dark plum-coloured velvet, rose-coloured breeches and white hose. She recognised the clothes as belonging to her father. Not only had he made free of the château, but her father's wardrobe as well. She shrank further back behind the pillar, her heart beating in her throat.

A few moments later, they parted company; Canard went into the courtroom and her uncle found a bench and sat down presumably to wait for her. She stepped out to stand before him.

'Ah, Lisette, punctual, I see.' He patted the seat beside him. 'Sit down, my dear, and tell me what you have discovered.'

'I'm afraid I have not been able to discover anything at all. I am not sure there is anything to be discovered and you must be mistaken.'

'I am not mistaken. It is your loyalty which is a mistake, Lisette. Do I have to repeat all the reasons I gave you for helping the Department of Justice to eradicate traitors and those who help them?'

'No, I remember them perfectly.'

'Good, because your brother's trial is set for tomorrow and the evidence against him is overwhelming. Henri Canard is in Paris with the two prison warders.'

'It is manufactured evidence. Canard knows nothing of my brother.'

'But he does know you and he knows James Smith.'

'Mr Smith is in England.'

He laughed. 'Oh, my dear, that was a nice try, but you do not deceive me. Nor will you deceive Citizen Canard and the gaolers who will easily identify him.'

'Henri Canard has taken over the château and my father's wardrobe and no doubt the apple harvest, the cider-making and the Calvados distillery, so what can he possibly gain by Michel's death?'

'He believes the estate is his by right.'

'Right through confiscation,' she said bitterly.

'No, my dear, it is more than that. He tells me the Giradet estate once belonged to his grandfather and that it was taken from him by a trick. He was temporarily in financial difficulties and your great-grandfather lent him the money to pay his debts. Unfortunately he could not find the exorbitant interest, so Giradet took the whole estate in lieu. Canard is anxious to have back what he believes to be his. The easiest and cheapest way to do that is to put an end to the existence of every Giradet who might challenge him.'

'My father is alive and well and out of Canard's reach.'

'But the Comte is an old man. You and your brother, on the other hand, are young and pose a threat.' He paused to let this sink in. 'Come, enough of your prevaricating. Tell me the names of Drymore's confederates and you and your brother will be given safe passage to England.'

'And my husband?' She was becoming so used to referring to Jay as her husband, it was almost as if their marriage were a fact and not fantasy.

'The Commodore? Yes, him too. The French

would hardly harm an accredited government envoy unless he were caught red-handed.' He laughed suddenly. 'Like the coward he is, he has managed to protect himself, but where does that leave you?'

Do not hurry, she told herself, pretend to be considering his request. 'I do not know any names,' she said slowly.

'Then you will condemn your brother to death.'

'He is your nephew, too.'

'So he is and that is why I am doing my best to save him. Isn't that what you asked of me? Without your co-operation, I cannot do it.'

'My husband and I have passes to leave France this evening. I want Michel to be with us.' Even as she spoke she wondered if Robespierre would provide the passes if she refused to do as she was asked.

'Only if you supply the names.'

'I know that.'

'Then you had better make all haste to find them. It is not I who wants them, believe me, but stronger forces than either of us can conceive are at work here. I can promise you the British Government will thank you.'

'I will try to find out what you want to know.'

'Good, but do not take too long about it. Citizen Robespierre is waiting for your answer and he is not a patient man. Meet me here in an hour's time.'

'Here, not La Force?'

'Michel has been brought here in readiness for his trial. He is, at this very moment, in the dungeons beneath our feet.'

She gasped; she did not doubt his information had come from Henri Canard. She was sure Jay did not know that and his plans were centred on La Force. It changed everything. Jay himself had said they could not free Michel from here. Her mind was working like an over-wound clock; she had to think of something. 'I have a condition...'

'What, in addition to your life and that of your brother?' He laughed again, enjoying her discomfort. 'You are hardly in a position to make conditions, my dear.'

'Nevertheless I am making one. I want you to arrange for me to see my brother and talk to him. Once I am satisfied he is in good health and has not been ill treated, then I will do my best to obtain the names you want.'

'But you will see him when he is released—is that not soon enough?'

'No. How do I know he is alive even? I might give you what you ask for and then you might tell me he died weeks ago. I do not betray my husband's countrymen for a dead body.' How she managed to say that with such calmness she did not know.

'It will require an order signed by Citizen Danton.'

'I am sure you can obtain it for me. You told me you had the ear of Robespierre and Danton too.'

'Very well. I shall see what I can do.'

She was silent. It had not been an easy decision to make; the risks involved didn't bear thinking about and she was truly frightened. Had she gone too far to turn back? Could she retract? Could she confess everything to Jay? But she would not see him again until the evening when they were supposed to leave. It would be too late then. In a dream—or was it a nightmare?—she heard the man beside her say something and then get up and leave her. She sat on, shaking so much she did not think she could stand, let alone walk away.

But time was slipping by and she had to make

a move. She stood up and hurried from the building, surprised that her feet carried her.

Jay concluded his business with Messieurs Martin, Robespierre and Danton and they parted on good terms, or so it seemed on the surface; underneath there was deep-seated mistrust on both sides which was not helped when Jay spotted Wentworth on the other side of the road as he left the building. Luckily the man was too busy shouting at a small boy who was taunting him for his extravagant clothes to notice anyone else and Jay slipped down a side road without being seen.

He did not go back to the Embassy, but hurried to the Cross Keys to meet Harry and the other two, knowing he would have to tell them about Lisette's treachery. Angry as he had been, he could not help feeling a twinge of sympathy for her. He could understand her overwhelming need to rescue her brother; in similar circumstances he would feel the same, but it was a pity she could not trust him and had gone to that mountebank, Wentworth, and, what was worse, believed the lies he had fed her. Had she already betrayed them?

Had Wentworth been on his way to convey the information to Robespierre?

The other three were waiting for him in a private room at the inn with two bottles of wine and glasses in front of them. They were cheerful and eager to put their plans into action. He sat down, poured himself a glass of wine and took a mouthful.

'Why so glum, Jay?' Harry asked. 'You look as though you are about to go to the scaffold yourself. Quarrelled with Lisette, have you?'

Jay paused before answering, took another mouthful of wine and told them of his fears. 'You three had better make all haste to leave the country,' he ended. 'Leave the matter to me.'

'And what do you think you can do on your own?' Harry retorted. 'Are you tired of life?'

'If Lisette betrays us all, it is for no other reason than she expects Wentworth to use his influence to have Michel released. If he keeps his word, then all I have to do is take the pair of them to England. I have safe conduct for Commodore and Mrs Drymore to leave the country, but I cannot do that with a clear conscience if you three are all still in France.'

'And do you honestly believe Wentworth will keep his word, or even that he has enough influence to do so?' Harry said. 'I would not put it past Robespierre to play him like an old fiddle. And your safe conduct can easily be cancelled.'

'I know, but I have no choice but to hope for the best.'

'Supposing, instead of freeing Giradet, Danton arrests Lisette? You will have two to rescue then and I do not give much for your chances.' Harry turned to the others who had been silently listening. 'What do you think? Do we turn our back on our friend here and let him be the hero on his own?'

'He'll be a dead hero if we do,' Nat said.

'If you think I am going to leave you alone in this Godforsaken country, Commodore, you are wrong,' Sam said. 'I would never be able to look Lord and Lady Drymore in the face again.' He turned to Harry. 'You may do as you wish, my lord, and you too, Nat and Joe, but I am staying here.'

Harry laughed. 'You are outvoted, Jay.'

'Then what do you propose to do?'

'Carry on as before,' Harry said. 'We do not know that Lisette will betray us. She may be relying on us to put our plan into action before it becomes necessary.'

Jay breathed a sigh of relief. They were all brave men, fools, but brave. 'Then it might be wise to bring everything forwards. Can that be done? I have told Lisette to be ready as soon as the carriage comes for her. I do not think she will let me down. After all, she is expecting us to reunite her with her brother and telling Wentworth about us would be a last resort, should we fail.'

'Then let us hope you are right,' Harry said.

'Nat, do you think you can bring it off?' Jay asked him. Nat had been chosen to take Lisette through the barrier to the rendezvous because he was about the same height and build as Jay and younger than the others.

'I reckon so, if the lady plays her part.'

'She will when she understands the necessity.' Jay gave a wry chuckle. 'We are so out of sorts with each other, you will not need to be pleasant or even speak much.'

'I have been schooling him to act like you,'

Harry said. 'He is not much of a thespian, but he will do in the dark.'

'I don't see why we have to change places at all,' Nat said.

'Because I have no intention of leaving this city until I have secured Michel's release and I will not sit back and let you do it. I have told you that half-a-dozen times. If they do make an attempt to arrest you, you must say I forced you to change places with me. When Wentworth hears of it, he will tell everyone it is the sort of cowardly trick I would play and you will be allowed to go.'

'As for the rest of us,' Harry went on, 'I have obtained a tumbril and a skinny old pony and our disguises are ready in the corner there. We will plan to be at La Force at half past four and, give or take a few minutes, here soon after five. Horses will be waiting for us here with fresh clothes and we will only be minutes behind the coach. Timing is everything if we are to be convincing.'

'Then I had better go back to the Embassy and tell Lisette to be ready.' Jay rose to go.

'Do not quarrel with her,' Harry called after him. 'We want her compliant.'

* * *

Jay strode down the street, ignoring the cold wind which threatened to lift his hat off his head. Above him the sky was dark with impending rain which might be a godsend later that evening. Darkness and bad weather could hide so many things. He was feeling more optimistic. The plan was intricate and daring. The tumbril would arrive at La Force to take the prisoner to the Conciergerie for his trial, but it would disappear on the way. That would be the most risky part, spiriting it down an alley and changing it into a common farm cart full of cabbages under which the prisoner would be hidden. They would not risk taking it through the barrier like that; the guards were wise to such tricks and always searched such loads. Remembering how they had fooled the guards at Honfleur, it was Jay himself who suggested that they should dress in the uniform of *maréchaussée* and pretend to be in hot pursuit of the carriage. The change of clothes, which had been purchased by Nat from a corrupt army quartermaster at great expense, would be made at the Cross Keys. After they had left, Madame Barnard would destroy all evidence they had been there and would have the added bonus of a cartload of cabbages with which to make soup.

If they could pull it off, all might yet be well. So much depended on Lisette. His earlier anger had evaporated; he could not stay angry with her for long and he admitted to himself he had been rather dictatorial, not telling her everything. His vow never to trust another woman seemed vain and pointless in the face of her courage. The way she had tended his sore feet, the way she had returned his kisses, her tears and her concern for his safety even when they were arguing, had all seemed genuine, not the act of a woman out to deceive. He desperately wanted it to be genuine. He wanted to trust her. You could not love without trust.

Lisette let herself in the Embassy and hurried up to her bedchamber, fetched out the masculine clothes she had bought earlier and stood breathing deeply to calm herself. Then she stripped off her own clothes, put on the shirt, breeches and stockings and her new blue-silk gown over them, lacing the bodice tightly over the shirt. She had planned to put the coat over that, but it was much too tight and she abandoned it; Michel would be wearing a coat and she could use that. Taking the scissors to her hair, she cut it to the length Michel wore his and tied it back with a length of thin black ribbon.

That done, she sat down to write a letter to Jay. That was the most difficult part of the whole proceeding. It was damp with tears by the time it was done. Having signed it and dusted it, she tucked it into the top of her bodice. Then she pulled another sheet of paper towards her, sat a moment with her pen poised over it, wondering what to write. Smiling to herself, she folded it and inscribed the outside with Mr Wentworth's name. Finally she slipped into her own shoes, stood up and looked in the mirror at a woman laced too tightly into a gown that appeared too small for her. A man's shirt filled the square *décolletage* and its sleeves protruded from the sleeves of the gown. If it had been a game she was playing she might have laughed at the apparition, but this was in deadly earnest. Topping this strange ensemble with her burnous, she went downstairs to seek out Madame Gilbert.

'If the gentleman who was here yesterday should call after we have left, will you give him this?'

she said, handing her the second of her missives.
'Do not give it to him before that.'

'*Oui, madame.* Am I also to shut up the house?'

'Yes. We will not be needing it again.' She re-
trieved a bundle of *assignats* from her purse and
gave them to her. 'We are grateful for the trouble
you have taken to look after us.' And with that
she left the house for the last time. There was no
time for regrets, no time for anything except to
go back to the Palais de Justice and her *rendezvous* with her fate. Outside she stopped. Go in or
turn away? It was the decision of a lifetime because whatever happened as a result of what she
did now, it would colour the rest of her life, however long or short that might be. Regret or glad-
ness, remorse or satisfaction that she had done
what was right? Did she have a choice? Could she
let them all die? She took a deep breath and made
her way into the building.

Her uncle was waiting for her in the anteroom
just where they had met before and for one heart-
stopping moment she wondered if he had never
left and the whole thing had been a trick. 'You
have courage, I will give you that,' he said. 'I

was afraid you would persuade Drymore to leave at once.'

'And leave my brother behind? You do not know me very well, if you thought that, sir.'

'Then he means more to you than your husband.'

She let that pass. It was her deep love of both that was the driving force behind what she did now. 'You have permission for me to see Michel?'

'Yes.' He handed her a sheet of paper signed by Danton. 'The list?'

'It has been left with the *concierge* at the Embassy with instructions to give it to you after we have left.'

'You do not trust me.'

'I am simply being cautious.'

He laughed. '*Touché*. Come with me, then.'

He led the way across the floor and through a door on the far side, along a series of corridors and down two flights of stairs. The grandeur of the upper rooms was left behind and there was nothing but bare stone walls and worn stone steps, lit only by lamps in brackets at intervals which only made a small pool of light in their immediate vicinity. The deeper they went the colder it became and Lisette shivered.

At the bottom they were stopped by an armed guard in front of a barred gate. From beyond it a babble of voices reached them and the stench of putrid food and unwashed bodies. 'The *citoyenne* has permission to see and speak to the prisoner Giradet,' Wentworth said in poor French.

Whether the man could read or not, Lisette did not know, but he certainly recognised Danton's signature on the paper she showed him. 'Come with me,' he said, taking a bunch of keys from his belt and unlocking the gate.

'You will forgive me if I do not come with you,' Wentworth said, putting his handkerchief to his nose. 'Urgent business elsewhere.' To the guard he said, 'She may have ten minutes alone with him, then send her back up to me. I shall be waiting in the foyer.' And with that he scuttled away.

Lisette smiled, glad she did not have to suggest he might prefer not to go any further. She followed the guard along a corridor and down more steps, and with each step the noise grew louder and the stench stronger. She was more convinced than ever that no one could ever be rescued from there.

She found herself in a long room lined with cages, each of which was filled with humanity, men, women and even little children. Some who had been there the longest were filthy and dressed in rags; the more recent arrivals still wore the finery they had on when brought there. As the warder and Lisette passed them hands reached out to her, some in supplication, others to grab at her cloak. Some to swear, some to moan. She had eyes for none of them, being more concerned with searching out her brother.

'Giradet!' The turnkey shouted. 'Giradet, come forwards.'

There was a general movement in the far cell as people made way for a ragged skeleton to come to the front. The turnkey unlocked the cage and pushed Lisette inside. She turned back to him in consternation. 'I am not to be locked in here and I am to speak to the prisoner privately.'

'You may make what privacy you can there,' he said. 'When you have had enough, let me know and I will escort you back.'

Lisette turned to face her brother. She hardly recognised him. He was thin, his face grey, his eyes lifeless and his hair matted. Her heart sank;

this was not going to be as easy as she had thought. Michel was staring at her in disbelief. 'You too, Lissie,' he murmured.

'No, I am not a prisoner and you will not be for much longer, but you must listen to me.' She took his arm and almost dragged him into a corner. 'Can these people be trusted?'

'Depends what you have in mind.'

She turned to a woman in a faded pink dress and a girl of about thirteen whom she supposed to be the woman's daughter. She did not think they had been incarcerated long; neither was as thin or ill kempt as the rest. She held out a handful of *assignats,* knowing the money could buy extra food and comforts and perhaps even a good lawyer. 'Will you stand guard?'

The woman snatched the money and stuffed it in the top of her stays and took up a stance between Lisette and the rest of the cell's occupants. Lisette took off her burnous and handed it to the woman, who beckoned to the girl to hold one side of it to make a screen. Everyone else began to laugh, imagining what might be going on behind the cloak. Well, let them laugh, she did not mind that.

Michel was standing with his back to the wall in

a kind of daze. Lisette smiled at him and reached over to kiss his cheek. 'We are going to change places, you and I,' she whispered. 'Take off your coat.' She began undoing the bodice of her gown as she spoke. 'Remember the games we played as children when we pretended to be each other to deceive our friends? You are going out of here as me.'

'And leave you behind! Never!' It was said vehemently in a hoarse whisper.

'There is no risk. I am to stay here for an hour or two after you are gone, then someone will come and let me out. Have no fear.'

'Who? Who has the power to do that except those monsters who put me in here?'

'My husband is an envoy of the British Government and has a great deal of influence here in Paris. They will let me go.'

'Are you sure of that?'

'Yes,' she lied. 'I am certain. The French Government cannot afford to make an enemy of the British. They have too much to lose.'

Once the lacing of her gown had been undone, she was able to take it off; the petticoat underneath was easy to step out of, leaving her dressed in a man's shirt and breeches. Trusting her, he removed his once-fine coat of burgundy silk, which was now filthy and torn, and Lisette helped him into the petticoat and gown and laced the bodice.

'Now put the cloak round you and keep the hood up,' she murmured. 'You are Mrs Drymore, remember, and expect to be treated with respect, but don't speak unless you have to. If you see an Englishman, flamboyantly dressed, on the way, avoid him at all costs. He is our uncle, but he is not to be trusted. Go to the British Embassy and wait for my husband to come. Give him this.' She tucked her letter to Jay down the front of his bodice. 'It will prove I have sent you. And this is the permit for Madame Drymore to visit the prisoner, Giradet. You may need it.' She gave him her gloves. 'Better wear these, too, or your hands will give you away.' Then she slipped his ragged coat over the breeches she wore and the transformation was complete. 'I will come to the gate with you.'

'Better not,' the woman said suddenly. 'You are altogether too clean and well fed. Better crouch against the wall and put your head in your hands in despair. I will summon the turnkey.'

The occupants of the cell watched the woman

and Michel make their way over to the gate. Lisette did not think they were deceived for a minute, but no one raised a voice in betrayal. Everyone of them would have taken advantage of such a means of freedom had they been offered it.

The turnkey came slowly along the corridor when he was summoned and unlocked the gate. 'Had enough, have you?' he leered, because Michel was holding the edge of his hood to his face.

As Lisette watched, Michel's whole demeanour changed and he became her; he had not forgotten their childish game which had always ended in laughter. No one was laughing now, even the occupants of the cell had stopped their ribaldry. Accompanied by the turnkey, he walked away, past the other cages and up the stone stairs and was lost to her sight. She did not have to pretend her despair. It enveloped her like the cloak she had wrapped around her brother's slight frame, it swamped her like a great tide running in from the sea, it overcame the euphoria of her success and left her in tears.

Jay's optimism lasted no longer than his walk to the Embassy. Mrs Drymore had come in and gone out again, Madame Gilbert told him.

He swore under his breath. 'Did she say when she would be back? Did she leave a message for me?'

'Not for you, sir, but she left one for her gentleman visitor.'

'Give it to me.'

His stony face and angry eyes told her it would be wise to obey. She went and fetched it for him.

He broke the seal and unfolded it. If he expected a list of names, he was wrong. The paper was blank. He was puzzled for a moment and then began to laugh. His laughter was verging on hysterical and the *concierge* became alarmed.

'Sir?' she queried.

'Oh, do not mind me, *madame*.' He refolded the letter and handed it back to her. 'When did my wife expect her visitor to come for this?'

'She did not say, but to give it to him after you had left this evening.'

'I see. Thank you, *madame*.'

She turned to go, changed her mind and turned back. 'Sir, there was another thing...'

'Go on.'

'When we went shopping for clothes, *madame* bought a man's suit of clothes—for her brother, she told me—but this afternoon I noticed she was wearing the breeches herself under her cloak. I saw her legs as she came down the stairs. And she had cut her hair.'

He groaned, knowing perfectly well what it meant. 'How long ago was this?'

'Half an hour, maybe a little longer.'

'If she comes back, tell her to get in the carriage when it comes for us and not to wait for me, do you understand?'

'Yes, *monsieur.*'

He turned on his heel and went out. He was almost running as he made his way along the river bank and up Rue St Antoine to the Rue du Roi Sicile. He had to catch her before she reached La Force, knowing what she intended. It was madness, utter madness. He was angry, angry with Lisette for her foolhardiness, even more angry with Wentworth who was using Lisette to destroy him, but most of all angry with himself for assuming she was like Marianne and not to be trusted. She was nothing like Marianne, who thought only of herself, loved only herself. Lisette loved her father and brother with the kind of single-minded, selfless devotion his dead wife had been incapable of. If only she could spare some of it for him, but why should she? He had been at fault for not taking her into his confidence and explaining exactly how they were going to free Michel. If he had done so, and if he had told her the whole truth about Marianne, she would not have trusted Wentworth and this whole sorry mess could have been avoided.

Not until his flying feet took him within sight of the prison did he stop. There was no sign of Lisette. A few people moved up and down the street, a one-legged man sat in the gutter begging, a child played with a hoop, a skinny dog foraged in the gutter down the centre of the street. The door of the prison was shut and apart from the sentries there was no activity in the yard. He looked about him and caught sight of Sam, who was hurrying away from the prison. Jay shouted at him to stop.

Sam turned to wait for him to catch up with him. 'Commodore, our plans have been set at naught,' he said. 'I am on my way to tell the others.'

'Never mind that. Have you seen Mrs Drymore?'

'Miss Giradet, sir? No, I have not.'

'She hasn't come along here or gone into the prison?'

'No, why should she? Her brother ain't there.'

'Not there?'

'That's what I were going to tell you. He's been moved to that place on the island where the trials are held.'

'The Conciergerie. Oh, my God! That's where she is.' He slapped his forehead with his palm in an effort to untangle emotions which threatened to engulf him and think clearly. 'Go and tell the others I think Lisette has gone to the prison to change places with her brother. I cannot, for the life of me, see her succeeding. She will be arrested in the attempt. We must stop her. There is not a moment to lose.'

'Aye, sir, but what are you going to do?'

'I am going to the Palais de Justice. Tell Lord Portman to meet me there. Go on, man, don't stand staring at me.'

Sam went off at a trot and Jay dashed back to the Île de la Cité. His anger had gone, replaced by remorse and an overwhelming love that filled his head, his heart, his whole body. He ached with it. Somehow or other, he had to get them out of the fix they were in and then he would never let her out of his sight again. But how?

He was about to cross the bridge leading to the

Conciergerie when he saw a cloaked figure coming towards him. 'Lisette, thank God.'

She did not appear to hear him and he took hold
of her arm. A head came up from the hood of the
cloak and he saw it was not Lisette, but someone
very like her. 'Michel Giradet,' he said, his joy
evaporating.

'I don't know you.' The voice was uncannily
like Lisette's when she was trying to be haughty.

'No, but I know you. You are so like Lisette I
could not be mistaken. I am Jay Drymore. I am
sure, when you changed places with her just now,
she spoke of me.'

The young man visibly relaxed. 'Thank God.
She said you would rescue her, otherwise I would
never have fallen in with her scheme. I don't know
how you could subject your own wife to such
hardship and squalor, even for a few hours. I
never should have agreed, I should have sent her
back and stayed where I was, but Lisette can be
bossy when she chooses and I was not thinking
clearly...'

Jay did not think it was an appropriate time to
go into why Lisette was posing as his wife. 'It was
entirely her own idea. I would have forbidden it

had I known, but now we are left with the problem of rescuing her from her folly.'

'She said they would let her go, that your influence would save her...'

'I believe that was said to persuade you.'

'You mean you cannot? That she is giving up her life for my sake?'

'That may have been her idea, but it is not mine.' His voice was clipped.

'I will go back, give myself up, then they will let her go.'

'Do you think so? I do not. I think it is more likely you would both be incarcerated. No, I must find a way to rescue her.'

'Then you must make haste. It is far from pleasant in there and my trial is fixed for tomorrow morning.'

'I intend to,' Jay said. 'Now you must do exactly as I bid you. There must be no taking matters into your own hands, do you understand?'

His vehemence made the young man smile. 'So you have been subject to her bossiness too, have you?'

'Never mind that. Have I your word?'

'To be sure. I am in your hands.'

'Then make your way to the British Embassy, stay there and do not move until I come. I do not want to find one of you and lose the other. You may come across a Madame Gilbert, the *concierge*. Do not let her see you too closely. Go straight upstairs to the second room on the left. It is Lisette's bedchamber, you will not be disturbed there. If a carriage comes to take Commodore and Mrs Drymore to Calais, you are to get into it whether I am back or not. Do you understand?'

'I understand, but...'

'No questions. Just do as you are told and trust me.'

'Very well. By the way, take care if you are going in there.' He jerked his head at the building behind him. 'I think our uncle is there. Lissie described him to me and told me to avoid him at all costs. Luckily the foyer was crowded. He was pacing the floor, but then he was hailed by someone who knew him and they stopped to talk and I slipped out. I am sure he did not see me.'

'Good. Now off you go. Keep to that disguise.' He smiled. 'It is very good. You could deceive almost everyone but me.'

'It would be strange if her own husband could

be fooled. Oh, I nearly forgot...' He fetched Lisette's letter out of his bodice. 'She bade me give you this.'

Jay took the letter, stared at it for a moment and put it in his pocket. As soon as he had seen Michel hurry safely out of sight, he strolled over the bridge and into the Conciergerie, curbing his inclination to rush. The court had finished sitting for the day and the place was crowded with people leaving. They were all discussing the trials and took no notice of him as he sat on the bench so recently occupied by Lisette to read what she had written.

Chapter Eleven

'My dear Jay,' he read. 'If you are reading this, it means Michel is free and I am in prison in his place. It was the only thing I could think of to keep you all safe.

'I told you the truth when I said my first meeting with Mr Wentworth—I will not call him Uncle—was by chance. He talked to me of you, but I told you that, did I not? What I did not tell you was that he persuaded me to confide in him, claiming that he would use his influence with Messieurs Robespierre and Danton to have Michel freed. What his connection is with those gentlemen I did not think to question. Nor did I tell him the whole truth.

'I said that I had met a French Comte and his daughter at the home of Lord and Lady Drymore and the young lady had begged me to see her brother and persuade him to return to England with us. I said I had, since coming to Paris, discovered he had been arrested and I was at a loss to fulfil my promise to her. He asked me the name of the prisoner and I told him. It was a terrible mistake and put everyone—me, you and your friends—in great jeopardy because, of course, he recognised the name. He was allowed to see Michel and immediately realised who I really was. He came to see me at the Embassy and that was the beginning of the blackmail.

'I was instructed to discover the names of the Englishmen who were helping the *émigrés* to escape which, you recall, Robespierre had asked of you. He said if I gave him the names, Michel would be freed and we would be given safe passage out of France. He gave me until today to meet him and deliver the names. I would never do that, Jay, never, but I did keep my rendezvous with him, hoping to stall him until you had effected Michel's release and we had left. It was then he told me that Michel had been taken from La Force to the Conciergerie for his trial and that Henri Canard and the two Honfleur gaolers had arrived to give evidence. I knew then it was too late to rescue Michel in the way you planned and I had to think of something myself.

'I told Mr Wentworth I wanted to speak to my brother before I gave him what he asked for and the list would be given to him by Madame Gilbert when we had safely left. He agreed to arrange it and that was how Michel came to be with you now. I commend him to your care. Take him to England. My father will be overjoyed to be reunited with him.

'Jay, I am so very, very sorry. I have been a fool, a miserable pig-headed fool, who has brought you nothing but trouble. I would much rather have brought you lasting happiness, for I do not believe the lies Wentworth told me about you. No one could be kinder, more chivalrous, more truly good, than you are. I shall, in my heart if not in fact, always be your devoted but inconvenient spouse. Take care of yourself and return safely to England and your children. My prayers are with you.'

Jay, the stoic, the man who kept calm no matter what, found his eyes brimming with tears. She had made this sacrifice to save Michel, to save him and Harry and the others, and expected to die for it. And she loved him. He screwed the letter up in his hand and sat numb and unmoving, his sight too blurred to see who came and went about him.

'Jay.' It was Harry standing in front of him, dressed in a smart suit of black cloth with a pristine white shirt and cravat and a wide-brimmed black hat, the garb a priest or a lawyer might wear.

Jay scrubbed at his face with the back of his hand and gave him Lisette's letter without speaking.

Harry smoothed it out and read it. 'Now we are in a pickle,' he said, folding it and handing it back. Jay put it in his waistcoat pocket.

'I know, but I can't leave her, Harry, I simply can't.'

'She means that much to you?'

'She does. She is not like Marianne, is she, Harry?'

'Not a bit,' his friend agreed cheerfully. 'But there is no need for anyone to die. Do not despair, we will think of something, but we might have to wait until the trial. Michel Giradet will be brought up for that, provided, of course, his accusers do not tumble to the ruse before that. Shall we take a stroll? I want to be able to find my way round this building.'

They walked unhurriedly through the public rooms where there was no ban on who entered and poked their noses into private rooms, noting their function and apologising in a mixture of French and English when they were challenged. They went down some of the stairs to the prison itself, which struck cold and airless. On one landing between one floor and the next, they were stopped by a turnkey. 'Your business, gentlemen.'

Harry put his handkerchief to his nose, for the stench was overpowering. 'No business,' he said in execrable French. 'We have become lost.'

The man laughed. 'You will be even more lost, *Anglais,* if you try to go any further, lost to the world.'

'How many prisoners are you holding here?' Jay asked him, going along with Harry's pretence of being two bumbling English sightseers.

'A thousand, give or take a score or so.'

'As many as that? How many are due for trial tomorrow?'

'Sixty, I am told.'

'Methinks we will come and listen,' Harry said. 'Will we find seats, do you think?'

'If you come early enough.'

'Do you have lists of who is to go when and what they are being charged with?' Jay asked, producing *assignats* from his pocket and holding them where the warder could see them.

'What do you want to know that for?'

'We want to choose the most interesting to witness,' Harry put in. 'Something melodramatic and juicy. We are not interested in run-of-the-mill thieves and harlots.'

'Do they go up one by one when they are called?' Jay asked.

The man took the *assignats* from Jay's unresisting fingers. 'No, I send a dozen up together, under armed guard of course. Here, take a look.' He turned away from them to open a cupboard behind him. Jay raised both hands above his head, ready to strike while the man's back was turned, but Harry grabbed his arm and shook his head, just as the warder faced them again with a sheaf of papers in his hand.

Jay took them and scanned the list until he came

to the name Giradet. 'Who is this?' he said, pointing. 'I think I have heard the name.'

'Oh, he is just another *aristo* who thinks he can overthrow the republic and take us back to the dark ages. He will die.'

Jay handed the papers back. It was plain Lisette's real identity had not been discovered and probably would not be until the following day. The two men returned to the cleaner air of the foyer.

'I could have knocked him out and seized his keys,' Jay said. 'Why did you stop me?'

'If they have a thousand prisoners and more, those dungeons must fill the whole of the lower floors and there would be other turnkeys guarding them. How could we be sure which of them holds Lisette? While we were trying to find her, the man would have come to his senses and the alarm been raised. I know how impatient you must be, but we must wait until tomorrow when she is brought up for trial.'

'My God, Portman, you are not suggesting we leave her in that stink hole overnight?'

'That is exactly what I am thinking. She might, by then, realise that she has to trust you.'

'You mean to grab her while she waits for her turn to go into the dock?'

'Yes, the place will be crowded. We will stage a diversion, start a rumour, and while everyone is milling about we can spirit her away.'

'But if they have already realised it is not Michel, but Lisette?'

'I have no doubt they will try her in his place. One Giradet is as good as another in their eyes.'

'You may be right, but then they will be searching for the boy and—' Jay stopped speaking and grabbed Harry's arm to pull him behind a pillar. 'There's Wentworth. And he's with Danton.' He peered out at the two men. 'They seem to be arguing.'

'No doubt Wentworth is at the receiving end of a drubbing for letting Lisette slip through his fingers.'

'I hope they do not send for the prisoner.'

His fears were groundless, at least for the moment. The two men parted and Wentworth hurried past the pillar without looking either to right or left. 'If he goes to the Embassy, there will be trouble,' Jay said. 'Lisette left him a blank sheet of paper instead of the names.'

'She has courage, that inconvenient spouse of yours,' Harry said, laughing.

'Too much courage,' Jay added gloomily as they followed Wentworth out of the building.

They had kept on his heels all the way to the Embassy.

'I shall have to waylay him. You keep out of sight.' Jay increased his pace to catch up with the man before Madame Gilbert answered the door. 'Wentworth, were you looking for me?' he called out.

The man turned at the sound of his name. 'Drymore, there you are.'

'Yes, here I am. To what do I owe this visit?' It was an effort to remain polite.

'I came to wish you and your good lady *bon voyage*. Is she at home?'

'She will be resting before our journey, I think. The carriage will be here at any moment.'

'Then allow me to say goodbye to her.'

'Why the courtesies, Wentworth? You were not always so particular.'

'She is my niece, but you knew that, did you not? Mind you, I'll wager you didn't know she married you to use your name as protection in a country where she is wanted for counter-revolutionary plotting. Or did you? You are not innocent in the affair, I think. Do you think you can keep her safe, Drymore?'

'Go,' Jay said, trying to keep his voice level although it was an effort. 'My wife will not see you.'

'Oh, I am sure she will.'

The window above them was opened and Lisette's head poked out. 'Is that you, Jay, darling?' she called. 'I have been waiting this age for you. Who is that with you?'

'It is Mr Wentworth come to say goodbye and *bon voyage*,' Jay called back, his heart in his mouth.

'Oh, Mr Wentworth, how civil of you. I am afraid I cannot receive you. I am *déshabillée* and do not have much time to dress before we are due to leave. A thousand pardons.' And with that she withdrew her head and shut the window.

'I must go in and make sure all is ready,' Jay said. 'Good day to you, Wentworth. I will not say I hope we meet again because I am not given to untruths.' He paused, watching a twitch in the man's jaw which told him the other man was even more nervous than he was. Fear, perhaps? Danton must have threatened him. 'If you are thinking of forcing your way in, you will regret it, I promise you,' he went on. 'I will not spare you a second time. The only reason I tolerate your presence at all is in deference to my wife.'

Wentworth hesitated, opened his mouth and shut it again, then left. Jay breathed a sigh of relief.

'How did she manage it?' Harry asked, joining him on the step.

'She?'

'Lisette.' He jerked his head towards the upper window. 'Back here.'

'She isn't. That was Michel. He is as bad as Lisette for acting on his own account. I could cheerfully throttle him.'

'My God, he was good. He fooled me.'

'Come in and meet him. You will see the difference when you are close to him.'

'I do not think we dare wait until the morning now,' Jay said as he ushered Harry into the vestibule. 'Wentworth will not believe Lisette would leave without her brother. He will check that Michel is still in the prison. We cannot risk him recognising Lisette.'

Michel was peering over the banisters above them. 'Did he go away?'

'Yes, thank goodness,' Jay said. 'Come down and meet my friend, Lord Portman.'

Michel descended the stairs, every inch of him an uncanny imitation of Lisette. 'And you can forget the charade,' he added. 'Lord Portman knows all about it. Harry, this is Michel Giradet, Lisette's twin.'

The two men shook hands. 'Your mimicry of your sister is extraordinary,' Harry said.

'Thank you. We often used to change places when we were children. Sometimes we could even fool our father. Never our mother, though.'

'Is your sister as good as you are?' Harry asked. 'Would she fool Wentworth as easily as you did?'

'If they are not too close, she might. She is an inch or two shorter than I am.'

'No,' Jay said firmly. 'I am not going to risk it. We must do what we have to do tonight.' He turned to Michel. 'Giradet, I want you to go to the Cross Keys on the corner of Rue St Honore and speak to Monsieur Barnard, the proprietor. Tell him our plans are to go ahead, but there might be some delay. Tell him to be ready to move at a moment's notice. You will also meet a man called Sam Roker. Tell him he is to bring the carriage to the Île de la Cité and wait for us as near the entrance as he can get without arousing suspicion. You stay at the inn until we come. If you value your sister's life you will not stir from there, and you will not try any of your childish games on anyone, do you hear? Keep hidden.'

'Is it safe to send him out on the streets?' Harry queried. 'Especially as a lady without an escort.'

'I am wearing my breeches under this gown,' Michel said. 'And I found this in the bedchamber.' He held up the coat Lisette had decided not to use. 'I can be a man again. I will not be recognised in the dark.'

'That's a much better idea,' Harry said. 'We can change your appearance with a little make-up, soot and carmine, a wig and a Phrygian cap.' He pulled one out of his pocket as he spoke. 'I always carry one, in case I need it to convince people of my loyalty to the Revolution.'

'Then let us make haste and do it,' Jay said. 'I cannot bear to think of Lisette in that place a moment longer than she need be.'

'You might be able to make use of this,' Michel

said. 'It's a pass for the bearer to visit Michel Giradet, signed by Danton. Lisette gave it to me.'

Twenty minutes later Michel was on his way,
looking like a man of middle years, not ragged
but certainly not dressed in any way that would
excite suspicion.

'You have not said how you intend to effect Lisette's release,' Harry said as soon as the young
man had gone. 'I presume you have a plan.'

'Yes, but I don't know if it will work. If it does
not, God help us all.' He pocketed the pass and
picked up the gown discarded by Michel, folded
it and put it into a leather satchel he had found in
the Ambassador's office, the sort a lawyer might
use to convey documents.

Harry watched him put the burnous round his
shoulders. 'Come on, out with it.'

'I will tell you as we walk.'

Lisette looked down at the greasy bowl of so-
called soup she had been given and thought she
would be sick. She supposed it was night. She
had no way of measuring the minutes and hours,
everyone who had a timepiece had had it confis-

cated. Someone who had been in the cell longer than the rest had scratched a mark on the wall with a piece of stone as each day passed, but only the turnkey could tell them if it was accurate. The hours and minutes ground slowly by and each one left her more desolate than before. Now the excitement of what she had planned and the euphoria of freeing Michel herself without betraying the others had worn off, she was left with no hope, no prospect of anything but a travesty of a trial and at the end of it a tumbril ride to the guillotine.

Had she really believed Jay would come and rescue her as she had told Michel he would? If she had, she believed it no longer. How could he? The plans he and the others had made would not work here; it was only a short walk to the law court, not a tumbril ride. Once there, under the gaze of hundreds of people and surrounded by guards, it would be impossible to extricate her. One half of her wished he would try, but the other half knew the futility of it and hoped he would not.

'Don't you want that?' Madame Collier indicated the soup. *Madame* was the woman who had helped her when changing clothes with Michel and she seemed to have taken her under her wing, explaining about the routine of the prison and what would happen when she was called. Lisette tried not to think about it, tried to divert herself by taking an interest in the stories of the others in the cell, all of whom seemed anxious to tell them and grumble about the injustice. Innocent and guilty alike, they were all awaiting trial and it was the only thing on their minds; it did not matter what the conversation was about, it always reverted to that.

'No, I cannot eat it,' she said.

'I'll give it to Christiane then, shall I? She needs to keep up her strength.'

'Yes, do.'

The bowl was handed to the woman's daughter, who drank the thin liquid hungrily.

'Why is your daughter in here with you?' Lisette asked. 'She is surely not accused of being a counter-revolutionary?'

'She refused to give evidence against me, kept her mouth shut when I would as lief she saved herself. I still think she could, if I could only persuade her.'

'Then she is very brave. Perhaps her tender

years and her devotion to you will persuade the courts to let her go.'

'Perhaps. I mean to plead for her. I care nothing for myself.' She paused. 'She is not the only brave one. You have done a selfless deed yourself. Do you think they will let you go when they find out?'

'I know they will not, but they will not find out unless someone betrays me. I must maintain the deception to the end, to give them time to leave France.'

'You will have lost your head long before then. Your lifeless body will give away your secret and then there will be a hue and cry.'

Lisette shuddered. 'How quickly do they carry out the sentence?'

'Sometimes the same day, sometimes the next, rarely longer. But perhaps you have a good defence? It has been known for the court to be lenient, especially if you denounce other traitors. Imprisonment and not death.'

Lisette thought about that and the idea of being cooped up as she was now for years and years would be unbearable. She would not want to live under those circumstances, especially if she had to betray Jay and his good friends to do it. She could not, would not, do that. She would defend herself, there was no one to speak for her, and if that did no good, which was most likely the case, then she would try to be brave.

Their supper done, everyone began to settle down for the night. There was only a scattering of straw for bedding and not enough of that. The prisoners simply lay down wherever there was space enough. Lisette went to the corner, which she had somehow come to think of as her own, and sat down with her back propped against the wall. She was weary to the point of exhaustion, but the wall was hard and rough, the floor likewise and both were damp. Her fingers and toes were numb with cold and she could not stop shivering. Michel's coat was little more than a rag, its lace in tatters; it did nothing to warm her. She shut her eyes against the feeble light from a single oil lamp at the entrance to the cell and prepared to wait for the dawn.

The rest of the inmates settled down too, but they were not silent. Some, unable to sleep, talked in low tones, some shouted out in their sleep, some wept, others snored. Gradually those sounds faded from consciousness and she dozed.

She was running through a summer meadow, bright with daises, buttercups and dandelions, and she was hand in hand with Jay. Edward and Anne skipped beside them, picking the flowers as they went. Above them the sun warmed their backs. They were all laughing. On the far side of the field a carriage was waiting and they all climbed in and were driven down a country lane, past hedges full of may blossom. The scent filled her nostrils. And there was Falsham Hall ahead of them, outlined against a cobalt sky, its windows gleaming, its front door open in welcome.

'Home at last,' Jay said.

'Home,' the children said.

'Home,' Lisette echoed and felt unbelievably happy.

'Giradet! Giradet!' The sound of the name penetrated her sleep. She opened her eyes and, for a moment, did not know where she was; the dream was still with her, enveloping her in its rosy glow. Then it all came back and she knew exactly where she was and why. The stench and the cold seemed to have penetrated right through her flesh to the bone and she could not move.

'Giradet! Michel Giradet!' She heard the name again and realised it was the turnkey who stood by the open gate. 'You are wanted.'

His raucous voice roused everyone else and they began noisily to protest at being woken. Christiane, who was lying beside her, whispered, 'You had better go.'

Lisette forced herself to her knees and then to her feet and hobbled over to the gate as the blood began to flow through her cramped limbs again; the pain was excruciating. 'What do you want of me?' She remembered just in time to lower the timbre of her voice.

'I don't want anything of you, *aristo,* others do. You are to go for interrogation.'

'Interrogation?'

'Yes. Come with me.' He grabbed her arm and pulled her out of the cell so that he could lock the gate again.

She limped after him past the other cells to the stone stairs. Who wanted to interrogate Michel? What were they expecting to learn from him? Would they see through her disguise? Did they already know it was she and not her brother, locked in the dungeons? If that were so, then what they wanted from her would undoubtedly be the names. Mr Wentworth must have gone to the Embassy and been given that blank piece of paper. Would they torture her? How long could she hold out? Had Jay and the others left? Were they safely on their way to Calais with Michel? If all her tears had not already been shed and if she had not felt dried up, wrinkled like a stored apple, she would have wept afresh at the thought that she was now entirely alone.

At the bottom of the stairs she was handed over to a new guard and the turnkey returned to his station and the pot of ale and pie that were waiting for him.

'Where are you taking me?' she asked her new escort as they climbed two flights of stairs.

'You will see.'

At the upper level she was ushered along several corridors. Her legs were working properly now and she looked around her, wondering whether to make a bolt for it. If she died in the attempt, would that not be a better end than the guillotine?

The guard, as if reading her mind, grabbed her

arm and held it in a painful grip until they stopped outside a door. He opened it and pushed her inside in front to him.

'Stand guard outside,' a voice commanded him.

Lisette found herself in a small room which contained a table, on which lay a leather satchel, and two chairs. There was a window opposite the door. A man stood looking out of it with his back to the room. It was he who had spoken.

The door shut behind her and a second man came out from behind it. 'Lisette.' It was spoken quietly.

She whirled round to face him. 'Jay!' Then she was in his arms, being hugged and kissed and she was crying all over him. 'Oh, Jay.'

'We have very little time.' Harry turned from the window. 'Save your embraces for later.'

Jay held her at arm's length and looked into her face. 'Are you ready, my darling?'

Her spirits soared at the endearment, but she was worried too. 'Do you mean to try to take me out of here?'

'Of course.' As he spoke, Jay pulled her gown out of the satchel, the one her brother had been wearing. It was sadly grubby and creased.

'You have seen Michel?' she queried, realising the significance of it.

'Yes, now take off that disgusting coat and put this on. Michel is waiting for us at the Cross Keys. Commodore and Mrs Drymore will leave Paris a little later than planned. Be quick before that guard becomes impatient.'

Lisette stripped off the coat and flung it on the floor. Jay helped to lace her into the gown, for her fingers were all thumbs. Then he wrapped her in the burnous. 'Go behind the door,' he said.

She did as she was told. Harry rapped on the door and when the guard opened it, delivered a punch to the man's jaw which felled him instantly. He dragged him into the room and took his keys from him. Jay took Lisette's hand and ran with her into the corridor. Harry paused only long enough to lock the guard in the room before following.

All three hurried along the deserted corridor and were soon in the foyer of the building, which was lit by oil lamps at intervals that cast a pool of light in the vicinity, but left the rest of the space in darkness. At the outer door they were stopped by a night watchman. Jay tucked Lisette's hand under his arm and squeezed it. 'Courage, my sweet,' he whispered, giving her his handkerchief. 'Pretend to be weeping.'

'What are you doing here so late?' the guardian of the door demanded. 'There is no business being conducted this night.'

'We have been allowed to visit a prisoner, kin to my wife, who is due for execution in the morning,' Jay said, waving Danton's pass at him. It was a document which had already proved useful. 'A last goodbye.'

He looked from Lisette, who was blubbering into the handkerchief, to the two men. 'All of you?'

'I administered the last rites,' Harry said, crossing himself. 'There are still some people who hold to the old ways and seek absolution before the hand of death takes them.'

'Off you go, then.'

Harry stopped to bless the man before following Jay and Lisette.

'Now all we have to do is find Sam and the coach,' Jay said as they crossed the bridge, trying not to break into a run.

They found Sam standing beside the coach a few yards away along the quay. As soon as he saw them, he jumped up on the box. 'Cross Keys, Sam,' Jay said, helping Lisette into the vehicle. 'As fast as you like.'

Harry climbed up beside Sam and Jay joined Lisette in the coach. In no time the horses were whipped up and they were on the move.

Jay took Lisette into his arms and kissed her. 'So far so good,' he said.

It was almost dawn; there was a pink light in the sky in the east and early risers were already going about their business on the street. 'Oh, Jay, I never thought I would see the light of day again except on my way to the guillotine.' She was shaking, not with cold this time, but with nerves and excitement and the realisation that she was free and in Jay's arms and he was kissing her with every appearance of fondness.

'Do you really think I would leave you in that place, you foolish woman? Did you not know I would move heaven and earth to fetch you out? I love you. You mean more than life to me, I would rather have died.'

'You love me?' she queried, not quite able to believe it.

'Yes, I do. Did you not guess?'

'No. I thought I was a hoyden, an encumbrance, and inconvenient spouse who would not do as she was told.'

'Well, of course, you are all those things,' he said, laughing. 'But it did not stop me falling in love with you. I believe you love me too, just a little, do you not?'

'Not a little,' she said. 'A very great deal with every fibre of my being.'

'Then if it pleases God to spare us, will you do me the honour of becoming my wife in fact, not fiction?'

'Oh, Jay, you know I will, but I thought you had vowed not to marry again.'

'I was a fool. I had no idea when I made that vow that I would meet you. You have cancelled it.' He paused as they drew up in the yard of the Cross Keys. 'We have a long way to go before we can truly say we have escaped and there will be many hurdles and pitfalls on the way, but we will overcome them together.'

He was kissing her again as the coach came to a stop and Sam jumped down to open the coach door. He coughed. 'Are you going to leave the coach, Commodore?'

They trooped into the inn to find Madame Barnard cooking breakfast. The smell of the bacon sizzling in the pan reminded Lisette that she had had nothing to eat since her previous breakfast and she was hungry. But first she must change; it was time to become Mrs Drymore again. She was conducted to an upper room where she found her portmanteau and some hot water. Hurriedly she washed and changed into the rose-coloured taffeta, repacked her portmanteau and returned downstairs.

They were all in the kitchen: Jay, Harry, Sam, Nat and Michel. Only Joe was missing, being already on his way to make sure there would be horses all along their route. Harry was in the uniform of a superior office of the *maréchaussée,* Nat and Michel were dressed as troopers. She hardly recognised her brother; he was sporting a moustache and a little pointed beard and thick eyebrows. Make-up made his face look fatter and older.

'I'm to stay in disguise until we reach the coast,' he told her as she hugged him.

'Come and eat,' Jay said. 'Then we must be on our way. I do not know how long it will take for the gaoler to be missed and let out of that room, but there will be a hue and cry when he is. It may already have happened.'

Lisette ate some of the bacon and swallowed some wine and then she and Jay returned to the coach and, with Sam driving, set off for the barricade at a normal pace. Impatient as they were, it would not do to hurry.

'The others?' she queried. 'What are they going to do?'

'They are going to follow and block any attempt to stop us once we have passed through the barrier.'

'Even Michel?'

'Yes. We are Commodore and Mrs Drymore returning to England with safe conduct. We cannot risk having your brother in the coach with us if we are stopped—not even my diplomatic status would save us. My father told me if I were caught, the government would deny all knowledge of me.'

'You never told me that.'

'No, you had enough to worry about. Michel will be safe enough with Harry. No one would expect him to be one of those sent in pursuit.'

'He is chasing himself.' She laughed. 'Oh, Jay, how clever of you.'

'That was Harry's idea. I only hope your brother is strong enough for the ride.'

'He will be.'

'And you?'

'I am ready for anything, as long as you are by my side.'

'Good, because here is our first test.'

There were two lines at the barricade, one to enter the city and one to leave. There was only a perfunctory search of those coming in to make sure they were not carrying forbidden imports like tea, coffee, tobacco or sugar, which could command ridiculous prices from those who could afford to pay. Vehicles waiting to leave the city, from handcarts to grand carriages, were thoroughly searched for *aristos* fleeing the country, taking gold and jewellery with them. Both were against the law and punishable by death.

They sat waiting their turn, moving up as the people at the front were either allowed through or taken away. Jay looked at Lisette and squeezed her hand. 'Don't look so apprehensive, my love. You must appear relaxed.'

She smiled at him as they jerked into motion and found themselves at the head of the line. A guard opened the coach door and put his head in. 'Out, if you please,' he said.

'I do not see the necessity for that,' Jay said haughtily.

'I need to search the coach.'

'I am an envoy of his Britannic Majesty and I refuse to be treated in this fashion. I shall inform your superiors.'

'Nevertheless...' the man began.

'Oh, let us humour him,' Lisette said, smiling at the guard. 'We have nothing to hide and the poor man is only doing his duty.'

'Thank you, *madame*.' He was disposed to be polite.

They left the coach while two guards pulled out all the cushions and two more opened the boot and inspected their luggage. They even bent to search under the vehicle in case anyone should be hanging there. Finding nothing out of the ordinary, they allowed the travellers to return to their seats.

'You may go,' the first man said. *'Bon voyage.'* And with that he waved them on.

Lisette let out a huge sigh of relief and Jay

laughed. 'You continue to surprise me, madam wife,' he said. 'Suggesting so coolly that we humour the man left me with my heart in my mouth.'

'But it worked. He was polite and waved us on our way when he might have delayed us for hours while he sent someone to check on us.'

'Yes, but I am glad they did not find the *livres* I had hidden in the false bottom of my trunk.' He let down the window in the door and put his head out. 'Once we are clear, Sam, tickle the horses into a gallop. I shall not breathe easy until we are well away from Paris.'

'You expect to be pursued?' Lisette asked as he settled back into his seat.

'Yes. It will not take them long to realise who is responsible when they discover they have neither Giradet in custody.' He smiled suddenly. 'I would not like to be in Wentworth's shoes.'

'Jay,' she said slowly. 'We have a long ride ahead of us, so do you not think that now might be a good time to tell me about Mr Wentworth?'

He put his arm about her shoulder and drew her to him. 'It is not a pretty tale and not one I am proud of and I suppose I should have told you before asking you to marry me. You might have re-

fused me under the circumstances. If you want to
change your mind when I am done, I shall understand. It will break my heart, but I will not hold
you to our engagement.'

'It would take something very dreadful indeed
for me to do that,' she told him. 'I am convinced
Mr Wentworth was lying.'

'Not altogether,' he said. 'But I will tell you everything and you may be the judge.'

She took his hand and cupped it round her cheek
before kissing the palm. 'Go on, I am listening.'

So he told her everything. How Marianne loved
life, how she attracted people round her like moths
to a flame, how she loved company, going to the
theatre and balls and card parties, that he ought
to have known from the outset that she would not
like the quiet life at Falsham Hall, especially when
he was away at sea and she could not indulge her
fancies. 'She took a lover,' he said.

'Wentworth?' she queried, half-guessing what
he was going to say.

'No, he came later. This was a stripling of an
earl's son who had more money than sense. His
father put a stop to the affair when he heard of

it, threatened to cut him off without a groat. He was followed by a baronet she met at a hunt ball.'

'You knew about it?'

'Not at the time. That came to an end when the baronet died suddenly. Then came Gerald Wentworth, the second son of Earl Wentworth and prodigiously rich. I was away at sea at the time. She left our home and our children to live with him.'

'Oh, Jay, how dreadful.'

'There was the most awful scandal. They didn't seem to care about it. I could not let it pass, so I challenged him.'

'He told me that. He said he spared your life.'

'I spared his. I cannot kill another human being, Lisette, not even when I am as angry as I was then. In a battle at sea it is different, it is done in the line of duty and I rarely saw my enemy at close quarters. Wentworth and I were well matched and the fight went on some time, but then I managed to knock his weapon out of his hand and he fell to his knees. I had him at my mercy, even held my sword above him, but I could not bring myself to plunge it into him. I threw it down and turned my back on him, expecting him to finish me off, but there were too many witnesses for him to do that. He has hated me ever since.'

'And your wife?'

'I left her to him and went back to my children.'

'But she died.'

'Yes. From time to time I heard that her life was not happy, that he treated her cruelly.'

'Would you have taken her back, had she asked?'

'No. Any love I had for her had died, but when a messenger came to tell me she had had an accident and I was wanted, I could not ignore it. I rode to Wentworth Castle, but I was too late, she was already dead. All I was needed for was to remove the body.'

'Oh, Jay, I am so sorry.'

'I have no one to blame but myself. I should have stayed at home with her, then perhaps she might have settled down.'

'Do you really believe that?'

'No, I do not think I do,' he said slowly. 'I realise now it was always in her nature to be wild.'

'Then you are not at fault.'

'Oh, Lisette, do you still say you will marry me?'

'Of course I do.'

He laughed and kissed her again and went on kissing her until they were both almost carried away by their passion. They might have been if the coach had not come to a stop.

Chapter Twelve

It was broad day and they had covered over a
dozen miles and the horses needed to rest. Sam
had driven off the road into a clearing in a wood,
where stood a little cottage with smoke issuing
from its chimney. They stirred their cramped
limbs and, while Sam saw to the horses, Jay and
Lisette went inside to be greeted by a tiny old lady
with a clay pipe clamped between her lips. Jay introduced himself and presented Lisette.

'The young man told me to expect you,' she
said, referring to Joe, who would have been flat-
tered to be described as young, but to the bent old
lady he probably was. 'Did all go well?'

'Yes, but later than we intended.'

'You will be in some haste, then. I'll pack food
for you to take with you while your man changes
the horses. I have obtained a spirited four for you,

but they are not well matched. I hope your driver can manage them.'

'I am sure he can. You may have a visit from three *maréchaussée* shortly who will not be all they seem. Do not be alarmed. Their leader calls himself Harry Portman—'

'Oh, I know that gentleman of old. He always stops here on his way to and from Paris. I never know what guise he is going to adopt next.' She cackled and took a kettle off the fire and poured boiling water into a pot containing tea leaves.

'If anyone else asks after us...'

'I shall send them in entirely the wrong direction. You may trust me, *monsieur.*' She poured tea into tumblers for them and for Sam who came in to say the new horses were ready to go. A few minutes later Jay and Lisette took their seats again, each clutching a package of bread, cold chicken and ham. Sam climbed on the driver's seat and they were off again.

The horses had never worked together before and the ride was an erratic one and Sam had to work hard to keep them in line. Lisette clutched Jay, who put his arms round her. They laughed, glad to be together and free and they did not care how rough the ride was. But they were slower on this section than they had been on the last.

'They should have caught us up by now, surely?' Lisette said. 'You do not think something dreadful has happened, do you?'

'No, my darling. They may have been held up at the barrier, but you may trust Harry to see them safely through.'

'Supposing Michel became ill and could not ride? He was starved and beaten in prison and is very weak.'

'He is stronger than he looks. Be patient.'

'I remember you saying that to me before.'

'Yes, but this time you are going to heed me because you have learned to trust me, is that not so?'

'Yes, Jay,' she said meekly, making him laugh.

Their second stop was at a posting inn where the proprietor laughed at their horses until the tears ran down his face. 'I've never seen anything like it,' he said. 'Where did you find those beauties?'

'In a field,' Jay said. 'Ours were spent. You should have fresh cattle for us, bespoken by my servant, Joe Potton.'

'That I do. You are late.'

'Are you surprised?' Jay said, nodding towards the horses that were being unharnessed.

'That I'm not. Do you want to eat? Boiled fowl and onions, very tasty it is, too.'

Jay looked at Lisette. 'What do you say?'

'Yes, let us rest a while. It might give the others time to catch up.'

'Not only our friends,' he said.

'Can't we risk it? We are a long way from the capital.'

'Very well. Landlord, we will have some of your fare.'

They were sitting down with Sam in the dining room when they heard horses galloping into the yard. The landlord went out to greet the newcomers, while the three diners looked at each other, hardly daring to breathe. Jay reached out and put his hand over Lisette's.

'How goes it, Jean, you old rogue?' The voice was undoubtedly Harry's and the listeners broke into broad smiles of relief. The next minute he came into the room with his arm about the shoulders of the landlord. They were followed by Nat and Michel.

Lisette ran to embrace her brother and dragged him to sit beside her at the table where they were joined by Harry and Nat.

'What happened?' Jay asked Harry as the landlord brought more food. 'Did you have any trouble?'

'Only from the mob. The news is all round Paris. The King is going to be put on trial for treason. It's all to do with that *Armoire de Fer* business. Even those who were against trying a monarch have come round to the idea. The population, or at least the noisy half of it, is ecstatic. They are out on the streets, singing, dancing, looting and carrying effigies of Louis and models of a guillotine. We could not get through. And when the crowd saw our uniforms, they crowded round and wanted to know if we had been at the Temple, guarding him.'

'He told them we had,' Michel put in. 'He made up a tale about how Louis had received the news weeping into his beard.'

'They wanted to drink our health,' Harry went on. 'What could we do but comply?' He laughed suddenly. 'If I had wanted to create a diversion to cover our tracks, I could not have chosen a better one.'

'So we have been forgotten?' Jay queried.

'Not entirely. By the time we had extricated ourselves, the authorities were rounding up anyone who had ever had any contact with Louis to force them to give evidence. I heard Michel's name mentioned, but not that he had escaped from gaol.'

'When they do find out, you may be sure they will soon know who was responsible,' Jay said. 'Wentworth will be all too ready to tell them.'

'Wentworth is no more, Jay. The vain fool went out in all his finery and the mob took offence and strung him up on one of the lanterns, after they had stripped him of anything worth having. I beg your pardon, Miss Giradet, I had forgot he was your uncle.'

'I barely knew the man and certainly never thought of him in that way,' she said. 'He was a traitor, prepared to betray his countrymen, Jay and Michel too, for gain and hanging was a kind of justice.' She paused. 'Does that mean we are safe? No one will come after us and make us go back now, will they?'

'Of course not,' Jay said. 'You will be my wife and your father and brother my kin.'

'I thought that was a ruse to fool the French,' Nat said, looking from Jay to Lisette and back.

'So it was,' Jay said. 'But Lisette has promised to make it a reality. We are to be married.'

This led to congratulations all round and Harry called for more wine to offer a toast. 'We'll stop at the next town and find a priest,' he said. 'We'll have you married before the night is out, just to make sure.'

Jay looked at Lisette. 'What do you say, my love?'

'I had dreamed of being wed at Highbeck with the children and family about us.'

'We can still do that. Do you think being married twice to the same man will make the bond stronger?'

'It could not be more strong than it is already,' she said, realising that to return unmarried after all their adventures might set the tongues wagging and Jay had already had enough scandal to contend with. 'But let us do as Harry suggests.'

* * *

The next stage of the journey was made with the coach drawn by four good horses. 'If anyone wants to know, we are escorting the British Envoy to his yacht,' Harry said. 'I hope Joe has managed to alert Lieutenant Sandford to be ready to sail as soon as we arrive.'

Jay and Lisette were married at the ancient church of Notre Dame in Louviers, which they had reached very late that night. Harry knocked up the incumbent and induced him to perform the ceremony for a handful of *assignats*. The priest was anxious to return to his bed and it did not take above a few minutes. Lisette could hardly believe she was married. 'I don't feel married,' she said to Jay as they returned to the coach.

'Now isn't that strange,' he said. 'I have felt married ever since our first night in France.'

'But nothing happened.'

He chuckled. 'No, but you will never know how hard that was for me, lying beside you and wanting you and knowing it just would not do.'

'As long ago as that?'

'Yes. And now I can properly and legally make

you my wife, we cannot stop. We are not safe yet and must ride through the night.'

'Then let us make haste.'

Two days and two nights later, poorer by thousands of *assignats* and several hundred gold *livres,* they arrived in Calais and there was the *Lady Anne* waiting at anchor. But they still had one more hurdle to overcome. Everyone's passports were being scrutinised. Harry, Nat and Michel had discarded their uniforms and left them behind in a woodman's hut. They were all English travellers returning home. It was then they learned that King Louis had been tried and found guilty on a whole host of charges and sentenced to death and those who had been loyal to him could expect the same fate. Not until they were safely on board and under sail did Lisette relax. It was over. They were going home.

The vessel was crowded, but Jay and Lisette, ensconced in the main cabin, were oblivious of what the others were doing. 'Now I mean to make up for lost time,' Jay said, untying the lacing on her bodice. 'I love you, Mrs Drymore.'

'And I love you, Mr Drymore.'

Her gown, stays, petticoats and stockings were taken off and thrown aside along with his coat and breeches, his waistcoat, shirt and cravat. Naked, they fell on to the bunk, locked in each other's arms.

Jay was a thoughtful and gentle lover, content to take her slowly and carefully, but when the time came their union was consummated in an explosion of passion that left them both blissful and exhausted.

They arrived at Blackfen Manor on Christmas Day to find the whole family gathered for the festivities: Lord and Lady Drymore, the Comte, who was frail but well, Sir John, Jay's sisters and their husbands and children and, of course, Edward and Anne. All were overjoyed to see them safe and sound and there were hugs and kisses and not a few tears. What had been perceived as a muted festival on account of the absence of the loved ones became a joyous celebration. It was, so everyone said, the best Christmas ever.

A week later Jay and Lisette were married again in Highbeck church, which was crowded with family, villagers and well wishers and afterwards there was a feast at the Manor. Looking at the loaded table, Lisette realised just how lucky they were compared with the people of France and she prayed the troubles of that country would soon be over.

The next day they took Edward and Anne home to Falsham Hall. It was not the summer of her dream because it was snowing, but the house looked just as beautiful in winter as in summer, with its roof sparkling white and smoke coming from its chimneys in a kind of welcome.

'Home at last,' Jay said.

'Home,' the children said.

'Home,' Lisette echoed and felt unbelievably happy.

* * * * *

THE UNIVERSITY OF WINCHESTER

Martial Rose Library
Tel: 01962 827306